SALLY BURTON

THE BARREN PATCH

VIKING

VIKING

Published by the Penguin Group
27 Wrights Lane, London w8 5tz, England
Viking Penguin Inc., 40 West 23rd Street, New York, New York 10010, USA
Penguin Books Australia Ltd, Ringwood, Victoria, Australia
Penguin Books Canada Ltd, 2801 John Street, Markham, Ontario, Canada L3R 1B4
Penguin Books (NZ) Ltd, 182–190 Wairau Road, Auckland 10, New Zealand

Penguin Books Ltd, Registered Offices: Harmondsworth, Middlesex, England

First published 1988
Reprinted 1988

Made and printed in Great Britain by
Richard Clay Ltd, Bungay, Suffolk

Filmset in 11/13 pt Sabon

British Library Cataloguing in Publication Data

Burton, Sally
The barren patch.
I. Title
8 23'.914[F]   PR6052.U7/

ISBN   0-670-81876-3

CHAPTER ONE

> Cat Food
> White Wine
> Milk
> Yoghurt
> Lean Cuisine

'Oh, shit,' she groaned.

Louise put the list aside, let out a troubled sigh and then bit her lower lip. She sat very neatly on the edge of the sofa, almost as if she didn't want to disturb any of the deep feather cushions. Her eyes scanned the small cheerful sitting-room, which was full of light and colour. The clever mixture of fabrics, the curtains and tie-backs toning with the cover of the sofa, the needle-point cushions scattered on the two chairs, the mirror above the fireplace and the basket of dried flowers in the grate gave her no comfort at all. The room was delightfully decorated and, although everything had been chosen with care, it had been chosen by someone else, and she felt like an intruder. As she twirled the fringe of the antique shawl draped over the back of the sofa, she longed to be back in another time and safely in a room that was familiar to her and full of her own memories and plans.

She sat feeling that life was utterly bleak and wondered how on earth she was going to summon up the enthusiasm to go out shopping. It was the only thing she had to do today, so she could afford to leave it for a while. But not for too long. She had meant to go shopping yesterday, but somehow the outing had got left until late in the afternoon, and when she had thought about it, it had not seemed worth the effort.

Gone were the days when Louise used to dash into the supermarket, throw things into a trolley, think on her feet about what to cook and for how many, spot the bargains and even have time to smile at the butcher. 'A full day's work, a lovely house, and dinner too. So clever, so much fun, how does she do it?' they said. She knew only too well that she wasn't doing it now and, what was worse, she could not imagine that she could ever do it again. She wanted to, she desperately wanted to, but it all eluded her and she was left to wrestle with her faltering concentration and her middle-of-the-night anger. Some fool, who should have known better, had gone so far as to tell her last week that she would soon be finding her old self and that it was only a matter of time before she would be back on her feet. What a joke, and what the hell did he know? If he had all the answers, why couldn't he see that she had unwillingly left her old self behind?

She reached out and touched the tabby cat safely curled up on a white-painted wicker chair stuffed with cushions. 'Patrick, I think I am becoming altogether too gloomy,' she murmured. The cat looked up, yawned and stretched, but didn't say much as he had heard it all before.

The cat might have reacted with more interest had he seen the two fragile fish being carried carefully into the flat on the ground floor. They were lying very low in the bottom of their aquarium, having had a disruptive experience as they were jogged around in the back of a truck during its all too long and tortuous journey across London. So far, it had not been a pleasant morning for two fish of distinction, and the day held little promise.

Their owner, Kate, who had a positive disposition, was of the same opinion. Plan as you might, moving was always difficult. Along with all that exhausting organization came the disbelief and guilt at the amount of human clutter accumulated over the years. Resolutions to do better the next time could, of course, be made, but there would always be that niggling doubt when the bulging carrier bags were assessed and counted. Still, things were definitely going to change for the better for Kate. Everyone had told her so and they should know. She had given Nick the boot three weeks ago and, in a fit of well-meant independence, she had refused to give him the telephone number of the new flat. The truth of the matter was that she missed him like hell, though when she tried to analyse the longing, she wasn't at all sure why, because when all was said and done (and after two gin and tonics she was the first to admit to anyone who cared to listen) their ten-year affair had been off and on, and really far more off than it had ever been on. Vague though the arrangement had been at times, it had served that useful purpose of providing a little comfort until something better came along. It hadn't so far.

At the age of thirty-eight, Kate harboured fond hopes that this would be a new beginning. At the age of thirty-eight, she also knew herself well and reflected, as she unscrambled an unyielding mess of wire coat-hangers, that it was just as well she hadn't got carried away and thrown out all her flowing, comfortable, elastic-waisted, generous-sized clothes. They would come in very handy during the next few week while she got the flat sorted out and before she embraced *Cosmopolitan*'s 'Diet for a Lifetime' one more time. Though this time it would be for the last time. This was definitely going to be the final thrust, because from now on she was going to be perfect.

Louise decided that this was the moment, and it was going to be the supermarket for her shopping, not the little twenty-four-hour shop two streets away. She had thought hard. The risks were great in either direction. The supermarket and the women with their children filling their trolleys for whole families or the tiny shop and the chance of someone speaking to her and having to respond. On balance, the supermarket won. If she was clever, she could keep her head down, her mind set, and ignore those bursting trolleys with their images of continuity and commitment, whereas it would be difficult to ignore a direct question and an inquisitive face. She would be forced into conversation, and in the confines of the shop someone might even come close, touch her, invade her territory. No, it was much safer at the supermarket. Eyes down and everything taken at a run. The decision was taken, all she had to do now was act upon it.

She picked up her basket, handbag and extra carrier bag, just in case, all of which she had assembled with great care, not because she was overly meticulous by nature, but because she knew that otherwise she would surely forget something. She glanced at the mirror over the fireplace and checked the black bow which firmly anchored her long, dark brown hair. She knew that her grey flannel trousers were looser than they should be, but on the whole she was pleased that she was getting thinner. Her body was the only thing she possessed, and every day she was becoming more angular. Her shape echoed her thoughts, finely honed and like a weapon. She knew that she was doing it to herself, and she knew why she was doing it: because it would really show him.

As she moved hesitantly towards the front door, she told herself that all she had to do was go out and buy a few groceries. It really wasn't that difficult. But it seemed difficult. It seemed like agony, yet somehow she got through the door and, as she descended the stairs and confronted the fact that she was going out into the open air, she saw several packing-cases crowding the hallway and spotted two burly individuals attempting to ease a sofa into the ground-floor flat. Her path to the outside world was emotionally difficult, and it was now physically hazardous as well.

'Give us a smile, darlin', it might never 'appen,' said the larger of the two, apparently delighted with the range of his wit and human insight. Turning to his companion, who was younger by twenty years and could be relied on to praise him loudly when required, he foolishly forget that he was supposed to be supporting the sofa and relaxed his grip, only to find this object crashing to the ground and landing on his foot. Self-satisfaction quickly turned to pain as he yelled. ''Ell's teeth! Me foot!' Had he been of slimmer build, he might have been able to bend down and massage his wounded extremity, but such was his physique that he had to put up with hopping and shaking his foot, which did nothing to alleviate the pain, but did serve to bring out beads of sweat on his brow due to the unfamiliar excessive exertion.

Standing on the bottom stair, Louise found her habitual

frown turning rapidly to a smile and she positively purred as she said, 'May I get through to the door? Thank you so much. Goodbye, gentlemen.' She stepped through the packing-cases and made her way to the door. As she closed it behind her, she heard the injured man being comforted by his colleague. 'Are you all right, Perce? Do you want to sit down for a sec?'

'Course I'm all right, Tone. No problem. Blimey, we've got a right one there,' observed Perce and as he did so he was probably adding a knowing wink and a nod of his bald, sweaty head towards the front door.

Outside in the street Louise noticed that it was cold, but that the sun was shining and she realized that she hadn't registered the weather for a long time. What she then saw, to her immediate horror, was the form of Doug Soper, her next-door neighbour, a tweed jacket stretched taut across his back, as he busily unloaded boxes from the boot of his Ford Fiesta. She hoped that she could walk briskly past and that he would continue to be thoroughly occupied with his boxes. She should have known that Doug had never been one to miss an opportunity for a little enlightening chat, and it was unlikely he would change now. Hearing the click of the closing door, he turned, lit up with recognition and took one step forward, a move that released in Louise that unmistakable sinking feeling.

'Hello-o there.'

'Good morning.'

'Well, well, well.'

She attempted to smile, but it was without success.

'Lovely day, I must say. I thought I'd give my kitchen a coat of paint. Mustn't let the old standards slip, you know, got to keep on the go, that's what I always say,' and then, as he changed his expression to one of studied seriousness and stood with hands clasped in supplication, two gallons of Dulux gloss in sunshine yellow forgotten for the moment, he said, 'And how are you feeling? Optimistic, I hope?'

'Yes, I think things are getting a bit better.'

'Oh, the trials and tribulations. The important thing to remember is that life goes on no matter what problems we have to face. I know, of course, from the most bitter experience of all.'

Louise doubted that he did know and thought that this kind of encounter on the pavement, following quickly as it did on her brush with the heavies at the bottom of the stairs, was enough to convince her that she could hardly cope with her own trials and tribulations, let alone with Doug's bitter experiences.

'I must get to the supermarket, Mr Soper. Goodbye.'

'Call me Doug, my dear, you know you can always rely on me. Always ready and willing, if you'll pardon the expression.'

For one long and awful moment Louise thought he was going to move even further forward and try to clasp her hand, but he bounced back and forth on his leather brogues and backed off with a parting, 'Well, goodbye. You know where I am, right next door.'

Yes, I am afraid I do know where you are, Douglas, and I wish you were anywhere but here. God, he makes me angry, everything makes me angry, life makes me angry, screamed Louise to herself. The walk would take her about ten minutes, which would be sufficient time to cool down. It was much easier to walk though she could have taken the car. If anything, the walk was a way to kill time and it certainly was a lot safer, as she wasn't awfully good at driving these days. She tended to misjudge distances and then get into one of her panicky states, and all in all it was *something* she could well do without.

'People,' she snapped.

Kate was delighted with the morning and the way it had gone. Perce and his cohort, Tone, had just taken their leave, and not before time. They had been a help with the heavy stuff, but they had entrenched opinions about the position of the television set and video equipment and could not understand why Kate wanted them in her bedroom and not dominating the sitting-room. A great many sideways looks and muttered 'we've got a right one 'ere' lines had passed between the two, and they were probably just as delighted as she was that their assignment was over.

A lot had been achieved during the morning, and so Kate felt that it was about time she stopped and that it wouldn't be a bad idea to reward herself for her outstanding humour and the considerable amount of work she had put in during the past few hours. Although it was only 12.30, she decided that she might as well take care of herself, as no one else was about to do so, and have a spot of lunch. Since she had taken the precaution of packing some provisions to see her through the day, it was the work of an instant. Although she did not immediately find a plate, she did lay her hands on a bottle-opener and a bottle of Sainsbury's Côtes du Rhône. She delved down into the basket containing the delicacies and located a lump of brie and a chunk of wholemeal bread. The plate was obviously not going to materialize, so she balanced the picnic on a piece of kitchen towel, which she held aloft in one hand while she cleared a space on the kitchen table with the other. The table stood in the middle of the kitchen surrounded by boxes; once the boxes were unpacked, she would be able to move the table into its allotted position up against the wall. The two chairs that were to do duty in the kitchen were stacked in the sitting-room. It had the potential of being a memorable meal – the first in her new home.

Louise studied the pale and ugly young couple in the queue at the supermarket check-out. The fact that they had somehow managed to produce a smiling and beautiful child proved beyond doubt that there was no justice in this world. She had negotiated the aisles without incident, had miraculously found a trolley without a squeaking and rocking wheel at her first attempt and was patiently lining up, ready to pay. Rather than annoying her, the blip-blip of the cash register was having a hypnotic effect and was efficiently lulling her to sleep. To relax and sleep seemed to be the most desired thing ever. She knew that tonight, like all other nights, she would fall into bed at nine o'clock, utterly exhausted, only to wake with her mind and body rigid three hours later. Then would come the darkened conversations, the pain and anger, intense and bitter. By 7 am she would drift off to sleep and have to force herself into action in the middle of the morning. If only she could sleep a natural sleep for eight hours, surely things would look better.

By the time she approached the semi-detached houses in Vaucluse Road, built by a shark to accommodate returning soldiers after the First World War, Louise felt her by now customary enervated state overtaking her. She was relieved to see that Doug Soper was nowhere in sight and was thus unlikely to pounce, oozing goodwill and fortitude. Louise opened the door of number eleven and noticed that the packing-cases had gone, as had the removal men, leaving the door of the ground-floor flat firmly closed. Since she didn't feel at home in the house anyway, it did not seem to matter much if there was someone else living there, who they were, or how she got on with them. Louise couldn't understand why she didn't feel peaceful in this house, for she knew it well. She had frequently visited it when her sister, Jill, had lived there. The first-floor flat was a safe haven until she got herself sorted out, until the crisis passed, until she had somewhere to go, whenever that might be. She was in transit from one life, but was unclear of where the future might be found. Louise had moved into the flat just four weeks previously with several suitcases of clothes, which had caused her to remark with some obvious bitterness that it was a wonder she had been allowed to keep them. Those clothes and her glazed expression were an inadequate disguise.

She slowly climbed the stairs and turned the key in the lock with difficulty, not quite understanding why all the simple things seemed so hard. She felt exhausted and decided that an afternoon nap would fill the void until six o'clock. She sank into one of the chairs and pulled out a cushion from behind her back to clasp in front of her for comfort. She was pleased that she had gone to the supermarket and she felt brave. Even though shopping for a few groceries should have been essentially a trivial matter, for her it represented a mountain conquered. It was, she told herself, amazing what you can do when you try.

Kate worked with considerable fervour during the afternoon through a combination of enthusiasm and an overwhelming desire to burn off a few extra calories, given the excessive intake of bread and cheese for lunch. She convinced herself that she had read in some informed journal that housework was a much underrated form of exercise and that a Victorian parlourmaid burned more calories per hour than an average squash player. She unpacked the new dinner service, which she had found at the Reject Shop, and filled her kitchen cupboards. She found the old and familiar table linen and began to fill drawers and shelves. She arranged, changed her mind and rearranged, all to good effect. She lined up her Habitat cutlery in a drawer, which she had previously lined with bright-blue lining-paper. She was thrilled that she could be so precise and hoped that she would continue in this vein. She found her book box and sat cross-legged on the Spanish rug while she filled the bookshelves, which ran on either side of the mock log fire in the sitting-room. She hung up her clothes in the large wardrobe and at the end of it all deliberated for quite some time about where the hell she was going to put the ironing board.

At six o'clock Kate decided to have a bath. She would very much have liked to have used the new pretty pale-blue towels she had bought from Frette last Saturday. They had been particularly chosen for the occasion and were the result of a zealous morning on Bond Street when the desire to do well by herself was strongly upon her. All she could locate amongst the carrier bags and packing-cases, however, was a soiled item she had pinched some months previously from the Leicester Holiday Inn. It certainly was not the time to make a crusade out of finding the new towels, because she knew that if she kept on trying it would only make her cross, and tonight was a night she really wanted to savour.

Realizing that she must not let her temporary inability to find her new luxurious towels put her off her course, Kate turned on the bath and poured in a lavish amount of bath oil. She eased herself into the bath and looked around the room. It really was an incredibly pretty bathroom, papered in a delicate sapphire blue design. In fact, it was the bathroom that had first caught her eye when she had viewed the flat. In most of the flats she had seen, the bathroom had been overlooked and was very unappealing. She had the feeling that whoever had converted this flat had started with the bathroom and that it was the core of the place. She planned to put in lots of baskets, which would hold cosmetics and soaps. There would also be some plants and perhaps some photographs in antique frames. There was plenty of room, and she hoped she could find a pine washstand to fit under the window. The festoon blind, an exotic and out-rageously expensive purchase, was a definite success and it was just perfect with the wallpaper. Kate was quite sure that she would do some of her best thinking here. To start picturing Nick right now, however, in the shower, laughing, having made love, was not the sort of thinking she had in mind.

Wrapped in a towelling robe, feeling warm and content, Kate poured herself a gin and tonic. She plonked herself in her new and comfortable armchair, pulled her knees up under her chin and smiled a broad and pleasing smile. What a good day, she told herself. Kate wanted to relish this evening on her own. She was going to plot and plan, to think about the future and banish all thoughts of the past. But before any of that, her immediate concern was what to eat for supper. One thing was for sure and that was it should be a treat, something she really enjoyed, so she decided to leave the rack of lamb and frozen creamed spinach until tomorrow. She simply had to give in and acknowledge that a fitting tribute to a day well spent was surely a bowl of pasta, a bottle of red wine and, as she was on her own, a generous quantity of garlic bread. She took a sip of her gin and tonic, put a tape of Vivaldi's *Four Seasons* into the player and did a happy dance and spin around the sitting-room, where all was more or less in order, before heading for the kitchen. After supper she thought she would have a quiet evening with a book, or perhaps curl up in bed and watch a video.

Louise was awake, but was not sure if she had or had not slept. She seemed to have hung in that half-awake state, hearing voices and sounds, plunging into dreams and spinning out of them again. It seemed that the only thing to pull her round would be a kir, so she got out of bed and gathered a silk kimono around her shoulders. Louise thought that she was drinking altogether too much at the moment, but as her wise sister, Jill, had said, better that than Valium. The truth was that if she was forced

14

into a corner, she would have to admit that she had done more than her fair share of that as well. She had eased off the sleeping pills and perhaps it was being unrealistic to think she could do everything at once. With that comforting rationale in mind, she poured herself a drink. In ten minutes she would feel better and then she would think about what to eat. She frequently thought about what to eat, but rarely did anything constructive about it. Sometimes she even went so far as to cook a chicken, only to leave it abandoned in the kitchen. Patrick, the cat, was an efficient little chap with the leftovers, and so there was seldom much incriminating evidence in the morning.

As Louise sat on the sofa, sipping her kir and staring at the wall, things were hotting up downstairs. The gentle strains of Vivaldi had given way to the Beach Boys at their best, and they were now blasting out of the stereo. Pasta was bubbling on the cooker, the garlic bread was ready and Kate was munching a large dripping chunk of it as she bopped the night away to 'Barbara Ann'.

Upstairs, Louise finished her kir, reflected a while, poured herself another one, wondered about turning on the television, but didn't think she could handle it, thought about the kitchen and food, but dismissed them and decided that after this kir she would have another one, and if that didn't do the trick, what the hell? – she would have a fourth.

CHAPTER TWO

There were times when things at work got to be a bit too much. On a day-to-day basis most things were under control, and there were a few laughs in between, but Michael Major, head of Major Events, that wonderful team, which could arrange anything from a business meeting for half a dozen to a conference for a thousand, was basically being a pain. He had always been given to excess and saw his company as one of the most creative and innovative, but since his return from a convention in Chicago he had slipped into the realms of fantasy and there was a marked change in his vocabulary. In the forefront of conference organization was where he wished to be, but his creative team of Ned, Geoffrey, Martin and Kate were lagging behind him. They had endured two hours of Michael droning on and on about his most recent triumphs (he was quick to assume all praise was for him) and his present philosophy on company strategy, which had induced at first boredom, then acute restlessness and frustration. It was more than Kate could stand, and how the wretched man had the nerve to go on about some pathetic conference in Bradford, allocating roles to each of them, seeking Ned's creative input and asking a bewildered Geoffrey about things technical, was difficult to imagine. Poor Michael had unwittingly made the wrong career choice, for instead of entering the world of public relations and conferences, he should have run for public office. He would have made a tremendous councillor, a mayor or even an MP. Who knows where he could have gone from there? He certainly would have been a welcome asset on the hustings, where he could have practised his extraordinary ability to thrash an idea to death, talk about it, turn it inside out, approach it from all directions and keep going with it long after it was decent to do so. It was against his rules to let anyone else get a word in, to make a suggestion or deviate from his prescribed line of thought. If there was the merest whisper of dissension, it gave him the opportunity to go all the way back to the beginning and present his case with added verve. What a loss. He could have spent a busy and contented life doorstepping little old ladies, conning union leaders, shaking hands in supermarkets and selling bum ideas to the unemployed.

Looking around the room, it seemed that everyone else was also failing to get the point, whatever it was. Occasionally there was an 'Absolutely' or an 'I couldn't agree more' thrown in as a goodwill gesture whenever Michael intimated that he was seeking approval, and, to give Martin his due, he had talked coherently for three and a half minutes about the advisability of including a contingency fund in the Bradford conference costing. For her part, Kate had tried to appear interested and behave like the production manager that she was, but for the past hour she had lapsed and had only stayed awake by keeping a tally of how many important names were dropped. Several had been, and some had been repeated quite forcibly whenever it had been felt by Michael that their full significance had not been completely appreciated. Try as she might, there seemed to be no adequate way to deal with a situation that seemed to be getting rapidly out of control. Casting a quick glance in Ned's direction, she had to work very hard at suppressing a fit of the giggles as he mouthed, 'Don't worry, we can have a drink soon. You'll feel better then.' Well, he was probably right, and Kate would not be the only one to feel better. Geoffrey, who had never had much of an attention span, except when studying the form of the runners in the three o'clock, had clearly long gone, and it was touch and go as to whether Martin could maintain any semblance of paying attention for many more minutes. Never known for his sensitivity, it took the awesome sight of four pairs of glazed eyes before Michael finally took on board that he was losing control of the meeting and that perhaps he would be well advised to assert himself as rapidly as possible.

'Well, I think that was very useful,' he said, smiling

generously around the room and then smoothly leaning back in his chair as he gave his tie an artful tug, stretched his neck and undid the top button of his shirt. Kate had never been quite sure what the performance meant, but it never failed to fascinate her. Why was it that a man could be thoroughly loathsome one minute and then do something utterly captivating the next? It really was amazing how attractive and sexy the ritual was. Did men feel the same way about women kicking off their shoes? It was something to do with the stretch of the neck, combined with the masterful dexterity of the fingers. Still, it was probably best to keep quiet about it, because if they ever caught on and found out just how appealing it was, they would be doing it all the time.

'Who would like a drink?' asked Michael. Geoffrey woke up with a start, Ned turned swiftly in his chair, Martin grinned in happy anticipation and Kate knew all too well what was coming next. 'Kate, be a darling, and get some wine, would you?' cooed Michael.

Answering his call, Kate left his office and hastily made her way across the main office, through the reception area and into the small kitchen, where she found a tray of glasses prepared in expectation by Vicky, their secretary, who had quite rightly decided that six o'clock was a good time to leave work. Two bottles of Sancerre were cooling in the fridge, and these Kate grabbed and put on the tray together with a bowl of peanuts, which she knew from past performances would be hoovered up in a trice by Geoffrey. In the midst of all these preparations it did cross her mind that it was always down to her to get the wine and that Michael never asked one of the chaps to do the decent thing. After all, not that anyone was counting, but they all drank it and some drank more than others. Why did she always respond immediately, jump up and meekly walk to the kitchen and get the beastly stuff? Never once had she declined, suggested that someone else muck in for a change, or, worse still, up until that moment actually considered that something sinister was afoot. Something, she said to herself seriously, will have to be done about this. She had thought that it was supposed to be different out in the real world, in the cut and thrust of the private sector. It was precisely because of this sort of behaviour that she had left her previous job with a large and groaning television company, the deciding factor being six months spent researching a documentary, working from a cupboard-like office, the only distinguishing feature of which was that it was on the right-hand side of the corridor and two doors past the ladies' lavatory.

Thinking it best not to become bitter, she nevertheless realized that it would not come amiss to try and infiltrate a few changes over the coming months. With this high on her list of priorities, she returned to the office and the gratifying sight of four men positively beaming at her, and was, for a fleeting moment, quite overcome. Sadly, it soon became evident that she was not the object of their admiration and desire.

'Let me make a space for you,' said one, jumping up and trying to be helpful.

'Put it down here,' came the joyful cry.

'Now, who would like a drink?' asked Michael, brandishing a bottle-opener.

'Yes, I would. Thank you,' said Geoffrey, first as always and not at all ashamed.

'Cheers!'

'Cheers!'

'Your health, Michael. Damn good meeting,' said Martin, who was trying to ingratiate himself.

'There's no need to open that second bottle, Kate, I think there's just enough left in here for you. Oh, sorry,' said Michael.

'No, it's all right. Half a glass is fine for me. Besides, I prefer red,' mumbled Kate, resolve going out of the window.

Geoffrey roused himself, sat up and grabbed his glass, didn't spill a drop and got it to his mouth all in one motion. With his left hand he scooped up some peanuts ready to pop them into his mouth as soon as he had drained his glass. It wouldn't be long. Martin and Michael launched into an intense conversation about Michael's new BMW, and it was all that Kate could do to stop herself from suggesting that it would be much appreciated if he would get in the damn car right now and sod off to Kingston.

Kate wandered over to Ned, who was looking particularly fetching in his lean and rugged way and was filling in time by draping himself rather elegantly in a leather-upholstered chair discreetly placed in the corner of the office.

'What was all that about, Ned? Can you explain to me why we all sat around like sheep for two hours listening to that nonsense? I mean, all we're trying to arrange is a one-day conference in Bradford. It shouldn't be that difficult. Now, I know Michael's image of himself as a successful man has been building up for some considerable time, but I think he's finally gone over the edge. Things are getting way out of proportion. That trip to Chicago did him no good at all. Any moment now I expect him to invite me to join him in a corporate awakening experience, and the way things are I'm terrified I'll say yes. All I want to do right now is get the hell out of here, go home and soak in my new bath. Have I told you about my new bathroom? It's absolutely wonderful.'

'The thought of the working day, and I use the phrase in its loosest possible sense, but the thought of it drawing to a close is infinitely appealing. However, the thought of your excessive proportions wallowing in foam in your new bath, which indeed you have mentioned once or twice, doesn't do a lot for me. But you are right, I too hope that we can leave soon, as I'm meeting James for a drink in Covent Garden before we go to Covent Garden, if you see what I mean.'

'Are they dancing or singing tonight?' queried Kate, a great one for the arts.

'You are not going to annoy me by being crass. Anyway, look lively you old has-been, it seems that our leader is about to make a move and head off homeward,' whispered Ned.

Whatever was said about Michael, and there was a lot to be said, he was a good dresser. Of course, it was difficult to know if he chose the clothes or if his wife, Andrea, did the shopping, but he certainly looked good in a pin-stripe, and he looked awfully good this evening as he went through a bit of riveting business with his tie and grabbed his Gucci briefcase. Perhaps he had something planned. Issuing a smile around the office, he said oilily, 'Well, thanks for everything all of you. I think we're now really on top of Bradford. I must be off. It'll be hell on the A3.'

'Oh, bound to be,' agreed Kate, and, anticipating that any minute Michael was going to touch her elbow, smile and ask her to be a darling and take care of things, she offered to clear up and then lock the offices. Clear up she would, but she did not think it was a good idea to go as far as to wash everything. There were limits, even for a willing soul. Vicky or Tillie, cleaner of offices, could do that in the morning.

'Goodnight, Kate,' said Geoffrey. 'Sorry I can't help, but I've got to dash over to the Turf Club.'

'Goodnight, Geoffrey. See you tomorrow.'

'I'm off, Kate,' said Martin.

'Are you playing squash tonight?' asked Kate out of politeness, as he was standing there with his kit much in evidence and he played every night.

'Yes, it's a club match. We should see some very good play this evening,' said Martin, who became quite fervent when discussing his favourite subject.

'Well, good luck.'

'Thanks awfully.'

'Goodnight. See you tomorrow.'

'Goodnight, Kate. You know, you really must come to the club some time.'

Kate wandered into Michael's office and looked at the mess they had made. While she was busily stacking newspapers and magazines, desperately trying to bring some semblance of order, she heard the telephone ring. After a pause she heard Ned say in what could be called a stage whisper, 'No, I'm sorry Nick, she's left.'

Kate didn't know whether to applaud Ned, or grab the telephone from him and tell Nick that she needed him desperately and that she hadn't really meant it to be over just yet. She went hot and then cold, bit her lower lip, ran her hands through her hair, took a gulp of air and thought how typical of him to telephone when he knew Vicky would have left and that she would be there on her own answering the telephone herself. Oh, but what a man was Ned, what a hero, and how fortunate that he was there and able to foil Nick's plot. He was to be relied upon and, having been briefed by Kate that no matter what she said, how she pleaded, he was not to let her talk to Nick, he seemed intent upon making sure she stuck to her guns. Although it was apparent that Ned was quite up to the situation, Kate felt the need to convince herself that she was too and so she rushed headlong towards him, furiously nodding her head from side to side while growling 'No, no, no.'

Actually, Ned seemed to be rather enjoying himself and was well into his stride as he purred into the telephone, 'She went home early, as she's leaving tomorrow morning for a two-week trip to Scotland. The North of Scotland that is. She said she might take in the Orkneys while she was there. I'll tell her you telephoned. Goodbye.'

'Oh brill, well played,' enthused Kate as she dramatically collapsed into the chair opposite Ned. 'Do you know, I think there's just the remotest chance that had I answered the telephone myself I would have gone weak at the knees and the game would have been up. I loved the inspired line about going away for two weeks. Do you think he believed it? Do you think he plans to try again? I hope he believed it, because it will give me some breathing space.'

'Come off it, old girl, who are you kidding? I don't think the chances of you going weak at the knees are in the least remote and the sooner I get you out of here and on the road the better it will be for all concerned. Do you want to come and have a glass of champagne with James and me? You know it always does you good, and as an added incentive we'll throw in a strong talking-to as well, in the hopes that you don't become feeble and give in when you get home. Just enough champagne to boost your spirits, mark you; too much and you become maudlin and uncontrollable.'

'You're absolutely right, of course. I accept. On balance, it seems like the only thing to do,' sighed Kate and then, breaking into a smile, she laughed, 'I'll just have to put on a brave face, won't I?'

Ned and Kate walked down the mews and past the overflowing dustbins surrounded by bulging, black plastic bags to the familiar gap where she parked her Renault Five. She found she enjoyed driving to work and liked the idea that the car gave her freedom and that she was able to pursue anything that might come up, though when you got right down to it, nothing had really come up for some time and returning home at dawn, after a night of passion, hadn't actually been on the cards. The car suited her, though once or twice she had tried the tube and had experienced the comfortable feeling of being a real worker as she hung on the strap and strained to read someone else's *Evening Standard*. On one occasion, when she had lived in Clapham, those many years ago, she had even gone so far as to try the proper train to Waterloo and had found the fringe involvement with dedicated commuters and travellers quite heady stuff. Anyway, one of the perks of her job and one of the things she had found most attractive when Michael had been trying to lure her to Major Events was a parking space. Kate recalled that her job had been described as having a wide brief, and there was the promise of executive potential. It seemed to her that the brief had got wider as she had co-ordinated everyone else's activities and that the executive potential had diminished to nil. But at least she had her parking space. So, every morning she sat in traffic jams, which, unlike all the fuming drivers around her, she found soothing, as it gave her time to think.

Gingerly edging himself into the car, Ned remarked that it was absolutely disgusting and why the hell didn't she clean it up.

'Christ, Kate, there's a tennis racket on the back seat and you haven't lumbered around a court in years. At least, I hope you haven't. Some legs look good in white shorts, but yours are not amongst them. What are you doing with a broken umbrella? And those old shoes are the most revolting objects I have ever seen.' With that he picked up an old carrier bag full of sheets destined for the laundry, but at that time occupying the floor space immediately in front of his feet. He briskly hurled it on to the back seat and suggested Kate consider seeking psychiatric help.

'You are so good to me, Ned,' murmured Kate. 'I love it when you insult me.'

23

As Kate turned on the ignition, the radio sprang to life at high volume and Ned immediately reached forward and turned it off.

'I can't bear rock music in cars,' he spat. 'It's a sign of an immature mind.'

'Don't be pompous, it doesn't suit you. Besides, I am immature and blissfully happy that way. It's part of my irresistible charm,' retorted Kate. 'Put it back on, but, just to please you, perhaps we could try Radio Four or, if you're feeling energetic, there are some cassettes in that box down there.'

'Which box, where?'

'There, you fool,' said Kate, turning around and looking out of the rear window as she reversed the car out of the parking slot.

'Now, concentrate on your driving, will you, and let's hope we arrive safely. Being involved in an unfortunate incident while a passenger in this heap would do my reputation no good at all.'

'I'm beginning to wish you hadn't come.'

'I'm the one who invited you, so remember that and don't push your luck.'

'I think you're really overstepping the mark. This is my car, and if you want to you can get out right now. I'll drop you on the next corner and if you can find a taxi at this hour with rain coming on, good luck. On the other hand, just think about it, you can enjoy my company all the way down the Mall. It's a treat thousands would be thrilled to accept.'

'You never were any good at statistics.'

'Oh, shut up.'

As Ned's contribution to the journey had been to feign terror, it was with considerable delight that on the first tour around the area, quite miraculously and quite out of keeping with the usual run of events, Kate found a place to park a mere hundred yards from the entrance to the wine bar. She even managed to reverse in neatly in one go, not mount the pavement, or leave her end sticking out.

She thought that they really looked rather fine as they entered the wine bar and she sensed that there were one or two appreciative glances, though they were all for Ned, who was, after all, so good-looking. Still, it was good to be seen in his company and he was a very true friend who was always ready with a funny line in a crisis. Kate thought that it was quite possible that he understood her better than anybody and she had found that he was one of the few people she could trust, who would really give her an honest answer and a dishonest one if he thought that was what she needed at the time. Tonight had been an example of him at his finest, of just how special and tremendous he was: dealing with Nick, making sure she didn't make a fool of herself and now about to fill her full of champagne and make her feel even better.

Then there was James. He was sitting in the darkened bar and was happy to see Kate, greeting her with a wide grin, and even happier to see Ned. It was just possible that James was that little bit more handsome than Ned, more in the classical mould, though it was Ned who was the most attractive. Casually put together in his Giorgio Armani suit, he was rugged and slightly flawed, a devasting combination always guaranteed to add appeal. James, urbane and and delicious, was a Turnbull and Asser man at heart. Some years ago they had met, seen something enduring in each other, and had been happy ever since.

About to launch into full flood and tell James that he would never guess what had happened, that she was having a traumatic time in the heart department, and hadn't it been awful, Kate was stopped by Ned, who told her that she was as usual being over-dramatic, that she should sit down, pull herself together and have some crisps.

'The trouble with you, Ned, is that you are too damned clever,' said Kate, attempting to look hurt.

'A glass of champagne?' intervened James at his gallant best.

'A far more pleasant attitude and one you might try and learn, you mean-mouthed, foul creature,' said Kate as she poked Ned in the ribs and tried to kiss him on the nose.

'Oh, stop it, Kate, there's a good girl. Have a drink and give me a break.'

Ned explained to James the intercepted telephone call from

Nick and the pressing need to get Kate into a jolly mood, full of resolve and determined not to give in. It didn't take too long to tell the story, and James was very good at making all the right noises in all the right places, suitably considerate and caring. Kate interrupted several times to explain just how thoroughly ghastly it all was, how desperate she was feeling, though she knew it was something she had to go through, that they were the most wonderful friends and she didn't know how she could ever thank them enough. Given that this was not the first time they had been through this with Kate, it was now becoming quite easy and was slipping into a ritual, in which they all played their parts very well and with a considerable degree of enjoyment and *élan*.

'What on earth would we talk about if we didn't have Nick? I suppose there's always Michael. Do you know, he's become quite impossible since he was mentioned in the *Financial Times*,' offered Kate. 'It probably went down very well in Kingston. I bet he's the hero of the cul-de-sac.'

'Does he live in a cul-de-sac?'

'I've no idea, but I think it would suit him,' said Kate, taking a contemplative sip of her champagne.

'Actually, it all started with that trip to Chicago, if you remember.'

'He was well on the way before he went to Chicago.'

'Yes, but things have got really bad since that convention. He was very impressed with all the hype and from that moment on he set his sights on bigger things. Take that meeting this afternoon. He's getting so carried away that I think he's in danger of losing sight of what we're there for.'

'What are we there for?'

'I've no idea. Anyway, back to Michael. He's happiest when he's having a meeting, so I am sure he will only find true fulfilment by having meetings every day and meetings to arrange meetings,' said Ned. 'The maddening thing is he'll probably get away with it.'

'Do you think he had a romantic encounter while he was away?' suggested Kate.

'It's possible. It's the sort of thing he'd think he should do.

26

You know, along with the gold American Express card and the BMW, the next step is a bit on the side.'

'Andrea won't like it.'

'Andrea won't like it at all. She doesn't strike me as the type to be crossed.'

'Imagine being married to him,' said Kate.

'Andrea married him.'

'Yes, but she was very young,' said Kate, sounding as if she was wise in these matters, and then turning to James she said, 'And what of you, James? Have you had a thrilling day in the City watching the dollar go up and down? Nice and bullish all day, were you?'

After two glasses of champagne and several laughs, which were at Nick's expense when they weren't at Michael's, Kate was all for prolonging the evening and having another one if they had time.

'No, we don't have time,' said Ned a shade firmly. 'And quite frankly, if you're going to negotiate your way out of here with any dignity at all, you'd better not. Besides, you've got to drive home and you're erratic enough on the roads stone-cold sober, so I don't think we should let you loose in a less than perfect condition.'

It was with some difficulty that Kate got to her feet, which was in no part due to the champagne, but because the strap of her handbag had somehow got caught under the seat of the gentleman next to her, quite how no one was able to tell. As she struggled to retrieve her bag, she noticed that rather a lot of crisp crumbs had become lodged in her ample knitted skirt, and, standing there as she did, wedged between three tables, there just was not sufficient room for any excessive brushing and flapping of the garment. James, being his usual genial self, was telling Kate that she must come over for dinner soon, to which Kate rather distractedly said that they must come over and see her new flat soon, as she had a simply stunning bathroom, which left Ned to remark that if they kept up this dialogue they would miss the curtain-up. The handbag was eventually dislodged, amidst a lot of apologies, and Kate did manage to shift some of the crisps with a quick flap of her skirt and a quick

27

stamp of her feet in the doorway of the wine bar, where they parted, Kate going to her car, James and Ned to the opera.

Driving home, Kate pledged to herself that she must never ever again become involved with a married man. Presumably Nick was by now home enjoying a bit of amusing conversation with his lovely wife, and Kate hoped he was feeling dreadful. It was the type of thing, she told herself, that she should have given up years ago. There is a theory that we are each in control of our own destinies and get what we want, in which case perhaps next time around she could find a rich admirer who would spoil her rotten and bestow lavish gifts upon her. Well, whatever happened in the future, she would be far more selective. Or did that sound too calculating? Perhaps it was better to put herself into the way of believing that she was going to fall passionately in love. It was easily done. One could fall madly in love four times a week with no problem at all. No, the problem always came with convincing the object of the burgeoning passion to agree, fall into line, and go along with the idea. Well, you never could tell, and the important thing to remember was to turn around and look at the future coming, rather than concentrating on the past flowing behind with all its unwanted debris. Enough of this rambling, she said to herself, it would be much better for all concerned if she concentrated on driving home, because there was quite a lot of traffic on the roads. Besides, it had started to drizzle.

The late-night grocery shop near Kate's flat looked inviting as she approached, so she decided to stop and pop in. Perhaps she might meet one of her neighbours, and there were a few things she needed. Since she had done so remarkably well with that business of Nick's telephone call, she thought she might pick up a bottle of wine, which she did before she picked up the milk. The wine was white and warm, but, never mind, she could always put a lump of ice in it. The great thing about having a home of your own was that you could do just what you liked, and perhaps that was one of the good things about not having Nick around any more; he was unlikely to telephone and ask to call round late at night, she could go to bed early, read, learn a language, eat what she liked and drink what she liked.

It took a while for Kate to open the door of her flat, partly because of the groceries she clasped in front of her and partly because she couldn't quite remember where the light switch was. How she loved this flat, which she considered to be a real home. It was a substantial and satisfactory conversion with two bedrooms and a garden. The semi-detached house had an established air about it, and her neighbours, from what she had seen on her brisk morning walks to her car, seemed to be made up of families with children and some older people who had probably been around since the area had been smart, gone down, only to come up again. She felt that she was really on the home-owning ladder now, this being her second purchase. There was nothing like the knowledge that she was no longer a first-time buyer to bring a glow of achievement to her features. Yes, of course, there were still some things which needed doing, the final touches, but they always took time to get right.

It was good to get home and see some mail lying on the floor: a letter from her mother wishing her well after the move and a postcard from her brother, who was on holiday with his wife and children in Brittany. Presumably they had got a cheap rate on a *gîte* in September. It was difficult to think of anything worse than a cold afternoon on a beach in Brittany with those revolting twins, Rupert and Rebecca, with their red hair and freckles, crying and sniffling all over the place. They had probably lost their buckets, got wet sand in their espadrilles and all they had to look forward to was the promise of a crêpe if it clouded over. Perhaps they were having freak weather conditions, but, no, there was quite a bit of rain, they were enjoying the break, managing to find lots of things to do, and were keeping on the go.

The answering machine flashed a number one, and, for a horrifying moment, Kate wondered if it was Nick checking up on her, until she remembered with relief that he didn't have the telephone number. She hoped that it wasn't going to be one of those frustrating messages when one heard the crushing rejection of someone hanging up. She flicked the machine to playback and heard 'Hello, Kate, it's Lizzie. The boys have gone back to school, so Peter and I wondered if you would like to come down and have lunch on Sunday. Give me a buzz tomorrow. Bye-ee.'

What a good idea. It would be lovely to drive to Oxfordshire and spend some time with Peter and Lizzie. They had been happily married for ever, it seemed, and Lizzie was always pleasant about her married state. She was quite inoffensive about the whole thing, unlike some people Kate could mention who came from humble beginnings and were likely to ram their husband's family silver down your throat at every available opportunity. She moved across the sitting-room and dipped her finger in the aquarium.

'Hello, boys. I'm home. Have you had a busy day swimming?'

In the kitchen Kate opened the wine and poured herself a glass. She didn't feel much like eating, but thought that she might heat up some soup from last night. There was some cheese that would do and some potato salad. It would make a nice snack. She could have an easy evening in front of the television and she also had a gripping novel on the go, where everything promised to turn out right in the next chapter. Later she would have a long bath. She had found a lovely stripped pine washstand at a shop in the Fulham Road, and it fitted beautifully under the window in the bathroom. If she could find just the right blue and white jug and fill it full of honesty, it would be perfect. She might let it be known around the family that she fancied some monogrammed towels, should anyone be thinking of giving her a present, though she did hope she wasn't making too much of this exotic bathroom with all her lovely bowls of pot-pourri.

CHAPTER THREE

It had come to something when the first thing a girl heard in the morning was Doug Soper's rumbling cough. A morning cough is never a pleasant experience and when it is part of the morning preparations of the gentleman one storey down and across the garden fence, it is liable to introduce a rather bad start to the day. Louise had just coaxed herself out of a turbulent sleep, and the habitual 7.30 am clearing of the vocal cords by Doug did nothing to help her make the transition from night to day. Not that this event had ever been witnessed – that was too much to contemplate – but as it was an extremely graphic cough, it was easy to imagine Doug opening his back door and sticking out his head like a tortoise in distress. Then would follow a long and productive clearing of the throat while he quickly turned his head from right to left in order to check the immediate neighbourhood and see if his dustbin had been stolen or if his perfect garden and display of dahlias had been vandalized in the night. Seeing that all was perfect and golden for another day, there would be a peremptory pursing of the lips, the hands would be clasped behind his back, he would rock forward on to his toes, back on to his heels and turn to go. A wavering whistle would then herald the fact that all was well in his world.

This was more than could be said for Louise's. The night had not refreshed her; she had plunged in and out of sleep and had laboured with her emotions. The anchor of reason had broken away and she was left to drift amidst relentless variations of despair and torment, which always brought her back to the question of what was wrong with her. Nothing she had ever learned had equipped her to deal with this inexorable chasm of loneliness. She tried to remember, but all her acquired knowledge had been used up.

Throughout the night her body had pitched and turned in different directions in its weightlessness. Now it was heavy, and she could not feel any part of it. She remained very still, unwilling to move at all, because she didn't know if she had a body or where the disconnected parts might be found. As the day came, her spirit returned from its bitter wandering, and bit by bit she was willing to try breathing. She pulled the blanket around her shoulders and moved slightly. Doug's cough had announced that the world was still there. As she stirred, the cat, which was curled up at the bottom of the bed, stretched and stealthily prowled towards her chin. He tapped her gently, nuzzled her and then returned to his guard-duty position near her feet.

Over the past few days Louise had given herself a severe talking-to and told herself that she simply had to get on with things and pull herself together. It would be good if she could do it for herself, but if that was insufficient motivation she would have to resort to convincing herself that she would really show him and make him suffer. Fine advice, but difficult to apply. It was all well and good to think of immersing oneself in the practical exigencies of the day, but what if none existed? How could she conjure up something out of nothing, and who would it be for, anyway? Myself, she told herself, but that just wasn't enough. As she tried to reconstruct her life she was constantly reminded of how things used to be and how joyful and easy it all was. How could she keep busy and occupied when the idea of making a telephone call left her wrecked and trembling? He had a lot to answer for.

If there was no one around to remind her of who she was, she knew that she had to try and do that for herself, and if luck held out there might just be something at the end of the day to carry forward as fuel for the days ahead. Louise knew that she had to feed herself, though she did it minimally and with little enjoyment. Gingerly she eased herself out of bed and wandered towards the kitchen, filled an electric kettle, switched it on, picked up a mug from the draining board and put in a tea bag. She sat down on a kitchen chair, closed her eyes and rolled her head in a circle in a vain attempt to offset the tension she felt already building up in her neck and shoulders.

It was one thing to have long conversations with herself and to plot strategies to overcome her despair, but all those illuminating middle-of-the-night thoughts didn't make sense in the morning. The blazing clarity that led to the thread that would unravel the whole of it was soon forgotten, especially when strength and hope could be instantly dashed by the tuneless whistle of Doug Soper as he continued his morning ritual. Louise knew that her anger was irrational and that she should not let a cough and a whistle get to her, but get to her they did, and it made her even angrier that they had this effect. She clenched her fists and remembered that the day before she had gone to the newsagent's shop and ordered a newspaper. She had come up with many plans to find a solution to her wild and wandering despair, most of which she immediately knocked on the head as worthless, but in a rash attempt to try and establish some minor structure and continuity to her day, she had ordered a newspaper to be delivered. Not in itself a profound move, and she had admitted to herself that this was not exactly a landmark victory, but if she could only work it out, it might just represent something important. The battle of the newspaper had taken quite a few hours to win, and in the end Louise had thought it best to start with the *Daily Mail* and work up. It might take some time to win the war, but it was far better and more realistic to start in the middle rather than open a serious newspaper, fail to understand anything and thereby catapult herself into a bout of inadequacy.

So, leaving the kettle to boil, she wrapped herself in a dressing-gown and tentatively edged her way down the stairs to the front door of the house to pick up her newspaper. As was always the way with these things, when she arrived at the bottom of the stairs, the door of the downstairs flat opened and Louise was thrust into contact with her new neighbour.

'Oh, hello. I'm Kate. How lovely to meet you. Actually I was thinking of shoving a note under your door and suggesting you might like to come down and have a drink sometime,' said the cheerful and beaming early-morning face.

'Hello. My name is Louise,' said Louise as she nervously tried to tighten the belt of her dressing-gown. She was feeling a complete idiot. What on earth had made her think she could quietly nip downstairs undetected?

'Well, how about tonight?'

'Tonight what?'

'For a drink.'

'Sorry?'

'Would you like to come down to my flat and have a drink, and sort of introduce ourselves?' said Kate spelling it out and trying to sound patient, but all the while thinking that she didn't usually experience so much trouble putting her ideas across.

'Oh, sorry, I'm a bit thick early in the morning. Tonight?'

'Yes, at about seven,' said Kate, who felt that she had gone too far down the road to change her mind with any decency. 'If that's all right for you.'

Faced with such an enthusiastic barrage, Louise found herself murmuring that it was perfectly all right for her, while she inwardly hoped that she would find a polite way to get out of the commitment later.

'Right then. I'll see you this evening. Well, I must get off to work and hit the daily grind. By the way, who is that ghastly chap next door? He always seems to be hanging around. Whenever I pass by he's cleaning his step or bending down to pick up his milk. Mind you, come to think of it, that's probably for the best. When engaged in conversation, he strikes me as the type who would like to stand very close.'

'Doug Soper. He has a way of making his presence felt, doesn't he? My sister, Jill, who owns the flat upstairs where I'm staying, insists he's not that bad really. She lived here for a couple of years and claims she managed to see a better side. I'm afraid I haven't seen it yet and I doubt if I ever will. I'm not sure I'm equal to the task.'

'Me neither,' said Kate, glancing down at her watch. 'Gracious, I must dash. By the way, red or white wine?'

'Oh, anything.'

'Quite right,' agreed Kate relieved that they were both now

34

on the right track. 'Bye. See you later.' And to prove that she really meant it this time, she tipped her hat and left.

Kate closed the door of the house behind her and thought how enviably slim, attractive and together Louise seemed, even allowing for the early-morning vagueness. But that could happen to anyone, and she had probably been out late the night before. She had looked great wearing a cashmere dressing-gown in a pale pink. It had probably come from Peal's. It had the look of Burlington Arcade about it. Kate thought of her own model, which had been a Christmas present from her mother several years ago and had shrunk in the wash so that it was now a chilly six inches above her ankles. That girl Louise had definitely looked good with the gold chains around her neck and wrists, not to mention the perfectly varnished finger-nails. Perhaps seeing her around would be an incentive to get slim and stick to a diet. What had happened to that diet she had started when she had moved into the flat two weeks ago? Strange how the days went by and nothing got done. Oh, well, a final blast and then start the diet on Monday. Still, there was one good thing, Kate seemed to be off the hook this morning for there was no sign of the ubiquitous Doug. Perhaps he was around the corner terrorizing someone else.

Louise held her newspaper in her hand and mounted the stairs, marvelling at how cheerful and together Kate seemed. Perhaps it would cheer her up having someone so positive and enthusiastic around. Kate had an open and engaging personality and clearly didn't give a damn what she looked like. That morning she had been dressed in many layers of bright and varying colours with an old Burberry raincoat thrown around her shoulders. She was topped out with a Tyrolean hat worn at a jaunty angle and carried a large black leather holdall, which was perilously full and likely to trip her up. She was thoroughly uncontrived and was undoubtedly the most attractive and sympathetic person Louise had met in a long time.

By the time she got back to the kitchen, the kettle had long since boiled, so she turned it on again and sat at the pine table feeling quite calm. She decided to pace herself gently through the day and definitely to go down and have a drink with Kate. It was about time she started to go out and mix with people. Not that going downstairs was exactly going out, in fact many would quite rightly consider that as an evening in, but the evening was to be spent with someone new and for once that prospect did not present a threat. On the contrary, Louise found herself looking forward to it. She made her tea and then sat down to peruse the newspaper. She flicked through the pages and sipped her tea. Every now and then she stopped to take in a headline, but she found that she really wasn't focusing on anything in particular. Nothing, that is, until she turned a page and stared at the Diary. A fiery, irrational and bitter anger surged up in her, and she groaned, 'Damn them, damn them, and damn her in particular.'

All the bitterness that she had ever felt poured out of her and was directed at the photograph of her ex-lover, David, and his new lover, Jacqui, who was smiling away in her abrasive blonde loveliness from the bottom left-hand side of the page. The day had not started too well for Louise, but she had overcome her initial distaste for the hours ahead. She had brought herself to the point of accepting that she was alive for another day and she had been anticipating an evening of gentle conversation, some smiles even, and a few glasses of wine with Kate, who might just turn out to be amusing company. How dare he look happy? And that awful Jacqui. What could he be thinking of? To consider what Jacqui represented completely destroyed the possibility of something good happening and any chance of the day being bearable. Louise knew that she had to talk to Jill immediately, that she had allowed David to hurt her too much, that she detested Jacqui and that she must not allow either of them to inflict any more pain, however unwittingly. She grabbed the telephone and dialled her sister's number.

'Oh, hello, Jill, it's me. I'm in one of my states. Galloping desperation. You know how I get. Something has just happened and it's set me off with a vengeance. I think I'm in danger of going over the top if I don't come and see you right now. I am so cross with myself. I'll explain all when I get there.'

She showered quickly and dried and in her furious haste nearly slipped on the bathroom floor, which was just what she needed at that moment, she thought to herself. She dressed in the same outfit as the day before: a pair of tan leather trousers and a beige cashmere sweater. She brushed her hair hard and swiftly, tossed her head forward and down to her knees, straightened up and ran her fingers through it. Scooping up her handbag in her left hand, she went to the wardrobe, where she lunged towards a hanger which, after a feverish tug, reluctantly yielded its burden of a classically cut tweed jacket. She slammed the wardrobe door closed and then kicked it when it failed to catch.

'Shut, you horrible door. Behave yourself.'

Luck might have been with Kate that morning, but, quite obviously, what with photographs in newspapers and wardrobe doors that failed to close, the gods were not on the side of Louise today. She did remember her front-door key and managed to double-lock the door without breaking a fingernail, but that was about the extent of it. Striding along the pavement with a basket of vegetables in one hand and a loaf of bread in the other came a purposeful Doug.

'Hello-o there.'

'Oh, hello, Doug,' mumbled Louise, who didn't even try to force a smile.

'Well, well, well.'

Louise stood looking at Doug, waiting patiently for him to continue, which, of course, he did.

'Lovely day, isn't it? Definite touch of autumn in the air today. I must say, you can't beat it. Mind you, it will soon be winter, you know. I've just been out to buy some root vegetables and a loaf of bread. Wholemeal of course. I find it's best. Got to look after yourself, you know.'

Doug's desire to state the obvious and to embark upon conversations about the merits of a healthy diet and his internal workings needed to be cut off at the pass on any day of the week, but particularly on this day of days when the very fabric of life had already been threatened with a serious setback by her ex and his present.

For what seemed like an age and a half to her, Louise stood

open-mouthed until she managed to collect herself and get out a forced 'Absolutely, I must dash.' And when it looked as if Doug was about to loom large and close with the idea of manfully linking her arm, always assuming he managed to cope with his wholemeal loaf and basket of roots, and escorting her to her car, she backed off and managed to say, 'I really am frightfully late. Goodbye.'

Doug was not the type to register a brush-off, even if it struck him down never to rise again. He was used to it, and it was quite possible that it had become an occupational hazard all those years ago when he had been a very junior insurance salesman in Pinner prior to his elevation to the giddy heights of Kilburn and Head Office. He was a man who knew his bran and his roughage, but clearly not his place.

Louise tried hard to apply herself to the task of driving, but found her angry thoughts wandering inevitably to Jacqui. What was it about that girl that so infuriated Louise, so enraged her and had her mind springing to extremes of irrationality? Just about everything, it seemed. Doubtless, at the age of three, Jacqui had been picked up by her doting father and eased lovingly on to his knee. He had then told her that she was the prettiest girl in the world and that she could have anything she wanted, and things had started to go wrong for everyone around her from that moment on, because the little princess believed him. She had carried his words like a banner before her into every situation for all the world to see, and the thing that made it even worse to stomach was that everyone seemed to be only too happy to go along with the notion and let her carry on with the fantasy. David included. The fool. How could he be so stupid? Louise shook herself out of the mire and realized that she had driven a long way and didn't quite know how. Somehow she had come along Ladbroke Grove which certainly wasn't the most direct route, so she must have gone on automatic pilot when she'd left Vaucluse Road and imagined that she was heading home to Bourne Street and the old days. She had negotiated Shepherd's Bush without incident and here she was all of a sudden about to surge over Hammersmith Bridge. The drive was familiar. From the flat, which Louise and Jill described as being down Ladbroke Grove, left and over a bit, quite a long way down and then quite a bit left and over, to Sheen took thirty minutes, which was good going in the morning traffic.

The tree-lined street of semi-detached houses looked solid and substantial. There were remnants of abundant summer gardens, which had had time and care lavished upon them. Roses bloomed, an LEB van was weaving down the road and a group of mothers and children were heading for play school. An idyllic setting in which it might be possible to be quite overcome with goodwill, were it not for acute anger and distrust of humanity. It was only to be hoped that all those involved in this surburban tapestry of delight were aware of their good fortune and were not given to attacks of smugness when they hit Safeway on a Friday morning.

Louise parked her car outside number twenty-six, nimbly emerged, and positively flew to the front door. Tubs of geraniums lined the porch and clematis poured over the wooden structure. It was not the morning to reflect on what a nice touch it was. It was the sort of morning when only an extended palm thrust at the bell and a muttered 'Oh, hurry up, will you?' would do.

Alerted by the telephone call that something serious was up, Jill was waiting for the doorbell to ring and answered it rapidly. She looked inquisitively at Louise while she held her baby, Rory, balanced on her left hip. Jill was younger than Louise by two years, was four inches shorter and was rounded in all the wrong places. They had always been close, but in the past two months Jill had spent hours talking to Louise, trying to help her as best she could, cajoling and soothing her through her mixed and depressing days. She told Louise time and time again that things would eventually improve and that she would understand, but there were times when she doubted the veracity of her words.

Louise kissed Jill lightly on the cheek, gave Rory a quick squeeze, and then marched straight through to the large kitchen at the back of the house.

'I feel lousy. You won't believe what happened this morning.

I can hardly believe it myself. I hate myself for being so angry. When is this going to stop? Have you seen the *Daily Mail* this morning?'

'Not all of it. I was just reading an article on teachers. It's having a real go at them and well it might. Teachers are such a pain. I agree with everything it says,' said Jill, following Louise into the kitchen and putting Rory down on the floor.

'But you're a teacher.'

'Yes, so I am. Or so I was. But there are teachers and teachers. Anyway, more to the point, what's happened that has so upset you?'

Louise looked as if she was going to sit down, but kept changing her mind and paced back and forth across the kitchen.

'I'll take a deep breath and start from the beginning. Any coffee on the go?' Louise went over to the kettle, tested the heat with her palm, and then flicked it on.

'Instant will do. Well, there I was feeling all good and prepared to behave and get on with the day. I was doing brilliantly until I saw a picture of you know who in the paper. You know who in the form of David and you know who in the form of the loathsome Jacqui. They've made it into Nigel Dempster, and the sight of her smiling out at me sent me plummeting to the depths. I know it's irrational, and that's what makes it so difficult and infuriating.'

Jill turned the pages of the newspaper. 'I see what you mean.'

'It's gruesome, isn't it?'

'It's a pretty frightening sight. What an awful dress she's wearing. What could she be thinking of? If I was to say she's obviously got a very distorted sense of her own femininity, since she finds it necessary to wear such an item in public, would that help?'

'Not really. David is standing alongside her. He seems to like her that way.'

'Oh, sorry.' Jill paused, tried to come up with a positive approach and to change the worn subject, but found herself drawn to the photograph.

'If I was to say that only awful people get their photo in

newspapers, would *that* help? Well, that's not strictly true, I suppose, because there's a charming photograph of the Queen Mother on the front page. No, how about only awful and pitiful people get their photo in the Nigel Dempster column? Is that nearer the mark?'

'But I've been in the Nigel Dempster column.'

'So you have. Well, in this piece about David and Jacqui, at least they haven't mentioned you, which shows they do have some sense of decency. It was probably written by a woman.'

'Don't get carried away, Jill,' said a bitter Louise.

'I'm not doing at all well this morning, am I? Do sit down. You're making me nervous marching up and down, and it's not going to help. The kettle has boiled. I'll make some coffee and try and think of something constructive.'

Louise bent down to kiss her nephew, Rory, who was sitting on the floor surrounded by toys, blissfully unaware that one day he would be a grown-up. He grinned up at her happily, and for a moment Louise thought that life really could be simple. She looked around the lovely kitchen and at her sister, who was making two mugs of coffee and putting out some biscuits on a plate. Jill had always had flair and style and had made a beautiful job of the house, as well as the flat in Vaucluse Road. She was also deceptively sharp and shrewd, buying the flat at the right time, doing it up cleverly for very little and then hanging on to it after her marriage, as she wanted some independence and her own investment. It had proved to be a providential move, since the flat, which had been rented, had become vacant when Louise needed a place to stay, and so she had moved in. Jill and Roger had moved into the house in Sheen shortly after their marriage, and again it had been decorated with skill and flair. Money had not mattered to Louise and David, and they had hired an interior decorator to do the house in Bourne Street. Louise was not sure which approach she preferred as she looked at the huge kitchen, with the wooden units, the Spanish tiles and the Aga, which she knew had taken Jill and Roger hours of work and thought to put together.

Jill returned to the large table in the centre of the kitchen, and Louise remarked, 'It's very clever of Rory to sit up like that on his own, but he's only eight months old – don't you think we should put a cushion behind him in case he suddenly forgets and crashes to the floor in a heap?'

'He won't forget. Anyway, they sort of just roll over in a ball and giggle, shove their bottoms in the air and lurch away into a crawl. Believe it or not, you used to giggle a lot. Roll on the day when you have a good laugh again. Look, Louise, I know that David and Jacqui hurt you, but I think you're destroying yourself with all this anger.'

'Well, if they're on overload, they damn well deserve it.'

'I think it would be a good idea to try and remember exactly who Jacqui is. You might also try and think along the lines that if David could fall for her, you're well shot of him.'

'But . . .' interrupted Louise.

'Let me finish,' said Jill rather sharply. She didn't like talking in circles and she had done a lot of it lately. 'I'll tell you something. She's a tart. Quite simply a tart. She has had three marriages, all of them disastrous, she's drifted from relationship to relationship, she has never been able to hold down a job, she has never done anything remotely constructive with her life. Quite frankly, she's a mess. Above all, she is not a happy woman. Think about it. She is not a picture of achievement.'

'Oh, really, Jill, are you suggesting that I should start feeling sorry for her? That I should start making allowances for her? At this point in my life I'm trying to make allowances for myself. I really don't have a lot left over for anyone else. Besides, she is living with David and I am not.'

'I don't mean that, and you know I don't. I think you're deliberately getting the wrong end of the stick. You are having to make a lot of adjustments at the moment; I know that whenever I say it will take time, you don't believe me. What happened this morning is that the photograph of David and Jacqui triggered off an outburst of anger, which, understandably, is just below the surface and likely to erupt at any time. But try and get things in perspective. David behaved like a pig, and because you are still in love with him and actually would go back to him like a shot, you won't allow yourself to get really angry with him. The result is you let rip at Jacqui. Quite frankly I'd be much happier if you put a photograph of David on a dartboard and invited us all round to see you score a bull's-eye.'

'I wish it was that simple,' said Louise with a sniff, for she was crying silently.

'So do I, believe me. No, it's not that simple. It takes a lot of understanding, but you have the desire to understand, and I know you will come through this and really show David what a mistake he made. I don't know what he could be thinking of.'

'I'm frightened that I'm jealous of her. I'm frightened because I don't respect her and therefore, if I'm rational, there is nothing to be jealous of. But I *am* jealous and increasingly bitter, and you are so right it *is* destroying me, yet I don't seem to be able to stop it. I don't want to be her, I really don't. I just want to be in her position, which is, with David. What on earth got into him? That confuses me as well. I'm beginning to think I never knew him. Look at them both, smiling, happy. It makes me sick.'

Jill and Louise looked again at the photograph in the newspaper.

'You know, I think he's thinner and his hair's longer. It doesn't suit him,' observed Jill.

'I thought he was thinner too. She probably doesn't feed him. She has to be taken out every night. You know, be seen at Annabel's and Langan's.'

'He'll get bored with that.'

'I hope so. I hope it costs him a fortune.'

'Well, she is awful. I mean, she is not going to surprise us all by changing her perfect record for wreaking havoc. Come on, now. Think about it. A series of husbands and lovers, barely conscious for most of her adult life, and, while I am at it, I might as well mention that awful business in the hotel in Bombay. I don't suppose we'll ever get to the bottom of what actually went on. I wonder what on earth happened to the rest of them? You are an infinitely more impressive character than she will ever be. I would like to think she's in awe of you, but as she's for the most part zonked out on goodness knows what, it's a subject which is unlikely to occur to her.'

Louise pulled a Kleenex out of her handbag and blew hard.

'You're right, of course. I can't stand her. In fact I detest her. I really don't know what David sees in her.'

'Well done. That's much healthier by far,' said Jill with a grin. 'I think you are coming around. Do you want to insult her? It usually does a girl good. You go first.'

'She dyes her hair,' tried Louise. 'She's actually mousy brown and has freckles.'

'How about she's got thick ankles?'

'Can't cook.'

'She's got dirty finger-nails.'

'She wears tips. They're very long. They look wonderful.'

'Does she?' asked Jill. 'I've often wondered about them, but thought I might lose them while making an apple crumble.'

'I think they stay on. It is difficult to hold a pen though.'

'Well, she wouldn't do that anyway. She's illiterate.'

'Quite. Where was I?'

'Insulting her. Your turn next.'

'Right. How about she can't sing?'

'Not strictly true, she made a record once.'

'I heard it, she can't sing.'

'She's got big hips.'

'She had a nose job,' said Louise, who was really getting into the swing of it.

'She can't ride a bike.'

'She's got knock knees.'

'She failed her O levels.'

'Failed her O levels? She didn't even pass the eleven plus.'

'She's riddled with cellulite.'

'She had breast implants.'

'Did she really? I didn't know that,' said Jill in a rather awed tone and then, getting straight back to the point, she offered, 'She's got no friends.'

'She's got David. She's living with him. I've said it before and I'll say it again: I really don't know what he could be thinking of.'

'Neither can I. Oh, Louise, you're hopeless, we're back at the beginning.'

Jill bent down to pick up Rory, who hadn't forgotten how to sit up, but was proving himself to be a very good baby. She put him on Louise's lap and suggested, 'Play with your nephew and think good and positive thoughts. Do you want to stay for lunch? I know you're bored with me trying to get you to eat, but couldn't you try? You are too thin.'

'I don't think I'm too thin. I like myself this way. At least allow me that,' snapped Louise, who was very touchy on the frequently mentioned subject of weight, because she knew she was indeed too thin. She hoped that she would bump into David somewhere and he would be horrified at her state and really feel bad.

'I am concerned about you. You seem to be deliberately getting thinner and thinner. I know you are under stress, but do be careful. Everyone who sees you remarks on how dreadfully thin you are.'

'At least they notice.'

It was the sort of remark that made Jill want to thump Louise, and she probably would have done had she not been her sister.

'You are not as isolated as you think. A lot of people care about you, though they probably don't know how to tell you. Well, I'm telling you now that I care about you and I love you, so does Roger and so does Rory. Now look at me.'

Louise looked up and bit her lower lip.

'Stop feeling sorry for yourself. Give Rory a big hug and if you feel like it, have a good cry.'

'Yes, I think I will,' sobbed Louise as she gave in to a huge gulp and some serious tears.

Jill looked around the kitchen in search of a box of Kleenex, while she tried to be brave herself, knowing that she was on the brink of a quiet sob. She moved her chair closer to Louise and put her arms around her. Louise clasped Rory tighter and he responded by gurgling, kicking his stubby little legs and trying to wave his arms, which were trapped amidst the sisters' arms and tears. Jill gave a gentle sniff.

'May I borrow your Kleenex? It's going to be all right, Louise. Honestly it is. I promise.'

Louise turned to her sister and took back the sodden Kleenex, as she needed to do a bit more mopping up and dabbing.

'Jill, what did Rory have for his breakfast? I think he's been sick.'

Chapter Four

It had been one of those mornings, and how! The photocopying machine had broken down, the artwork for the posters for the Bradford conference had got lost and when Michael had got to Heathrow to catch a plane to Chicago, his travellers' cheques had not been at the bank. Kate was extremely proud of herself for the way she had coped with the crisis, which had hit at full blast at 10.30 am when Michael had telephoned from the airport in a terminal panic, and of the way she had handled herself when under pressure, but the strain was beginning to tell. It wasn't just the mental effort involved in dealing with machines, printers and banks, but more the draining of her inner resources as she had been called upon to be pleasant and soothing to all the parties in each fracas. She had risen quite brilliantly to the occasion, but was now, at 4 pm, well able to give a fine impression of a woman about to faint. Aware that her star was rising high, she was mulling over just how she could capitalize on this good fortune and leave the office before she finally gave in to fatigue.

She stared out of the window at the afternoon sunlight and beavered away at the problem for a full ten minutes before she turned to Ned, who, having had a long and adequate lunch at Langan's, was looking fairly relaxed and feeling absolutely no pain at all. She straightened her back, fixed a smile and was pleasantly surprised at the level of chirpiness and confidence she heard in her voice.

'Ned, while things are quiet after the storm, and as I've finished everything I have to do, I think I'm going to slope off now and nip down to Fortnum & Mason's to pick up their Christmas catalogue. It might be an idea if I got a head start on the company presents this year. I don't want a repeat of last year's performance, when everything was left until the very last minute and Michael couldn't make up his mind between sending a bottle of port or an executive toy. You know how irritating he can be when he gets picky.'

'It's only October. It's a bit early, isn't it?' came his helpful response.

'You can never be too early. I've also got some ideas for Christmas cards, and, as you're supposed to be the artistic one, you might like to cast your eye over them and give your seal of approval. I thought we'd go for a bit of fine art this year rather than one of those crude cartoons. I am sure a nice snowy land-scape and a carefully worded goodwill message would appeal to Michael and all his friends.'

'Couldn't you phone them and ask for the catalogue to be sent in the post?'

Kate glowered at Ned with a look that said, 'I know you've rumbled me, but don't you dare say it out loud, otherwise I'll clobber you.'

'There's nothing like the personal touch. It's always a good idea to establish a relationship with some nice young man in the hamper department. It tends to come in handy later. When you're in a fix and not knowing what to send to your aunt, I can step in with the helpful suggestion that you call my young man in hampers, and before you know it a handsome farmhouse cheddar, gift-wrapped no less, will have been dispatched all the way to Bridlington. So, if you don't mind, my old son, I'll be off.'

Kate tried to flash a look at Ned to warn him not to say any more, but found her heart wasn't in it when he winked at her. She opened her large leather holdall and scooped her diary and address book off her desk and into her bag. She then looked around and spied a notebook and a clutch of felt-tipped pens, which she prudently banged on the desk in order to secure their tops before tossing them into her bag.

'Now, did I bring an umbrella today? Can anyone remember, because I sure as hell can't. Geoffrey!'

'He's gone out to the betting shop.'

'Martin, have you seen my umbrella?'

'He's gone out for a run.'

'Oh, well, I wouldn't like to disturb anyone!' snapped Kate, wondering just why she felt it necessary to construct excuses when she felt like taking a few hours off. It seemed to her that it was more extraordinary to find the rest of the company in the office.

'Oh, never mind, it will turn up later,' continued Kate. 'And I suppose if I didn't bring it with me, it'll be at home.'

'My, aren't we sharp today?' observed Ned.

'Thank you, Ned,' enunciated Kate in a very clipped manner. 'All I have to say to you is that I am off.' She put on her Burberry raincoat and her hat, noticed that she'd pulled a thread in her dark green woollen tights, but thought that no one else would notice and if they did they surely wouldn't think any the less of her. She checked her bag again and at the conclusion of her search she once again said that she was off. Vicky, their secretary, who had had a very exacting morning booking squash courts for Martin and phoning through to Joe Coral's for Geoffrey, looked up from the magazine she was reading. How much of the information contained therein she retained and would find useful later, was open to question. When Kate asked her to take any messages for her, the look of bewilderment that stole across her features convinced Kate that she was just about to say, 'Messages for you, you old bag? You've got to be joking. No one ever calls you.'

Polite to the end, Kate said, 'I'll see you all tomorrow then,' but got little response, as Martin and Geoffrey were both out and Vicky had returned to her magazine. Although Ned was deep in a newspaper, he did at least see fit to raise his left hand in a brief wave.

'Kate.'

'Yes, Ned,' she said, as she spun round, all agog with anticipation.

'You were brilliant this morning. Thank you.'

Oh, what a man. Not knowing quite what to say, she took a dramatic gulp of air, rested her forehead against the door, attempted a misty-eyed look somewhat unsuccessfully, mouthed 'bye' and blew him a kiss.

As Kate bounced down the stairs, she pondered on whether she should be true to her excuse and go down to Fortnum's to pick up a catalogue or whether she could get away with telephoning them in the morning and having one sent. At this time of day it would take a while to get to Piccadilly, and then, of course, she wouldn't be able to find a place to park. If she wrote a note in her diary telling herself that she had to telephone Fortnum & Mason re catalogue, that should do it. As soon as she got into her car she rummaged in her copious holdall, located her diary, and, to her surprise, a pen at first go and wrote, 'Phone F & M, don't forget'. She knew it was highly likely that she would forget and she did want to keep up the appearance of efficiency so recently established that morning. She looked again at the cryptic note and rewrote it, putting in the words 'Fortnum' and 'Mason', because in its original state she thought it quite possible that she would think she had to phone Fiona and Malcolm. She hadn't seen them for quite a long time – not since their dinner party last autumn, in fact, when there had been that embarrassing incident with the Beaujolais *nouveau* and the quiet young gentleman from the Austrian Embassy seated to her left. Come to think of it, she had him to thank for her Tyrolean hat. Poor thing, he had been so confused and in such a rush to leave that he had forgotten that fine specimen of his august heritage and had left it there, all alone and abandoned in the hall.

She had only to stop at an off-licence and buy some wine on the way home and perhaps a few nuts and nibbles. It was always nice to offer nuts, but usually Kate found herself eating all of them. One cashew and it was impossible to stop. She wondered if it would be the same with caviare and suspected it might well be. Perhaps she was not destined to be the sophisticated type, the sort of person who would delicately play with a piece of smoked salmon and refuse an olive because she instinctively knew that it was impossible to deal with the stone with any degree of decorum or dignity. At parties Kate usually found herself with both hands full and nowhere to put a pip, a stone or a cocktail stick.

It was Wednesday, and all that appeared on the social horizon was drinks tonight with Louise, which Kate hoped wasn't going to be too onerous. Perhaps she had been a little too quick off the mark with her invitation and her desire to get to know her neighbour had been misplaced. Oh, well, one drink and then call it a day if necessary. She was planning to go and see Peter and Lizzie on Sunday, and that was about it. What she could really do with right now was a work trip somewhere interesting, or, on second thoughts, a trip anywhere. Not that the new flat was beginning to wear thin. No, that side of things delighted her. Something was missing somehow, and she was not quite sure what. There was the obvious gap left by not having Nick in her life, but they'd spent weeks, months even, apart in the past ten years, so it shouldn't really be any different now.

Kate thought, as she drove through Notting Hill Gate, which was bright and busy, about what the missing piece might be. Try as she might, her life seemed either to be in a turmoil, with too many things to do, or else distressingly close to the other end of the scale, when she had too few things to do and too much time to think about the missing piece of the jigsaw, the piece that would make sense of it all. As she turned the car into Vaucluse Road, she felt calmer and knew that here at least, behind her own front door, she didn't have to put on a show and could be herself, whoever she was at the moment. She could wait here until some greater force led her to her true self and complete understanding. The sooner it came along, preferably in the shape of a man, the better it would be.

As soon as she got through her front door she realized that she had committed the cardinal error of forgetting to buy the wine. Such had been her preoccupation with the larger issues of life that the main event of the evening had passed from her mind. Kate wondered if she shouldn't come to an arrangement with the local off-licence and have wine delivered by the case-load, but was not sure that the move was suitable for a single lady living on her own. Didn't it smack of a certain desperation? – no take it or leave it, but an attitude of wanting to know it's there, available and in quantity. In the case of other single ladies residing in peace, it would undoubtedly appear as being tremendously organized, and praise would be lavished upon their attention to detail, their foresight and capability. It was a sad fact, but Kate's vision of herself was such that she felt that if she pursued this line of action, it would result in raised eyebrows and knowing comments.

Betraying only the briefest flash of annoyance, she spun right around and walked to the local off-licence, which was a fast ten minutes' walk away, but as she had found a place to park her car right across the road from the flat, it didn't seem worth driving. There were very few people about so early on a midweek evening, save for the ever present and creeping Doug Soper, who had just embarked upon the thrifty purchase of a bottle of sweet sherry from the wood. The man serving in the off-licence seemed very friendly and helpful. He suggested a Muscadet and a Beaujolais Villages on the grounds that you couldn't go far wrong with those and that at a push they would appeal to even the most discerning of palates. He was the sort of chap who might well become a useful contact. He might provide a special rate for bulk purchases for parties and come good with the glasses. Such was the stuff of dreams.

In the fridge Kate had an opened bottle of white wine. It was a large green bottle and had started its life provided with a metal cap. In its present state, which was open with its neck stuffed with a piece of kitchen roll, there was no way it could be laid on its side to make room for the Muscadet, so she thought she might as well have a quick one now and drink it while she lay in the bath. It would help her unwind from the rigours of the day, and after all, if she didn't drink it now, she would only drink it later.

As she passed the aquarium, she said good evening to the fish, threw in some food, attempted to give them both a tickle and walked on to her lovely bathroom. She turned on the water and dribbled in some Floris Ormonde bath oil because she liked it and because it permeated the entire flat, lending an air of luxury and extravagance. She decided to change her clothes, as it seemed churlish not to make an effort, so while the bath was running she went to her bedroom and opened the doors of the fitted cupboards. There were a lot of clothes in the cupboards and it had taken an entire Sunday afternoon to arrange them in groups of skirts, shirts, dresses, jackets, smart clothes and clothes to dress up in for grand occasions, and yet the right thing for tonight did not immediately leap out at her. When in doubt, go for comfort, she told herself, as she selected a faithful old soft-denim skirt, a checked Viyella shirt, a wide cowboy belt, some big red wooden beads and a yellow sweater to throw around her shoulders. She spread the clothes on the double bed and wandered back to the bathroom, undressed, turned off the taps and slid into the hot and soothing water. As she lay back in the bath she sipped her wine and tried to think of nothing in particular.

Louise had also had a long bath and was now lying in bed trying to sink into sleep. Every now and then she did drift off, but she came winging back to consciousness with a bump, and, as it was clear that a fast thirty-minute nap was going to elude her, she decided to concentrate on what to wear to go downstairs to see Kate. It wasn't really a mighty problem and certainly not one that was going to defeat her, but as it seemed the only thing worth discussing with herself that erred on the side of having a logical conclusion, she thought she might just as well give it a try. The result of all this internal talk and imaginings was the decision to wear the same leather trousers that she had first put on that morning but to replace the sweater with a cream silk blouse and a string of pearls. Having got that far, she sank back into the pillows in order to summon up the energy to follow through with the actual dressing and then the walking out of the door, down the stairs and into a room with a stranger.

At seven o'clock Kate topped up her glass of wine and wondered just what she had got herself into. Her first impression of Louise had been that she was very nice, but, of course that impression had been based upon a few fleeting minutes of early-morning conversation in the hallway. She looked down at her comfortable shoes, which, although they had been an expensive and wise purchase at the time, were now scuffed and down at heel, and remembered the gorgeous pink cashmere dressing-gown wrapped around the very slim and stylish figure of Louise. She took a long sip of her wine, followed by a gulp, and reflected on her mother's words of encouragement when she left university and was about to launch herself on the working world. That piece of advice – looks weren't everything and she should always remember to be thankful that at least she had personality – came back to haunt her time and time again.

Louise seized a bottle of champagne from her fridge and hoped that by offering it to Kate it would get her over the first few awkward minutes. Not that she had always been like this. Far from it. She used to walk into a room with her head held high and there had been none of this reticence and stooping. Shakes, flutters and complete inability to speak were here to plague her now and she wondered for how long this was going to go on. It had hit overnight, and even though she told herself she was made of sterner stuff, it didn't seem to do the trick. She picked up her Chanel handbag and threw the chain strap over her left shoulder, reached for and clasped the champagne firmly and then scooped up her keys in her right hand. She was on her way and got down the staircase with only one pause.

Moments passed and Kate sank inside as she looked at the elegantly dressed Louise standing at her opened door with the proffered bottle of champagne. On the other side of the doorway Louise dithered and tried to remain calm as she looked at an open, welcoming and smiling Kate standing back and asking her to come in. Kate watched her guest glide in and neatly sit down, while Louise for her part was grateful to find the chair, as she thought her knees were going to give out and collapse.

'How kind of you to bring this champagne,' said Kate, who was inspecting the bottle and had discovered that it was Dom Pérignon. 'Shall we open it now?' she inquired and even as she did so she was concerned as to whether she had said the right thing.

'Oh, yes, I'd love a glass,' agreed Louise without hesitation, which seemed to indicate that there was a possibility that all was not lost and that the evening might not be too tortuous after all.

As Kate went to the kitchen in search of champagne glasses, she thought once again how slim Louise appeared. Actually, she was more than slim; she was thin, very thin indeed. Kate took the glasses down from the glass-fronted cupboard and returned to the sitting-room, where Louise presented a composed and altogether elegant picture. Kate opened the champagne with expert ease, which, she thought to herself, was pretty impressive, and poured two glasses. Handing a glass to Louise and then taking one herself, Kate said, 'Cheers.'

'Cheers,' returned a smiling Louise.

'You're wonderfully slim. I do envy you,' said Kate by way of an opener and then immediately wished she hadn't.

'I don't know. My sister thinks I'm too thin. She was going on about it today. She actually went as far as to tell me she thought I was anorexic, which is absolutely ridiculous.'

'Well, there's not a lot to be said for anorexia, other than it beats the hell out of being fat. I wouldn't mind a fast and efficient dose, I can tell you.'

'No, I don't think you would.'

They both sipped their champagne and thought a great deal about what to say next. They seemed to have exhausted the first topic of conservation. Louise looked around the cosy room and so did Kate. At one point their eyes met. Louise looked away quickly and Kate issued an encouraging smile. In an effort to keep the conversation going Louise remarked, 'I see you have some fish. How very interesting.'

'Well, they were given to me,' said Kate. 'They're not necessarily the sort of company I would have chosen for myself. Ned – he's a chap I work with – said I was getting very over-excited one day and that he was going out to get me something to calm me down. Well, I thought he was going to come back with a handful of Valium, but he arrived with two fish in a bowl and told me to sit down in the corner and watch them for an hour as it would soothe me and stop me from being such a pain around the office. I very nearly called them Val and Lib, but wasn't sure that many people would appreciate the joke. So the little dears ended up being dubbed Eric and Jimmy. Eric is the one with the black spots. He's the livelier of the two. Jimmy is very exotic and he tends to be a bit reserved. As far as they can be, they've turned out to be quite good company.'

'I've got a cat,' said Louise. 'Have you seen him? He seems to spend most of his time asleep, but as he gets used to the flat and his new surroundings he occasionally wanders outside and does a bit of prowling in the garden. He jumps out of the bedroom window, walks across the roof of your bathroom and then jumps down into the garden. He's a big fat tabby.'

'Oh, he's yours. Yes, I have seen him round and about in the garden. What's he called?'

'Patrick. I'm not quite sure now why we called him Patrick. I know there was a good reason at the time and I think it was rather funny, but I've completely forgotten.'

At least they shared a degree of dottiness about pets, thought Kate. They both sipped their champagne, and this time Kate took the initiative and was the first to start up the conversation again by saying, 'You mentioned this morning that the flat upstairs belongs to your sister and that you are just staying there. How long have you been there?'

This was quite a leading question, and Louise was unsure how to handle it, other than by telling the truth.

'Yes, I moved in about six weeks ago, four weeks before you. It was about two weeks ago, wasn't it, that you moved in?'

'Yes, that's right.'

Trying hard to deflect the conversation and to guide it in another direction, Louise said, 'And are you happy here so far? Is it a change from your previous place? Do you see yourself staying here for a long time?' Louise eased herself back into her chair and hoped that she had fed Kate with enough fuel to keep her going for quite a while.

'I love it here. I'm so thrilled with this flat. My previous flat was lovely, but positively grim compared with this. I have the most sensational bathroom. In fact, that's what appealed to me when I viewed the place and, quite honestly, I think that's the reason I bought it. Anyway, I also love the garden. I know it needs a lot of work, but it has so many possibilities. Don't you adore the garden? I'm hoping to do lots of things with it. But as

55

to the future, I'm not sure that I can bring myself to think about it in any long-term way. What about you?'

'I don't think I have a future,' slipped out from Louise, who had dropped her guard during the description of the rubbish tip that passed for a garden.

'I'll drink to that. I know exactly what you mean,' said Kate as she poured more champagne. They both seemed to have downed their first glasses rather quickly.

Thinking with an adroitness that surprised her, Louise calculated that it was better to let Kate do the talking, as she seemed to be extremely good at it and was in her element doing so. She could then just listen; she didn't feel like speaking, besides which she was all talked out after her morning with Jill. Toying with her champagne, which she was rather enjoying, she said, 'You don't want to think about the future? That usually means you don't think you have a present or, if you do, you don't feel part of it and it's not the present you want.'

Kate thought that this was very perceptive and really rather profound. It made her feel that there was someone who truly understood what she was about and it also gave her the strong desire immediately to tell all.

'Well, I've been involved with this man, you see, for absolutely ever. And just before I moved in here, I decided that it was about time I called it a day. The thing just wasn't going anywhere. You see, the problem is that he's married. Same old story, I know, and as boring as hell, but there you are. I wish I could say I feel on a moral high, but I don't. I feel absolutely wretched and if I don't keep a strong hold on myself I just know I'll have him back in a flash,' confided Kate in a rush.

'Is he wonderful?'

'No, he's a shit. Always has been, always will be.'

'He's fascinating then.'

'The most interesting man I've ever met.'

'Disastrous. Good-looking as well?'

'Delicious.'

'Oh, dear. It's a fatal combination.'

'I know. You don't have to tell me.'

'How long for?'

'Ten years, off and on. A lot of "off", but quite a bit of "on" too.'

'A long time.'

'My best years.' The conversation seemed in danger of taking rather a morbid turn, so Kate gallantly intervened by asking, 'Would you like a crisp?'

'No, thank you.'

Kate filled her palm with crisps and thought that Louise looked like the type not to indulge, but at least she wasn't holding back on the champagne, which was a good and encouraging sign. It would have been awful if she'd turned out to be a Perrier-water-and-exercise nut.

'More champagne?' offered Kate, bottle in hand, ready and eager to pour.

'Yes, please. I am enjoying it,' said Louise enthusiastically.

'So, will you only be staying for a while in the flat upstairs, Louise? Is this just a temporary measure?' questioned Kate, quite legitimately she thought.

'I really don't know. I'm in a bit of a mess at the moment, actually,' said Louise, thinking to herself that she was a fool for saying so, but somehow she was unable to stop. She was wounded, why not let them know, why all this bravery and pretending that she could manage? She couldn't manage and she needed to talk. She needed help, but she didn't know how to ask for it.

Kate said, 'Oh, I'm so sorry,' which seemed like the only thing to say and as often happens with such lines, it hung in the air while both Kate and Louise wondered if it was going to be answered.

'It's a frightfully long and complicated story. I won't bore you with it,' said Louise in a voice that pleaded to be allowed to tell everything.

'Oh, please do,' urged Kate, edging forward on her chair.

They both took a contemplative sip of champagne, sat back in their chairs, shifted their positions slightly to try and find a greater degree of comfort, as it was impossible to know just how long this story was going to take, finally crossed their legs and waited.

'Well, to start at the beginning, two months ago I discovered that the man I was living with was having an affair.'

'The beast.'

'Quite.'

'Go on.'

'Not only was he having an affair, but he was having an affair with someone I thought of as a friend, though, of course, now I can't stand her and can't imagine why I thought of her as a friend in the first place.'

'Isn't it always the way?' agreed Kate.

'Isn't it just?'

'Carry on.'

'Well,' said Louise, gathering her thoughts, 'we had been together for five years, so much of what I'm dealing with now is that I think I didn't really know him. I mean, how could he do that? Was he lying to me all those years?'

'Exactly. Men!' exclaimed Kate.

'Absolutely,' agreed Louise.

'Do you think he had other affairs while you were living with him?'

'Well, I don't think so, but how can I tell? I really am confused and sometimes imagine that David was at it all the time and that I completely misread him and what our relationship was.'

'Well, you would, wouldn't you? Have some more champagne,' offered Kate, as she needed more herself.

'Men.'

'They can be beasts, can't they?'

'They most certainly can.'

'When did you first suspect something was wrong?' asked Kate.

'Well, you won't believe this, but he told me about her. Over dinner.'

'He didn't!'

'Yes, he did.'

'The wretch. What a nice surprise that must have been,' said Kate, wishing that Nick had had a bit more courage, as it might have helped their cause along the way.

'The thing is,' said Louise, 'I should have guessed something was up when David asked me to marry him.'

'Well, yes, that should have made you think a bit. But you were probably busy saying yes.'

'Quite.'

'When was the wedding supposed to be?'

'November.'

'Reception booked, was it?'

'The Orangerie.'

Kate wondered if she dared ask, took a sip of her champagne, and decided she might as well take the risk: 'Your dress ordered?'

'Yes,' sighed Louise, 'almost finished.'

'What colour?'

'Ecru.'

'A wise choice.'

'It was a suit. With a peplum.'

'Quite. A long dress wouldn't have been right. Not in the circumstances.'

'Exactly. I was going to carry a single lily.'

'Very evocative. I've always hankered after freesias myself.'

'They wilt.'

'Oh.' Champagne, and more of it, seemed the only way to go at this point.

'Let's have another bottle of champagne,' said Kate, hoping that it might brighten up the proceedings. 'I've got a bottle in the fridge. It's a rather inferior variety, but I think champagne is the only thing to drink tonight. Oh, you poor thing, I can hardly bear it. Stay put, don't move a finger, I won't be a minute. That's awful, absolutely awful. Men! Do you know something? I really don't know what he could be thinking of,' confided Kate as she stood in the middle of the sitting-room, not knowing quite what to do or say until she remembered that she was supposed to go into the kitchen and get a bottle of champagne from the fridge. Well, that will teach me, thought Kate to herself, so much for my problems. She tried to imagine how Louise must be feeling, how deceived and used, and thought that she understood a bit. She knew that she had to snap out of her own despair and that there was nothing like listening to someone else's problems for helping to put one's own self-doubt into perspective.

Louise quietly sipped her champagne and felt much calmer. It was doing her good to chat and she recognized that she had to learn to let things go. She could exist in her own right, and living as someone else's shadow was no good at all. During the past two months, even though Jill and Roger had been very supportive, she had felt totally isolated. The telephone didn't ring very much. Did people think she didn't want to hear from them or was it simply that they didn't know what to say? It might be that. Perhaps the reality was that all those good friends had only wanted to be around her when she was with David and that they had never really wanted to know her for herself. So, rewrite the address book, said Louise to herself, and make sure they were all real people and not just fringe, good-time hangers-on.

Kate returned to the sitting-room, opened the second bottle of champagne and poured two glasses. She took a grateful sip and felt genuine remorse when she said, 'Oh, Louise, I'm so sorry, how dreadful for you. I do apologize for droning on about Nick.'

'Gracious, don't be,' assured Louise. 'It did me good to hear about it. We seem to be in much the same boat.'

'Yes, we do. And I don't suppose we're the only ones.'

'The trouble is that along with the hurt and the anger, I am going through so much self-doubt at the moment,' said Louise. 'Most of the time I am asking myself what is wrong with me. What is it about me that was wrong? Where did I fail? I would put it right in an instant if only I knew.'

'I ask myself that all the time,' admitted Kate.

'Isn't it ridiculous?' said Louise. 'Why can't I pick up my confidence and say to myself, "Well, it's his loss, my gain," and go off into the arms of someone else and get on with life?'

'I know, I know,' said Kate, and unfortunately she did know, only too well. 'Where did you live?'

'We had a house in Bourne Street. Well, I suppose the truth is, he had a house in Bourne Street, and I lived in it with him. She's there now, of course.'

'It's enough to make you sick.'

'Exactly,' agreed Louise.

'So, how did you come to be living upstairs?' asked Kate.

'Well, when everything went crazy, I decided to leave David and went to stay with Jill, that's my sister, and her husband, Roger. They were awfully good about it. It wasn't easy. All those telephone calls in the middle of the night, and I must have gone back to him half a dozen times during the first week. It was quite ridiculous. Lots of crying and lots of packing and lots of fights in between.'

'I can imagine.'

'Fortunately for me, the flat upstairs became vacant, and I was able to move in. Jill bought it about eight years ago, hung on to it when she got married and rented it out. She's a very sensible girl.'

'She must be.'

'Jill and Roger were very good to me, but I did feel that if fate had decreed I was to live on my own, I might as well get used to it, so I moved in and tried to get on with it.'

'How's it going?'

'I hate it.'

'It must have come as a tremendous shock.'

'It did. The awful thing is that I feel I've lost my future. I can cope with losing the past. I mean, that is the way of the past. It's over. But it's the losing of the future that is so difficult to handle.'

'If only we could think of it as being given our own future.'

'Well, I am trying.'

'So am I.'

'It's not easy, is it?'

'No, it's not.'

They both drank and were silent while deep in thought. Louise was thinking that it probably was best to get this off her chest and she did hope that she wasn't going to live to regret it in the morning. It was all very well being brave and dignified, hinting at nothing, but a good talk was a wonderful remedy. Kate was thinking that even though people looked terrific, it didn't necessarily mean that they felt terrific inside. It just went to show you.

Kate leaned forward to Louise and said, 'I know it sounds

frightfully gushing, but, honestly, if there's anything I can do, if you want to scream and shout in the middle of the night, just bang on the floor and come down, or I'll come up. Please, I mean it. Any time you need to talk or want to let rip, just let me know. To tell you the truth, I've done a good deal of letting rip in my time. I'm an expert. I bet I know some tricks you've never even thought of. You've done the obvious, I suppose, like thumping a pillow and shredding newspaper.'

'Oh, yes, I've done those quite a bit.'

'Have you thought of throwing old mugs into the garden from a great height? We could set up a target if you like.'

Louise managed to smile and said, 'Oh, that's awfully kind of you, thank you. Actually, it's done me so much good just to talk to you tonight. I've talked to Jill and probably bored her rigid, but I seem to talk in circles with her. Perhaps it's because we know each other too well. Talking to you so frankly was the last thing I intended, but it sort of slipped out, and now it's out I'm rather glad. There's a lot more, and maybe one day I'll get around to letting all of that out as well. In the meantime, I don't know if it's the champagne or what, but I do feel much better. The day didn't get off to a brilliant start, but it came good in the end. And the same goes for me. If you ever want to have a good old moan about your Nick, just call on me.'

'I most certainly will.'

'Ten years, you say?'

'Ten years,' affirmed Kate. 'Ten long years.'

'It's not right.'

'It's certainly not right at all.'

'Men.'

'The rotters. They've got a lot to answer for.'

'Can I ask you something?' queried Louise, inspiration lighting up her face.

'Fire away.'

'Would you go back to him?'

'Like a flash,' admitted Kate reluctantly. She knew that she could not get away with lying. She wasn't going to lie to herself, so why lie to Louise?

'I thought so.'

'And what about you, Louise? Would you go back to David?'

'Of course I would.'

'I thought so. Life can be a bitch sometimes.'

'It certainly can.'

They both looked at their empty champagne glasses and then gave them a twirl.

'Men,' they said together.

'How about another glass of champagne?' suggested Kate.

'Damn good idea,' said Louise.

CHAPTER FIVE

Ten-thirty on Sunday morning found Kate standing beside her car, marvelling at the gloriousness and promise of the day. For a girl who was given to swings of mood and fell prey to the odd depressing moment, she was definitely riding on the upward swing of the pendulum. At this particular moment she was content to enjoy long and deep intakes of invigorating air, which left her with the conviction that life was all right and that she would be well advised to switch into a happy and positive mood and, with all the tenacity she could summon up, hold on to it for as long as possible.

It was curious that fine weather brought out the best in people, and aware, though he had never been able to work out exactly how, that he sometimes brought out the worst in his fellow man, Doug Soper realized that today was the day to avail himself of the opportunity of a bit of fast footwork and a spot of enlivening conversation. Sidling down Vaucluse Road, as he did every Sunday at this hour after having checked in and done his turn at the Coffee Circle in the Crypt at nearby St Anselm's – such a nice group of people – he spied Kate idling by her car, apparently lost in thought and surely waiting for someone such as he.

'Hello-o there. Lovely day for it, I must say. Doug Soper's the name,' he said by way of introduction and then, seeing a rather vacant expression flash across Kate's face, rushed on with, 'Your next-door neighbour. I saw you moving in a few weeks ago, but didn't like to bother you until you were a touch more settled. I know how it takes a while to get things organized. However, may I say, on behalf of the other residents and myself, welcome. Marvellous community, truly marvellous, you take my word for it. Now, I know you working girls have a lot to do and sometimes need someone who can be relied upon to assist whenever needed. You know, the odd bit of plumbing, assistance with complicated paperwork, all sorts of things crop up. Well, just remember I'm your man, always ready and willing, if you'll pardon the expression. Whatever it might be, I can guarantee that you can rely on me and that I will carry out your instructions to the letter.'

And just so that there would be no doubt about his goodwill, he thrust out his hand and grabbed Kate's in anticipation of a grateful female shake. He may well have thought that she would then fall into a deep swoon right there on the pavement and declare that she didn't know how she could possibly have considered carrying on without him. It was one of the most maddening things about Doug Soper, and there were a lot to choose from, that over the years, for some reason known only to himself, he had done a thorough job of convincing his panting inner being of his supreme ability with the opposite sex. He therefore knowingly attributed Kate's lack of response to the fact that she was lost in admiration for his physical prowess – no one would have guessed he was in his late sixties, as he frequently told himself while considering an afternoon on the green – and his way with a blazer and Bowling Club tie. 'Can't believe her luck,' he said to himself and he accompanied his private fantasy with a contemplative downward turn of his mouth and a forward thrust of his chin.

'How do you do? My name is Kate Lanning. I'm delighted to meet you,' she lied through her clenched teeth. Wise in the ways of the world and registering a certain clamminess about Doug's palm, Kate knew that if she didn't act with decisive haste she would be held in the grasp of a prolonged conversation while he patted his pockets, produced a pipe and lit up.

'I must dash. I've got quite a long drive. It was nice to meet you. Bye for now.'

'Well, be careful, won't you? Let me help you. That's right. There you go. In you get.'

This joker really didn't know when to stop. It was a wonder he didn't lean across her and fasten the seat-belt, breathing heavily and pausing as he clicked the buckle into place.

'Let me do that for you,' he offered, closing the door on the second attempt and then adding a cheery wave.

In anyone else it would have been rather attractive, but there was something about Doug Soper's frequently voiced good intentions that induced a hollow feeling in the pit of the stomach, coupled with galloping revulsion. Wisely putting it all behind her, Kate applied herself to the business of the day, which was getting to the motorway and on to Oxfordshire in the shortest time possible. The thing to do was not to let minor irritations upset the balance of things. It was a beautiful day and it should be relished and enjoyed to the full.

Whizzing along the motorway, Kate found herself becoming quite lyrical about the intensely blue sky, the wispy clouds being whipped across the horizon by a cool and capricious wind, not to mention the stunning array of autumnal colours on the trees. It was the kind of day when a person might burst into song at the sheer joy of being alive; a girl might be foolishly inclined to make a rash promise, be convinced that quite obviously the only thing to do was to join an Outward Bound course, or, better still, sign up for a lifetime with the Mennonites on half pay; the entire nation with one voice might well stand up on the stroke of midday and say, 'If only the weather was like this all the time, living in England would be all right.'

All in all, life looked to be all right all round for Kate. Certainly her evening with Louise had brought her up with a start. Why was it that it took the lesson of listening to someone else's problems (and problems that were invariably far more complex and worse than one's own) to appreciate one's lot? For the moment Kate was into appreciation. Appreciation of her job, her new flat, her friends and her own future, which she could carve out for herself. As far as she was concerned, Nick could take a jump. He was excess baggage and not needed on the voyage of life.

Today was just the day to set the seal on her new approach. Good old Peter and Lizzie. Well, old *Peter* that is. Clocking in at seriously past fifty and not handling it too well, he had become a trifle moody of late. Lizzie was the same age as Kate, although, as everyone was fast to agree, you would never have known they were both in their late thirties, for they both looked frightfully well on it. Lizzie had always looked good, and Kate thought back to the time when they had been in their early twenties and had met Peter, the handsome hero and older man of thirty-eight. He had been so attractive, with his double-barrelled name, which was always guaranteed to get a girl going, and his allusions to an unhappy and unsuitable marriage made at an early age. He had cut quite a dash through Kensington and had been a wow with the ladies. He had gone straight to Lizzie's heart and had rather appealed to Kate, but when she saw that he only had eyes for Lizzie, she had graciously given way. The thought that he was the kind of chap who would have a mass of old school friends and amusing cousins waiting in the wings primed for an introduction had to a great extent appeased her sad loss. To date, Peter hadn't actually come up with any useful introductions, but it was best not to give up hope, and they were such a lovely couple that it was thoroughly reassuring to spend some time with them. Of course, since Lizzie had produced two sons and they had moved down to the country so that Peter could take up his rightful place in his father's firm, they hadn't seen quite so much of each other, but at least they had kept in touch and hadn't lost contact, which was the main thing.

Not much further to go, she thought to herself as she purred along. Even the car seemed to be responding to the weather and was running beautifully. Kate was also quietly pleased with the way she looked. That morning she had remembered that standards could sometimes be surprisingly high in the country, and, as you never knew with certainty who might be sprung on you at lunch, she had dressed with care in a calf-length pleated skirt and toning lamb's-wool sweater. She had toyed with her highly decorous red beads, but sense had prevailed and she had wisely decided against them and opted instead for a Liberty scarf, discreetly draped and knotted.

Realizing that she was at the point on the route when she usually went wrong, Kate yanked herself out of her reminiscences and flights of fancy and applied herself to her driving and navigation. She always thought that she knew the exit off the motorway and then went too far, only to have to double back. This morning she was bang on target and confidently recognized that she had taken the correct exit when she saw the sign to the RAF station. Mentally she went through Lizzie's often repeated instructions.

'Follow the RAF sign, go about a mile and a half, turn right at the Goat and Shuttle (we must have a drink there sometime), follow the signs for Ottley-on-the-Edge, twist and turn a bit and just when you're ready to give up because you think you've gone too far, you'll spot the telephone box on the right. Keep on going until you see the pond on the left, then it's a sharp swing and a turn left and there we are. You'll see the white wooden gates and the name, "Poolhead House" in black lettering.'

With a sigh of relief that she had pulled it off, Kate parked her car in front of the garage, where the doors were open to reveal Peter's Range Rover, several bicycles, a collection of cricket bats and Lizzie's hatchback, which was of Japanese origin and in need of a clean, but otherwise lacking in any distinctive feature. Sheba, the labrador, sloped around from the back of the house and launched into a loud and insistent bark, which belied the fact that she was an extremely soppy and friendly old dog who really just wanted to lie down on her back and stick her legs in the air.

Peter was doing a bit of Sunday morning tilling in the herbaceous border and yelled, 'Shut up, Sheba,' and then waved to Kate with both arms, which looked rather long and not altogether co-ordinated, calling, 'Hello, Kate, be with you in a sec.' And to prove that he was a man of his word, he abandoned what he was doing amidst the perennials, thrust his spade into the soil, and marched purposefully towards her.

'Lovely to see you, Kate. Come around the back. Good journey, was it? Stunning day, I must say.'

'Yes, it's glorious, isn't it? The drive was smashing and very fast.'

'Splendid,' he said as he put his arm around her shoulders and guided her to the back of the house. 'We've got a couple of friends joining us for lunch. Lovely people. Greville, our dentist, and his wife Asta. She's Australian, but she's all right once you get to know her. In fact, they're frightfully good value. You'll like them. Here we are.'

And indeed, here they were. Peter opened the back door of the house and stepped back as he ushered Kate in. He strode in behind her, and they made their way to the large kitchen, where Lizzie was whirring a food processor and peering into a cookery book.

'Darling,' called Peter in a happy 'we're going to have Sunday lunch with friends' voice.

'Oh, darling!' snapped Lizzie as she stared down and focused on his mud-caked green wellies.

Peter replied rather sharply and with a touch of aggression, which would have been recognizable even to those who did not know him well, 'Don't call me "darling" like that, darling.' Whereupon he did the only thing a man could do in the circumstances, which was to turn around and stomp off into the conservatory, kick off his wellies, fiddle with his woollen socks and leave the trouble and strife to stew.

Now, Kate became all agog at this moving bit of Sunday morning domestic drama and didn't quite know what to say. Should she remain on the sidelines and be polite, ignore what had happened and carry on regardless or could she trade on a friendship of long standing and ask the question she was dying to know the answer to? In times of stress, friendly concern will out and she launched in with a well-meant and heartfelt inquiry, albeit expressed rather bluntly.

'What the hell is going on here?'

'Perfectly normal behaviour. At least, at the moment it is. It's basically called getting on each other's nerves. Peter's become increasingly grumpy since his fiftieth. Every now and then he comes over all wistful and talks about his retirement. Any minute now I fully expect him to start on the not-living-to-see-his-grandchildren tack. I thought that when the boys were packed off to boarding school, we'd have a bit more time together – you know, return to the old romantic ways. What we've managed to achieve is constant bickering. I think it's called crisis time.'

'Oh, surely not?'

'Oh, surely yes. Mind you, I know a lot of it is my fault. Now that I have all this time on my hands I think I'm doing too much thinking and all I manage to come up with is that I've become thoroughly dumpy and boring, while Peter's out there in the cut and thrust of the business world, being brilliant at the office and charming all the secretaries.'

'Really?' inquired a quizzical Kate, looking at Lizzie, who appeared just as smashing as ever, and thinking about Peter, who had been well settled down for some considerable time and of whom the words 'solid' and 'reliable' sprang to mind.

'I think it's time for me to revamp my image. You know, cast off the well-worn and fraught "mother of two" look and replace it with an alluring "aren't you thrilled to come home to me" guise.'

Remembering Peter in his garden and as the crestfallen owner of muddy green wellies, Kate was not at all confident that he would know what to do if he came home to find Lizzie raring to go and all got up in a vampish number in red satin. Someone's perception was a bit off-key here, and she didn't think it was hers.

'Tell you what, let's have a drink and give this a bit of thought,' Kate suggested.

'What a good idea. Why didn't I think of that myself? Did you know that the latest statistics on alcohol have it that a woman on three bottles of wine a week has a problem?'

'How absolutely terrifying. I had three bottles yesterday.'

'Let's go into the drawing-room and have a gin and tonic. Perhaps that doesn't count. I'm sure Peter will come running in and join us when he hears the chink of ice. He usually does.'

'Peter said you had some other people coming. Greville and Asta, I think he said, though it sounds most unlikely.'

'Well, he's our dentist and she runs an aerobics class. She's desperately active and bright. Makes me feel like a complete wreck. Actually, I've been going to the class in a bid to get the body organized. It's such hard work. All that talk about physical exercise improving the mental powers means nothing to me. I'm so exhausted after a class that I have to have a Mars bar to pull myself round. My heart simply isn't in it. Here's your gin and tonic. Cheers.'

'Cheers. Well, why do it? Couldn't you take up a more passive activity?' suggested Kate as she collapsed into a large chintz-covered armchair.

'I don't know. It fills the time, I suppose, and it's the in thing, isn't it?'

'It might be in, but I'm not sure that is enough to recommend it. I do absolutely nothing to improve either my body or my mental powers. I don't think either department could handle the onslaught. Isn't it ridiculous? There's me, labouring away for the Mighty Major, imagining you leading the perfect existence in this idyllic setting, having a wonderful time playing house, knitting socks for the boys on winter evenings and being the loving wife and mother.'

'And I sit here imagining you are having countless brilliant affairs.'

'Nothing is ever the way you imagine and nothing could be further from the truth. It's all off with Nick,' sighed Kate.

'Again?'

'For good this time. I really mean that.'

'I hope so.' Rather like Ned and James, Lizzie adored Kate and had seen her through the many trials and tribulations of her on-off relationship with Nick; she did indeed hope that it was off this time, never to be rekindled again. She could see, as she had told Kate time and time again, that it was no good and that she was much too good for him. This line of thought usually provided some solace until Kate saw just one couple too many blissfully walking into the Ark two by two, when the notion that Nick was better than nothing at all would overwhelm her.

'Do you think if I had an affair it would make me more interesting?' mused Lizzie.

'Don't be ridiculous. Anyway, there aren't enough men to go round for us single ladies, so you putting youself on the market would be thoroughly selfish and upset the balance of things.'

'But it would be nice to get in a bit of practice. Perhaps I could start with Greville over lunch, and you could check my

71

progress. You know, tell me where I might be going wrong, keep me up with current trends and techniques and assess my potential.'

'Lizzie, what has got into you?'

'I don't know really. I think it might be that Peter and I are at the point when we're not actually in love any more and we've got to decide if we like each other and can be friends. I still love him – well, some days I do, I think – it's just that I'm not in love any more. It happens.'

'Oh, Lizzie, do be careful. It seems to me you should concentrate on what you've got.'

'Well, what have I got?'

'A devoted husband. He is devoted, isn't he?'

'Yes, I think so.'

'Two smashing children, a beautiful house, good looks, damn good figure, you always look wonderful, your clothes are great. You always did dress well.'

'I don't know about that. My idea of shopping these days is to go to London and find out if the Marks & Spencer's at Marble Arch has a better stock than the one in Oxford.'

'Clearly they do. Is that skirt from Marks?'

'Yes. It's two years old.'

'I never would have known. Now, where was I? I've been doing a bit of thinking recently – I know, it came as a shock to me too – and I really do think that we should live our lives knowing that there's no guarantee that at some time in the future there's going to be an opportunity to redress the balance and believing that every day we should get the show on the road and make the best of it.'

'That sounds frightfully wise and deep. You haven't got religion, have you?'

'No, I'm just trying to work things out.'

'It sounds as if you're dangerously close to working out that you should let Nick re-enter the picture,' observed Lizzie.

'Don't dodge the issue. This is supposed to be advice for you.'

It was advice that appeared to have had some effect, because when Peter sheepishly entered the drawing-room, wondering just how he was going to open the first round of negotiations with Lizzie, he was rewarded with a huge smile and the offer of a glass of red wine. He was even told to sit down, which he did, secure in the knowledge that he had successfully resumed his role as master of the happy home.

'How long is it since we saw you last, Kate?' he inquired, all affability and confidence.

'Last Bonfire Night. Don't you remember? Charles and Robert got carried away with the fireworks and frightened me to death. All I could do to keep myself calm was to eat baked potatoes and sausages. I shall never forget it.'

'Well, we must have another party this year, and, as the boys will be away at school, perhaps you won't be plagued with bangers. I think I hear a car arriving. It must be Greville and Asta. I'll go and meet them. You two get yourselves more drinks,' he hummed.

Lizzie watched Peter leave the drawing-room before asking, 'How is your new flat, Kate?' and, as she had had a trying morning and knew what was ahead of her over lunch, she poured two large gin and tonics.

'Wonderful. I like it so much. The sitting-room is almost right; it's very simple and cosy, but I do have the most stunning bathroom. It might seem ridiculous to get carried away about a bathroom, but it is quite something.'

Lizzie knew how easy it would be for Kate to get carried away about a bathroom, for when they had shared their flat in Holland Park they had had a particularly grim example and had never got enough hot water from the ancient gas appliance. Kate did eventually move on to better things, but that flat had not been blessed with tremendous facilities, and so it was hardly surprising that she was now relishing her new-found luxury. It was a subject that could have kept them well occupied for some time, but all talk of towels and tiles would have to wait, because, as they were just about to get really warmed to the theme, a feast for the eyes in baby-pink velour and false eyelashes bounced into the room. The lovely Asta, platinum blonde, flashing dozens of teeth, was determined to let them know that she was pleased to see them.

73

'Hi, Lizzie. How are you? You didn't come to class on Friday, you naughty girl. We all missed you. You've simply got to try harder, you know, if you're going to get in shape. I'll expect you tomorrow,' gushed Asta, pink all over and trying to be kind with it. It was a marvel she didn't go all the way and tell Lizzie that in a matter of weeks and with a bit of hard work and solid determination she could look just like her.

'Oh, you know how it is. There was a bit of a domestic crisis. The dishwasher broke down. I'd be lost without it. Now, do meet our friend Kate,' said Lizzie, hoping that she could steer Asta away from aerobics, cellulite and all attendant topics.

Asta flashed her teeth at Kate and told her that she was delighted to meet her, and Kate wished there could have been some truth in her reply that she was also glad to meet Asta. As Asta sat down on the sofa, to which Lizzie had guided her, it became evident that she was wearing a curious feather arrangement encircling a pony-tail at the back of her head. As she smiled, first at Lizzie and then at Kate, turning from one to the other just as she'd been taught in charm school, the feathers flowed and bounced behind her. Kate attempted to smile back, but all she could think of was that she wished she had worn her big red beads and that throwing gravy all down the pink velour might be fun.

'Would you like a drink, Asta?' asked Lizzie.

'I'll have a Perrier water. Alcohol and health do not go together, you know,' lectured Asta. She was wagging her finger. Kate was transfixed. 'I have just been reading about a most wonderful apple and date diet, which I'm sure you would both like to try. I'll let you have my copy. I really don't need it,' confidently claimed the vision in pink.

Given that Greville had been proposed as practice material by Lizzie and had been described as being frightfully good value by Peter, relief might have been thought to be in sight. However, as the perpetrator of Asta's teeth job was ushered into the drawing-room, it was all too clear that he fell several notches short of his billing. Perhaps he had hidden depths.

'Now, let's get you a drink, Greville. On the wine, are you?

74

Splendid. You sit down there, old chap, and tell us all about your golfing weekend in Spain.'

Asta beamed with pride at her husband, who was quite a short individual, though he looked better when he was sitting down. The heavy-framed glasses were a bit odd and, of course, the wispy hair around the balding head didn't look too grand, though the slight sun-tan from the recent trip to Spain had improved matters a great deal. Still, if you happened to be from Australia and had ended up teaching aerobics in Ottley-on-the-Edge, he might appear to be a good catch. Greville took a long and thoughtful slurp of his red wine, made sure that everyone was sitting comfortably and prepared to enlighten his audience.

'Well, the weather was very nice, which always helps, but things went wrong from the beginning. I told the organizers it was a mistake. You can never mix two groups successfully. It would have been all right if they'd kept it to the Dentists' Golfing Society, but there weren't enough of us to fill the charter from Gatwick, so we had to team up with the Chartered Accountants, which the committee did without referring the subject to any of the members, I might add. They were a very noisy lot. Now, as you know, we included our wives, while the accountants treated it like a lads' night out. Very embarrassing, I can tell you. So, as I said, things went wrong from the start. Now, one of the highlights was supposed to be Sean Connery, and I think I can say that was one of the main reasons for us going. We were told he was going to attend the dinner on Saturday night and then be around for the match on Sunday. You know, swap a few hints on technique and generally muck in. Well, something went very wrong with those arrangements. I don't know who was responsible and I'm going to get to the bottom of it, but we had to make do with Jimmy Tarbuck. Now, he's a very nice chap, and I won't say anything against him. I must say he gave it his best shot and was delightful company, but it just wasn't the same. The girls were very disappointed.'

'Oh, bad luck,' said Peter, always a good conversationalist and adept at keeping things on the move. 'Are you going to lodge a complaint with the committee?'

'Oh, I've already done that. It was one of the first things I did when we got home. We can't let that sort of thing go unnoticed. No. I've sent a written report.'

'It was a disappointment, I'll admit, and not quite what we'd planned, but we must look on the bright side,' trilled Asta.

'It wasn't all wasted. I got those girls out running in the mornings, and I organized a few aerobics classes too.'

'An experience like that can rather knock it on the head for the future, can't it?' suggested Peter, though it was not clear if he was referring to the unfortunate non-appearance of Mr Connery at the seventh hole, or to the sight of a mixed bunch of dentists' wives with thighs of varying size and texture on an early-morning run in Marbella.

'You're right. I'll have to give it some serious thought. But I can tell you one thing and that is this: it makes me wonder, it really does, just what sort of people we've got running things these days. I was going to keep this to myself, but I think I might as well let you know, as I trust you and I know I speak amongst friends who know how to keep a confidence. The truth of the matter is, I'm thinking of standing for election myself. Quite frankly, I think I can do a better job.'

Asta touched her husband's arm and beamed at everyone in the room and to its four corners as well, indicating that her Greville was the man to take this on and wasn't he wonderful. A sentiment that fell on stony ground as Kate was already convinced that Greville was an impossible little prig and unforgivably boring with it. Lizzie was thinking of her leeks *au gratin* which probably needed no more than another five minutes. And so it was left to Peter, who was frightfully well brought up and always polite in company, to make noises of assent and generously pat Greville on the back while murmuring, 'Good man.'

'Please excuse me for a moment. I must do a spot of organizing in the kitchen,' said Lizzie, getting up and heading off as fast as she could.

Kate assumed that Lizzie had had just about as much as she could reasonably tolerate of Greville and Asta, so she bounced up, saying, 'Can I help?' with the intention of seeking sanctuary in the kitchen herself. And before there was any chance of a reply, she had made her move and had joined Lizzie.

Asta, being a girl who preferred male company and who was convinced that they found her extraordinarily attractive and interesting, remained behind. She was last seen doing a bit of cooing and smiling while she flapped her false eyelashes in the breeze.

'Who are those people?' asked Kate, making sure that the kitchen door was firmly closed behind her.

'Yes, I'm sorry about that. It was Peter's idea to ask them. I think he's trying negotiate a good price for his bridge work,' said Lizzie as she efficiently dusted the top of an apple pie with sugar.

'Are we going to have whipped cream with that?' asked Kate.

'Certainly.'

'Oh, good. Asta will hate it.'

'What on earth could you have been thinking of, mentioning Greville in the same breath as that wonderful word "affair"?'

'It must have been a passing moment of lunacy. Stir the gravy.'

'Well, don't do it again, it's quite unnerved me. Is lunch under control?'

'Yes, it's all ready, I just needed a breather and made an excuse.'

'Going back to Greville, I don't think dentists are allowed to have affairs with their patients. It's unethical.'

'Oh, I'm sure they can, as long as they don't do it in the chair or while under the influence of gas.'

'No, I think you're wrong. I'm sure they're like doctors. You know, they can make their mistress their patient, but they can't make their patient their mistress.'

'Well, he might do for you then,' laughed Lizzie.

'Lizzie, please don't insult me. Let's get lunch ready. I don't think either of us could handle Peter storming in here and inquiring after his roast and potatoes.'

'All right. While I take things through to the dining-room, you go and tell them everything is ready.'

In the drawing-room, the conversation seemed to have kept going while Kate and Lizzie had been in the kitchen, and the three of them were now in the midst of a penetrating discussion on what to do about an afflicted rhododendron in Greville and Asta's front garden. Obviously, the delicate subject of bridge work had yet to be touched upon.

'We can go through to the dining-room. Lunch is ready,' announced Kate.

'I must say, I'm really looking forward to it. I had the most awful bout of tummy trouble in Spain and I haven't been right since. I've hardly eaten a thing. It's only in the last few days that things have really settled down and I've had any degree of comfort. The stuff I was given by the local chemist didn't work,' said Greville, who looked just the sort to be beset by gastric problems. It was only to be hoped that he did not return to the topic during lunch or give way to strange rumblings as the roast lamb slid down his less than attractive gullet.

At least all was not lost, for Peter was a man who knew his wines, and it was one of life's happy circumstances that he always served lashings of the stuff. It would certainly help to move things along, and they needed all the assistance they could muster.

'Asta, you sit to Peter's right, and Kate, if you would sit down there, and Greville, you're next to me,' said Lizzie.

Sitting opposite Asta, of the flashing teeth, and next to Greville, the protector of the same, would have given a weaker girl indigestion, but Kate was not going to let them put her off her food or her wine. She sipped her claret and thought that the best thing to do would be to eat a hearty lunch and then get on the road home. It was lovely to see Peter and Lizzie, but there were limits, and with her new-found philosophy of making every day count, there really didn't seem to be much point in making pleasant noises to Greville and Asta for the rest of the afternoon. Kate happily toyed with her wine glass and watched Peter carve the lamb.

'This is a delicious wine, Peter. What is it?'

'Glad you like it, Kate. It's a Château Tour Servan. 1982 actually. Quite a find, don't you think?'

'Wonderful,' said Kate, though she was none the wiser. All that she knew was that she liked the taste of it. Good old Peter: he'd got several bottles lined up on the antique sideboard.

'Asta, my dear, how do you like your lamb? Pink?' inquired Peter, which seemed the logical thing to inquire of a pink girl.

'No, thank you. I don't eat meat. I'll have some vegetables, that's all. And some water, please. No wine.'

Well, she would, wouldn't she, and had there been any lingering suspicion that she was going to come good and prove herself to be a startling and stimulating presence around the luncheon table, it was now irretrievably gone.

'I'll have some of the crispy fat bits, please, Peter. And some of the pink. Splendid wine, it's really delicious,' said Kate and then turning to Greville she smiled and murmured in an overly concerned fashion, 'I do hope this isn't going to upset your stomach, Greville.'

'Is that enough lamb for you, Kate?' asked Peter, attempting to maintain order.

'Yes, lovely, lovely.'

'Who said "lovely, lovely" first?' inquired Lizzie.

'Noël Coward. He said most things first,' replied Kate. 'How are your vegetables, Asta? Enjoying them, are you?'

'Yes, they're delightful, thank you,' said Asta with her feathers bobbing and pony-tail dancing as she got to grips with a parsnip.

'Good for you,' said Kate by way of encouragement. Looking at Lizzie, Kate saw that she was attempting to stifle a giggle and was making a reach for her wine glass, from which she took a long, obvious and very pleasant slurp. Perhaps if they carried on this way they could get thoroughly blotto and run the dentist and his sidekick off the premises. The afternoon might hold something in store after all.

As has frequently been found and proven throughout history in all circles, be they social, business or diplomatic, it is surprising what a drop of claret can do to smooth the edges in trying times. True to form, Peter piled on the wine, and, while Asta didn't exactly tuck in, being a picker by design, she at least kept reasonably quiet and sat back as the rest of the table, Greville included (though he would probably pay for it later), polished off their roast leg of lamb, roast potatoes, parsnips, *gratin* of leeks, apple pie and whipped cream, and then asked for seconds. And so the lunch ran its happy and mellow course until gone four o'clock, when Lizzie suggested that everyone might like to move into the drawing-room and have some coffee.

Kate realized that it was just as well she hadn't had a glass of port with her cheese when she almost collided with a round table, covered in a delightful and well-chosen print cloth with frills all around the edge and bedecked with several precious family photographs, all in silver frames.

'Oh, that reminds me of the time at that grand house in Pelham Crescent when you . . .' cried Lizzie, unable to get the rest of the sentence out because she was laughing too much.

'Oh, I remember that,' hooted Peter.

'Don't remind me, please. I was embarrassed about it for weeks,' said Kate, collecting herself and making a sedate, steady and graceful progress towards a big armchair, into which she gently lowered herself.

As Kate sat and focused on the room and its occupants, she acknowledged that she was quite aglow after all that wine and that a coffee would really be a very good idea. Lizzie was similarly inclined and was not sure that she could summon up the energy or the inclination to mount a thorough search for decaffeinated coffee, which had been requested by Asta. She would give her a cup of instant and tell her it was decaffeinated. Beans for the rest of them and instant for Asta – serve her damn well right too. Peter, who was a man who could usually handle his booze, looked as if he was about to join them on the glowing stakes, while Asta was a girl who glowed quite naturally. Greville was not quite sure how to look, but so far it seemed that the chances were he was going to be able to keep his lunch down.

Kate decided that having had her coffee, and another one for good measure, she had best be on her way. If she didn't make a move soon she would drop off to sleep, the wine and the roaring fire being thoroughly conducive to a late-afternoon post-luncheon nap. But it wouldn't do. She knew that she would wake with a start, wondering if she'd dribbled or snored or talked without discretion in her sleep, and all she would be left with would be an ache in the neck.

'It's been super, but I really must leave. You know how bad the traffic can be on a Sunday night. And, of course, I'm not very good at driving in the dark,' said Kate, as she stretched, smothered a yawn and got up from her comfortable chintz-covered armchair.

Obviously Kate had not made a big hit with Asta, and neither had Asta with Kate, as they said goodbye in the briefest way possible, with only one bob of the feathers, while Greville, in the grip of a cramp, managed a nod. Lizzie bounced about in the background making promises to telephone and come up to London within a few weeks and inquired as to whether Kate would like to take home some lamb sandwiches with a nice bit of pickle for her supper. In the midst of all this, Peter, the gallant host, offered to walk her to her car.

As they moved across the gravel drive, Kate became aware that Peter had his arms around her shoulders, which was quite normal, but what was a little different was that he was gently stroking the back of her neck and – surprise, surprise – it felt rather good. Perhaps they had both had rather too much wine. As they got to the car, he pulled Kate into his arms and, with the briefest look back at the house to check his tracks, he gave her a great big smackeroo, right on the lips, which – oh, dear – she found extremely pleasant.

'Oh, Kate, I've been wanting to do that for years,' said a fulfilled Peter.

'You'll regret it in the morning,' said Kate, wise beyond her years.

'Probably,' he agreed reluctantly.

Kate gave him a pat of prudent counsel on his right shoulder and then got into her car and, as she drove away down the gravel drive, she looked in her rear-view mirror to see him standing there, all alone and troubled, loath to move until she had turned on to the road and disappeared into the gathering twilight. She reflected that his legs looked thinner than they used to, or was it just that, front and rear, he had become a good bit bigger?

CHAPTER SIX

In life there are some pretty harrowing early-morning sights. Take, for example, a saucepan of congealed spaghetti floating on top of a sink full of cold greasy water, a spider dead or alive in the bath, or even an empty packet of Alka-Seltzer when what is required is a full one, and fast. But there really can be nothing quite so undermining as the sight of a double bed with only one pillow dented. To wake, turn and focus on a pristine pillow cosily nestling alongside can upset a girl and throw morale way off course. Some have been known to give up, occupy the centre of the bed and abandon the second pillow, others burrow down under the duvet and have a little cry, while the Kates of this world roll over and give the offending item a savage dent and, if that doesn't look good enough, swap it with their own.

On this particular fine and wholesome Saturday morning, Kate did a bit of denting, swapping, tossing and turning, before looking at the bedside clock and deciding that she could well afford to give herself an extra thirty minutes' doze before getting up and tackling the day. She might even try and think of some reasons for sleeping alone. Although it would take a bit of concentration, she was sure she could come up with some. And when she did get up, she was going to make breakfast (scrambled eggs on toast looked like a front runner), put it on a tray and bring it back to bed, just to make a point. Nick hated breakfast in bed, and, as he wasn't there to whinge and make disapproving noises, she might as well go the full hog and read the newspaper. If she got newsprint all over the sheets, so what? – they were hers, bought and paid for. As she and Nick had been so violently opposed on the breakfast issue, she did wonder why she had had anything to do with him in the first place.

After a thoroughly uneventful week at work, Kate reluctantly admitted that it looked like it was going to be an uneventful weekend at home. Later on she would do a bit of gardening, plant the daffodil and tulip bulbs she had purchased from the garden centre, and, with the guidance of a paperback on instant town gardens, establish her right of ownership and creativity over the neglected wasteland at the back of the house. Peter would be the man to ask for advice on all aspects of horticulture. Since Lizzie had telephoned on Monday and had told her, while giving in to a burst of rather uncharitable laughter, that he had confessed to his moment of weakness, there was no reason to feel embarrassed or wonder if he was going to telephone and suggest a spot of lunch somewhere quiet in order to talk things over or for her not to tackle the question of propagation – in the garden, that is. Of course, it would have been nice had Lizzie at least made an effort to sound slightly put out, anxious even, as if it was possible that Peter had concealed and nursed a burning passion for Kate over the years, instead of dismissing it as being the funniest and unlikeliest thing she had heard in months. There were times when friends could be altogether too understanding and not understanding at all. Ever conscious of her duties of friendship, however short of the ideal others might fall, and feeling quite keen to attack the garden, Kate grabbed a couple of thick paperbacks, which she thought Louise might enjoy reading, climbed the stairs and knocked on the door of her neighbour's flat. It was not a well-rested and composed face that appeared in answer.

'Oh, hello, Kate.'

'Hell, you look awful.'

'I don't feel too bright. Come in.'

'What's up?'

'I didn't sleep last night, but that's not exactly unusual. I kept going over and over things and getting nowhere. I kept having middle-of-the-night arguments with David and Jacqui. I do wish I could see some change, some way forward, but I seem to be absolutely trapped and, however hard I try, I can't seem to get out. I'm so sorry to keep going on about things. You must be bored sick with my problems.'

'No, really,' said Kate with conviction. 'I told you, and I meant it, any time. Why didn't you give me a call or bang on the floor? I would have been up here in a flash, probably with a bottle of brandy in hand. You know how everything always gets way out of proportion at night.'

'Yes, you're right, I know it does. You are kind, and I'll try to remember. The trouble is that sometimes I just get so wound up in everything that I can't see a way out and I don't even think of talking to someone else. I should try and remember that talking is such a help. Perhaps I've placed too much emphasis on keeping up appearances, dressing neatly at all times, behaving graciously, never saying the wrong thing and upsetting someone and keeping a stiff upper lip. I wish I was more like you.'

Kate, of course, wished that she could keep up appearances, that her face did not betray her innermost feelings at every turn, that she knew how to dress beautifully and that, instead of playing centre-forward in the school hockey team, she'd learned how to behave graciously. As for her upper lip – she'd never known how to control it.

'Well, I'm here now,' assured Kate. 'I've brought you a couple of books, which I thought you might enjoy. This one is called *Essence* and it's about two sisters fighting over a perfume empire.'

'Oh, I've read that one. I think it's over here on the coffee table,' said Louise, sifting through the pile of books on the low-level glass table. 'Here it is. Oh. No, this one is called *Aroma*, but it's definitely about two sisters fighting over a perfume empire. Isn't that odd?'

'Very odd.'

'No matter. I'll read it anyway.'

'Then there's this one,' said Kate. 'It's about an investigative reporter; she's very beautiful, and she's sent off to Sicily to do a report on the Mafia.'

'Don't tell me. She falls in love with the Mafia boss and renounces a life in Fleet Street for a life of international crime.'

'No, she falls in love with her photographer.'

'Well, you'd think for a journalist she would have had more initiative. I'll read it anyway. Thanks.'

'I was wondering,' began Kate. 'It's a gorgeous day, and I'm planning to do some gardening. Ridiculous, I know, but I'm going to give it a try. There's no point in giving in before you start and all that. So do you want to come down for an hour? We could have a bit of a talk and a chat, and get some fresh air and exercise as well. What do you think?' asked Kate, hoping that she could encourage Louise to open up a little and get out of the confines of the flat, as she really did look awful. A combination of tension and despair seemed to be pouring out of her and, if anything, she looked thinner than ever.

'Well, yes, I think I would. It would certainly make a change from hiding up here with only Patrick for company,' said Louise. On hearing his name, the fat, overfed and spoiled cat roused himself from his favourite spot on the wicker chair, where the sun was pouring through the window and catching his back nicely, and did a turn around the sitting-room.

'He is a handsome pussy. My Eric's off his food. There's not a lot you can do to bring comfort to a fish who's not feeling too well. I'm afraid it's a case of just having to wait and see. I hope he pulls around. Perhaps he suspects there's a cat lurking near by.'

'Well, I suppose he might. On the other hand, are fish that bright?' asked Louise, an animal lover herself.

'My Eric and Jimmy definitely are. They get very excited when I get home and rush around the aquarium flapping their fins. Of course, that might be because they know I am going to feed them, but even so it's an indication that something is going on between the gills. Anyway, at the moment Eric isn't eating, or flapping his fins, for that matter, he's being very quiet and just hanging around the corner of the aquarium looking peaky,' said Kate, quite concerned. Recognizing, however, that it might be injudicious to speculate on Jimmy's reaction, should Eric fail to hang on to the flimsy thread of life, with a girl who was confused by her own problems, she moved along to safer topics. 'This is such a pretty flat.'

'Yes, isn't it? Jill, that's my sister, I told you about her, didn't I? I know I sometimes repeat myself at the moment – I can't remember who I've told what to – and I forget things all the time. Where was I? Oh, yes. Jill. Yes, well, she did it herself. She's frightfully good at things like that. She even made the curtains herself. Actually, she's good at a lot of things. It's a wonder she didn't get around to the garden, but I think she must have met Roger shortly after she moved in here and only had time to do the flat.'

'Well, I'm sure she'd be thrilled to know you are working on the garden. Shall we make a start in ten minutes?' asked Kate as she made a move towards the front door.

'Absolutely, I'll be there. See you later,' affirmed Louise, for all the world looking as if she meant what she said. She then closed the door and sat down for five minutes very quietly making sure she did mean what she said, because inside what she really wanted to do was to lie down and never wake up.

Not being a gardener of experience (in fact, not being a gardener at all), Kate imagined that she was going to have the whole area cleared by lunchtime, her bulbs in by tea, and a few decorative urns in position before the sun went down. Digging, she found, was hard work and her plans for a town garden with several interesting features might have to be modified.

'If I can get this small patch cleared, it will be a start, won't it?' she panted in what was just a shade nearer a puff than a wheeze.

'Shall I take over for a while?' offered Louise.

'No, you do the raking and I'll do the digging. You never know, it might burn up a few calories, and I need all the help I can get. It's quite satisfying really, isn't it?'

'Yes, it is,' agreed Louise, though as she looked down at the small area they had managed to clear after thirty minutes of intense labour, she wondered for just how long it would continue to be so. 'Do you think we could really make a proper garden out of this?'

'I don't see why not. We can start this autumn and clear a bit and then carry on in the spring. By the summer, I'm sure we'll have a wonderful garden, and we can lie out in the sun and give barbecue parties in the evenings. We might become quite renowned for them,' said Kate, once again demonstrating her enthusiasm and refusal to err on the side of caution.

'I'm not sure it's that easy. I think a lot of digging, raking and fertilizing has to go on and I'm sure it takes years for plants to get established.'

'Well, I know it doesn't look like very much at the moment, but the important thing is to have plans and vision,' said Kate, taking a commendable stance, as was to be expected from a pillow denter of some expertise. 'I'm sure if we put in a bit of hard work, we will get results. It's almost guaranteed, isn't it? Put in the plants and they grow. Well, they do grow, don't they?'

'Not always.'

'Oh, dear. Shall we take a bit of a break and sit on the step and think about this?' suggested Kate, downing her spade.

Kate and Louise moved, Kate slightly slower and inclined towards a stooping position, in the direction of the three steps leading down from the french windows of Kate's bedroom and sat down with, it might be said, a considerable degree of relief. They then both fell into a contemplative silence.

'Do you think we should get a chap in?' attempted Louise.

'What for?' asked Kate, all ears.

'You know, to do a bit of the heavy work. To clear the ground.'

'Oh, I'm not sure. I think that might be an admission of failure.'

'You don't think it might be described as delegation and a sensible use of resources?'

'Good idea. I hadn't thought of that. You could be right.'

'Mmm.'

'I can think of one or two things I'd like to get a chap in for. Still, there's no point in dreaming. Oh, dear, I'm constantly making plans that all seem to come under the general heading of "how to overcome", and I seem to work my tail off with no end result. We never know what's around the corner, do we? I suppose you know that better than most. But wouldn't it be nice to think that if you did enough hard work, sowed all the right seeds, in the right order, the result would be a life blooming with colour and delight, which grew and grew and got better and better just like a garden? Except that I've just found out that even gardens don't do that. Am I getting carried away? I think I am. I'd better stop,' said Kate, full of contrition, wondering what to do about the garden and what to do about life and in which order and how.

'I agree with you that it would be nice to think that way. Right now I am going through all these mental and physical exercises in order to try and get back to normal, whatever that might be, and just when I'm almost there something happens to turn me back. It's almost like trying to swim in a flooded river, and every time you are near dry land a piece of driftwood, or a tree, comes floating by and sends you right back into the midst of the swirl.'

'And I suppose Jacqui is the biggest tree of them all. Tell me about her.'

'She's a most extraordinary character, really. She's very stupid, and you know how difficult it is to have a discussion with a stupid person. You have to make allowances all the time and you have to try and understand. It seems to me that the sensitive people of this world have to make all the allowances and the stupid people reap all the rewards.'

'Stupid people run the world.'

'I think it all started with me feeling sorry for Jacqui. She'd just broken up with her third husband – he was a Dutch businessman, much older than her – and I invited her to stay with us until she found a new flat.'

'How did you meet her?'

'Oh, she had always been around. She was a model at one time, then a bit of an actress, and she even made a record once. That's how we met her. David, for his pains, wrote the song. It was awful. Anyway, as I said, she sort of drifted around and kept popping up. She goes to all the parties and her photo is always appearing in the *Daily Express*.'

'It's not *that* Jacqui, is it?'

'Very likely.'

'Ah, well, I'm beginning to understand everything. She's a classic bitch. It's written all over her. It's a sad fact, but there are quite a number of them around,' commiserated Kate.

'Well, she's all of them rolled into one.'

'You know, things are suddenly falling into place,' said Kate, her mind suddenly clicking into a 'go' position and throwing up all sorts of useful information. 'Now, I might be wrong here, but wasn't there an awful business in a hotel in Bombay? There were several people involved, but it never became clear exactly what happened. There were a number of horrific versions. I wonder what really went on? Now, you'd think that after a thing like that, and all over the papers too, she'd have learned her lesson and vowed to stay indoors for the rest of her life. Nothing has ever been heard of the rest of them, has it? Perhaps they have stayed indoors,' speculated Kate, wondering if Louise was going to be able to throw any light on what really occurred on that steamy night in the East.

'Jacqui is invincible, I swear. I suppose it's a kind of tenacity that should be admired. I've never been able to work it out. She's so stupid that I expect she doesn't really think very much about the full implications of what's going on. She's wholly concerned with the present and her own self-indulgence. She's drifted from situation to situation, relationship to relationship, and from job to job, if you can call them that. She wasn't much of a singer, she wasn't much of a model and, come to think of it, she wasn't much of an actress.'

'I reckon the only thing she's interested in acting in is *My Own Life Story*!' enunciated Kate. 'A sweeping mini series, in ten block-buster episodes.'

'She was in an episode of *The Saint*,' offered Louise, who was beginning to smile.

'Oh, I know the sort of thing. Did she play one of those blonde girls whose father, a brilliant scientist, had been kidnapped by a hostile country and she took her cause to Simon Templar, who, with great derring-do, helped her unravel the dastardly plot?' asked Kate, getting quite carried away.

'No, she was type-cast. She played a barmaid,' cried a triumphant Louise.

'Oh, isn't life grand?' said Kate, happy that the conversation had turned around and that they had found something they could grin about. 'How did you meet David?'

'I'm frightfully self-conscious about it, because it sounds such a cliché, but I went to work for him as a temp, and, as the story-books would have it, never looked back,' smiled Louise, happy to remember and talk about it and for once not feeling in the least bit embarrassed.

'Oh, how romantic. I've got goose-pimples and gone all gooey,' sighed Kate. 'Why feel self-conscious about it? It's a lovely story.'

'Funnily enough, I don't feel awkward talking to you about it. And I've certainly never found if difficult to speak to Jill about it. I used to feel self-conscious around Jacqui, because she was forever saying things like "And when are you going to go back to work?" "How long will you be staying here?" and so on. The truth of the matter is, I never stopped working when I started to live with David. I kept right on going and I did everything.'

'You're crazy to take any notice of Jacqui. She sounds like a real cow. So, along with losing David, I suppose you feel you've also lost your job?'

'Yes, that's right. I'll have to start looking for some work soon. The trouble is, I had the best one going.'

'What sort of work do you want to do?'

'I guess I'll have to go right back to the beginning and work as a secretary.'

Two girls sitting on a step, having enjoyed a bit of Saturday morning gardening, and now deep in convivial conversation, was not the kind of scene that Doug Soper could pass by. As he emerged from his kitchen door into the bright sunlight, he heard the low murmur of conversation and then crept to the fence, where stooping down, bottom thrust out, hands on his knees, he closed his left eye, screwed up his right, focused and watched Kate and Louise. The more uncharitable would have said he licked his lips. Slowly his plan of action formed in his mind, and he straightened his back and made as if to stroll casually around his garden, happening upon the two, quite naturally, just like that, and as a delightful surprise for all concerned.

'Hello-o there!' he called out merrily and saw fit to accompany his words with a lot of hand gestures and nods of the head, which were supposed to denote surprise and an 'I bet you spotted me before I spotted you' attitude. 'Lovely day for it, I must say.'

'He says that all the time,' whispered Louise to Kate.

'I know. I've heard it once or twice myself,' muttered Kate.

'Well, well, well,' said Doug, trying to remember his script.

'Yes, yes, yes,' said Kate, who had well and truly got his measure.

'Doing a bit of gardening, I see. This used to be a splendid garden when old Mrs Parkes lived here. A splendid garden. Well, if you need any help just remember I'm always ready and willing, if you'll pardon the expression. I'm your man.'

'Do 'e 'eed 'elp?' whispered Kate, the ventriloquist, as quietly as she could, barely moving her lips.

'Not that badly,' answered Louise, masking her comment with a delicate ladylike cough into her right palm.

Thinking that it was a lovely day and that it wouldn't be a bad idea to make it even lovelier for two such lovely girls, Doug piped up with, 'I was wondering if you two lovely ladies would like to come round for a spot of sherry before lunch?'

As any old campaigner would be the first to admit, there are two lines of thought on this one, the first and obvious being to cut, run and deny all knowledge, the second being to attempt to infiltrate the enemy's camp and, with inside information, completely disarm him for ever more.

'What a lovely idea,' said Kate, seasoned in the social ranks. She did notice that Louise's brown eyes, which had been called beautiful in the past and were exquisitely made up in shades of cinnamon and peach for her gardening duty, had taken on a certain piercing quality. 'What time?'

'In about fifteen minutes. Would that be fine for you two?' hummed Doug, quite convinced that he had made a major hit across the garden fence.

'I think it's probably best to be very strong,' observed Kate to Louise.

'I am not convinced that strength alone is going to be enough,' replied Louise.

Dressed for the occasion in his Bowling Club blazer (well, it had never let him down yet), Doug was delighted when his two lady guests arrived at the front door. It was infinitely more fitting for the occasion than the back door and having to step through the kitchen and apologize for the cabbage. He had a toad-in-the-hole planned and he thought that they would go well together. It was with gratification that he realized he was going to be entertaining two ladies who had class and style and who instinctively knew that this was a front-door occasion. Already his spirits were soaring and they rose to even greater heights when he noted that, as a mark of respect, Kate and Louise had changed out of their jeans and gardening gear, and into rather attractive little numbers. What company.

'Come along in, won't you? Right on time, I see. That's something I admire. Punctuality seems to be out of favour these days,' said a grinning Doug, always eager to share his observations on the changing face of the nation. He welcomed Kate and Louise to his home and ushered them through to the sitting-room, the front room, which was all done out in the 1961 renaissance style and, as such, was a fine example of the men at the Co-op's efforts to bring good design to the high street at affordable prices for all to enjoy. A nice lady friend had helped him choose it. Still, that was another story.

'Sit yourselves down, won't you?' he said in a fluster, for he was anxious to get them in and pinned to their seats. 'Now, what can I get you? A nice drop of sherry? Cream would that be? Or perhaps a little taste of medium would be more to your liking?'

'Actually, do you have an Amontillado?' queried Kate.

'Yes, I think I do,' said Doug searching through the selection of bottles. Many of them had been hasty purchases in duty-free shops all around Europe and, although they had survived the journey back to Vaucluse Road, they had since languished unopened on top of a wrought-iron trolley, which was all twirls and bits of gilt and, of its type, quite fetching, but of limited general appeal.

'And for you, my dear?' he said, turning to Louise.

'The same, please.'

'Right-o, coming up as quick as you like. I think I'll stick to my usual tipple. Sweet. Well, well, well, cheers then.'

'Cheers,' said Kate.

'Cheers,' said a less than certain Louise.

'And how are you feeling, my dear?' asked Doug, fixing upon Louise and looking quite menacing with it. This was just what she had been dreading. 'I must say, you are looking much better, much better. Of course,' he said, now holding Kate in the grip of his gaze, 'I have had my own upheavals in life. I know from the most bitter experience of all. I don't often talk about it, but I lost my dear wife many years ago, and it troubles me to this day. She was so young, so very young. A tragedy, really. She was only thirty-one. Yes, Colin, our son, was only six when we lost Jean. That was in 1953. It hardly seems possible. The years go by so fast.'

'The year of the Coronation, just imagine,' said Kate, a history buff.

'But enough of me and my troubles. What about you two? Have you settled in yet?' he asked Kate, hoping he could get more out of her than Louise, who just sat there – but then, of course, the girl was troubled, and only someone such as himself could understand the extent of it. One day she would be bound to confide, and there he would be, for, after all, hadn't he said it himself, he was always ready and willing?

'Yes, everything is fine. I'm quite settled in now, thank you.'

'Well, if there's anything you need doing, just remember, I'm always ready and willing if you'll pardon the expression,' said Doug, little knowing that it was only with the utmost restraint that Kate did not join in the chorus and finish before him.

The three fell into a contemplative mood, each battling with their own thoughts. Doug wondered if he was going to crack it first with Kate, or would it be Louise, or would it be both at once? Louise stared down wistfully at the carpet and counted the twirls up one side, across to the middle and all the way back to her chair. Kate thought she recognized the print over the fireplace, but couldn't quite place it. It didn't go with the print of the girl with the big blue eyes and lots of eyelashes, which was hanging squarely in the middle of the wall opposite the bay window. She recognized that one too and could remember where she had seen it before. It had been in the cottage her parents had rented in Mevagissey when she was thirteen years old, still in socks and longing to be sixteen and staying out late with boys. There are times when a girl just has to accept her social obligations, so Kate stuck to the rule book and said, 'So you have a son, Doug. Does he live in London?'

'No, regrettably not. I would like to see more of him, naturally, but he's living near Huntingdon. He's a lecturer in social sciences and has made his base in the countryside. We don't have a normal father-and-son relationship, because of the sad circumstances. I couldn't cope on my own, you see, and so Colin was brought up by his Auntie Vera, who lived in Hatfield. I saw him most weekends, though. Poor Vera's gone now, of course.'

Kate would have liked to have chipped in with someone who had gone, but couldn't think of a recent loss so she queried, 'How long have you lived here, Doug?'

'Jean and I moved in in 1947, would you believe? How the years do fly. Colin was born in 1947. Yes, I was working in Kilburn at head office,' and lest the full impact of his early promotion to higher things had not been fully appreciated, he went for a second take. 'I'd gone to head office by then.' Foolish girls, they were not biting. Couldn't they see that here was the man of whom the upper echelons of management had said 'better get him to Kilburn as soon as we can?' 'Jean was working at Derry and Toms.'

'What did she do there?' asked Louise, rallying to the cause and raising her troubled brow from the carpet twirls.

'She worked in the corsetry department, actually. Of course, in those days a long apprenticeship had to be served. Jean put in her years, I can tell you, before she got her own tape measure. She was devoted to her job and devoted to Derry and Toms. In some ways, I think it was just as well she went when she did. I'm not sure she could have borne the demise of Derry and Toms. All that work on the roof-garden gone for nothing. Many of our courting days were spent on the roof-garden. My, it does seem sad. Kensington High Street has changed so much. I understand there's a club there now where the roof-garden used to be. It doesn't seem right to me. A Marks & Spencer. A British Home Stores. It doesn't seem right at all.'

'You must have seen a lot of changes in the area, Doug,' offered Kate.

'Oh, you wouldn't credit some of the things I've seen. But, quite frankly, between us, things are improving. May I say, it's a delight to know that two such lovely ladies are residing in such close proximity,' countered Doug.

And aware that a certain creepiness, tending to oil, was in danger of seeping into proceedings, Louise said, 'Does Colin come up to London very much?' It was dubious where this innocent question would lead them, but, with the benefit of hindsight, it might well have been the turning-point of the whole occasion.

'Every two or three months he manages to get up to see me. And occasionally, of course, I go to Huntingdon. Well, just outside, in the countryside. Colin likes to go around the libraries and museums, but he has such a busy life in Huntingdon. He has so many hobbies and pastimes. He's on several committees – I'm afraid he gets that from his old father. I've always liked to be involved,' Doug said conspiratorially. 'And, of course, there's his beer. He's a campaigner for real ale and he also makes his own at home. It's absolutely fascinating. You wouldn't be able to tell it from the real thing. In some instances I consider it to be superior.'

'Does he read the *Guardian*?' queried Kate, anxious to get the picture of Colin Soper in her mind absolutely spot-on.

'By Jove, you clever girl. Yes, he does. How did you know that?' said the proud father, while he gave his right knee a brisk thump.

'It just sort of came to me in a blinding flash.'

'Well, I'm blowed.'

'Is he married?' asked Kate, quite unable to quell her curiosity any longer.

'Strangely, no. He's a good-looking boy, and there was a young lady in the picture when he was in his mid twenties, but that romance came to a most unfortunate end. They were on a camping holiday in the forests of Bavaria, and she went off with a woodcutter. Just like that. No warning at all. She took her sleeping-bag as well. Very cruel. Well, you can imagine, it cut him to the quick. It took him years to get over it. Actually, to be perfectly honest, I don't think he has, even to this day. To come home after an afternoon's ramble to find the tent bare. It must have been a terrible shock. Still, we all have our crosses to bear.'

Kate looked down at her empty glass, raised her eyes, smiled, and looked down once again at her glass. Louise twirled her empty glass between two fingers and said, 'I saw Jill the other day, Doug. She sends you her best wishes.' Well, it wasn't strictly true, but it seemed like the polite thing to say, and really it was about time they moved off troubles of the heart.

'Charming girl, Jill,' said Doug to Louise and Kate, who began to wonder if they were just as charming, but came to the conclusion that they probably weren't, because if they were in there with the best of them he would surely have refilled their glasses by now.

'Oh, what can I be thinking of? Let me top you up. Now, let me see. Amontillado, wasn't it?'

Phew. They were back in favour!

'I'll tell you what,' said Doug, inspired all of a sudden, 'Next time Colin comes to London, we'll have a little get-together. I'm sure he would be delighted to meet you, and, if I may say so, he'll be quite impressed with the sort of company his old father is keeping these days.'

Well, wouldn't that be something to look forward to: young Colin, all real ale and cords, Doug, all blazer and *bonhomie*, and two young ladies of particular distinction, just trying to be true to themselves. It was a mixed bag from which to conjure up a successful evening.

'Dear, dear, dear,' said Doug.

'Sorry?' said Kate.

'No, I was just thinking what a fine time we'll have. All four of us together. Yes, yes, I'll get on to that immediately.'

Louise, concentrating on her swiftly disappearing sherry, was either lost in thought, or lost for words, and very possibly both. Kate was definitely lost for words and took refuge in her glass, as she frequently did when all else failed her.

'Well, well, well.'

'Mmm.'

'Mmm.'

Kate really would have liked to have kept a bit more on top of things than she had and felt that she had given rather a bad show. Poor Louise seemed to be failing fast, so it might well be a good move to get her home as fast as possible and give her a proper drink.

'Well, I'm sure you want to get on with your lunch, Doug. And we really must be going. It has been lovely,' said Kate, easing herself up from the chair upholstered in sea-green velvet and noticing a series of leather coasters scattered across the wooden coffee table. Funny that she hadn't noticed them before. They had a little red-painted figure and the poignant word 'Olé' emblazoned across them with a flourish. In a final decisive thrust, Kate added, 'Thank you so much, Doug. My turn next.' And then she stared right into his eyes, which was going altogether too far and was quite unnecessary.

'My pleasure, my pleasure. Believe me. Right, now. Let me show you girls out.'

Once Kate and Louise were out they immediately told each other how much they fancied a stiff drink and would it be Kate's place or Louise's, while Doug, ever the romantic, fell into thinking what lovely ladies they were. Louise was just as charming as Jill, and Kate was so alert and amusing. What would Jean make of it all? But then, what would Jean have made of a lot of things? – his lady friend, for example, the one who had helped with the decorating, and Vera, of Hatfield fame, gone now. Well, they'd fallen into each other's arms, Jean, that was the sum total of it. Doug was a lonely widower, and Vera was doing her best to care for young Colin, who was quite a revolting and difficult child. Sorry, Jean. Didn't mean to upset you. But what would be the outcome of all this? A man has his needs, Jean. Kate? Perhaps. Louise? Maybe. But then there was Colin. Would it be Kate and Colin? Or would it be Louise and Colin? On the other hand, what about Doug and Kate? Not forgetting the possibility of Louise and Doug. Or Doug and Louise. Which sounds better, Jean? Ah, but then, of course, there was Beryl to consider.

CHAPTER SEVEN

Michael Major was in his office and had assumed control of the thriving concern that was Major Events by 10 am. At 7.30 that morning he had left his desirable home in Kingston, which Kate had rather scathingly referred to as being in a cul-de-sac. It wasn't at all. It was situated in a very charming, neatly clipped and manicured close, where he and Andrea were very happily surrounded by like-minded neighbours, who also had their eyes on something a little bit more substantial in Virginia Water. Andrea had waved him off, conscious of her wifely duties and that Michael was travelling quite a bit these days. (For a girl who had been brought up living on a main arterial road headed in an easterly direction, she had adapted very well to Michael's fast-changing life-style and was in and out of Leonard's having her hair done twice a week.) Michael had pushed off up to town early because he had a breakfast meeting at the Savoy with some American businessmen he had met at the convention in Chicago. These days he was running with a very fast set.

So, the boss was in, but Martin had telephoned to say that he was just on his way and would be in as soon as he could. He also added that, should anyone telephone from the squash club about the ladder, would Vicky please take a message. Geoffrey had been in but had since nipped out to see his pals at Joe Coral's to lay his plans for the 3.30 at Chepstow. Ned was in, though only just, and was looking very cool in a Missoni sweater. He was reading the newspapers, feet up on the desk, cigarette on the go and just about to ask for a cup of coffee, though he would, of course, add that he only wanted one if someone was making one and that they shouldn't go to any trouble on his account. Tillie, cleaner of offices, would have been in and about her business by now, except that it was her day off. Kate was in and had been for some time. Which left only Vicky, who was not in. Her desk and chair were seriously empty. Kate kept glowering at them as she spoke on the telephone, which had its lights flashing and two calls on hold.

'Well, yes, of course, I do understand . . . Indeed, it is a fine opportunity and not to be missed . . . Yes, I will clear out your desk and send everything to your mother. And what about your mug?. . . All right . . . Well, yes, I'm sure everyone will be delighted to have something to remember you by. It is, after all, a very distinctive mug. I seem to remember we gave it to you for your birthday earlier this year, but if you don't want to take it with you, I won't press the point . . . Well, yes of course, I do wish you luck. Good luck . . . Bye.' With that, Kate put down the telephone, cut off the two calls on hold, once again glowered at Vicky's empty desk and added a snarl.

'Ned,' she said.

'Yes, I'd love one, thank you, but don't go to any trouble on my account.'

'I wasn't going to offer you a coffee.'

'Oh, weren't you?'

'No, I wasn't.'

'Oh, sorry. It must be that time of the morning.'

'Pay attention.'

'On my marks.'

'Vicky's leaving. Well, actually, the truth is she's left.'

'Is she pregnant?'

'Oh, really, Ned, that is quite disgraceful and wholly unnecessary!' snapped a defensive Kate.

'Only asking.'

'Typical of a man.'

'Sorry.'

'Well, she's not pregnant. Adventure calls. She's got a chance to work as a croupier for a cruise line and she's off to the high seas on Monday.'

'She can't leave without giving notice.'

'She just did leave without giving notice.'

'But she can't leave without finishing those letters I gave her yesterday.'

'She did leave, and I think she's given your letters the proverbial elbow. When choosing between "Dear Sir, Thank you for your letter of . . ." and "Place your bets, please, gentlemen", the spin of the roulette wheel and the chance to show off a bit of cleavage to the punters held more sway.'

'But does she know anything about being a croupier?' asked Ned and then as the truth began to dawn he added, 'You don't mean to tell me she's been a secret gambler all this time?'

'Those evening classes she was always nipping off to weren't for yoga and Spanish. Apparently it was blackjack on Tuesdays and roulette on Thursdays. She probably had a crash course in poker on Fridays.'

'Do you mean to tell me local councils are now spending the ratepayers' money on giving courses for budding croupiers? I call it a disgrace, an absolute disgrace, that's what I call it.'

Ned thought that this was just the sort of thing that merited a letter to the editor of *The Times* and would have started to flex his literary muscles and compose a few succinct lines right there and then, had it not suddenly dawned on him that there was no one to type what might become a long, drawn-out correspondence.

'Oh, do calm down, Ned, and help me think.'

They both sat for a ponderous few minutes, each hoping that the other would realize that a restorative coffee would go a long way to kicking the brain cells into action and into a fit state for dealing with this knotty problem.

'Would you like a coffee?' asked Kate, the first to break under the pressure.

'A coffee? Mmm, yes, why not? I hadn't thought of that.'

'Well, go and make it then.'

'Sometimes, Kate, you can be very disagreeable, and it doesn't suit you. You'll get wrinkles before your time. However, on this occasion I will go and make you one. I presume you will require it very strong?' he queried in an overly clipped manner as he made his elegant way towards the kitchen.

Geoffrey puffed his way into the office. He was not in the best of physical shape, in part due to lack of discipline and age, in no part due to pressure of work, and for the most part due to too many sandwiches in the pub at lunchtimes over the past thirty years.

'Where's Vicky? Where's she put my copy of *Sporting Life*?' he asked without preamble, getting right to the main thrust of his day with no hesitation at all.

'She's left.'

'What do you mean "She's left"?'

'What I said: she's left.'

'You mean she's stepped out for a few minutes to buy a pair of tights,' suggested a desperate Geoffrey.

'No, she's left,' snapped Kate.

'But she can't leave without giving notice. What about her leaving party?'

'She did leave without giving notice, and under those circumstances I don't think a leaving party is appropriate,' said Kate, who could be very censorious at times.

'Oh, I don't know. I think we all would have enjoyed a leaving party. We could have made it a surprise leaving party. We haven't had a good leaving party in the office for ages. We could have shifted all the furniture and had a disco. I could have run a video. The one for the Sunderland Tourist Board is very amusing. What's she going to do?'

'She's got a job as a croupier on a ship,' said Kate. She had a sneaking suspicion that this was a subject she was going to be forced to return to all day.

'Oh, good for her,' said Geoffrey. 'I didn't know she had it in her. Oh, well, I suppose I had better nip out and get my own *Sporting Life*. I hope they haven't all been sold. See you later. Oh, if Paddy from Newmarket calls, tell him I'll be back in ten minutes.'

Ned returned to his desk with two mugs of coffee and passed one of them to Kate. He had had the good taste not to use Vicky's mug.

'You know,' he said, as if it were a blazing revelation, 'we're going to miss her.'

'I know we are. That's why I'm so worried,' said Kate. 'She did a lot of work for all of us. We won't find her like again.'

'You could be right,' agreed Ned, who then silently began to think about the letters he had given her yesterday. How many had there been? Well, one had been to his bank manager, one had been to his stockbroker, one had been to his travel agent about a proposed holiday in Venice, one had been to his wine club about their special offer and he thought one might have been to Dermot Dessistropoulos of the Sunrise Group of hotels about a conference Major Events would like to stage in one of their fine establishments. Dermot the Greek could wait, but as for the bank manager, the stockbroker, the travel agent and the wine club, that was another matter.

They would have to get a temp, thought Kate, which meant that she would spend the next week explaining where everything was, only to hear that the girl had got a permanent job and that the agency was sending a replacement. The alternative would be to struggle on until they found a permanent replacement. After all, what was there to do? They would all have to chip in and split the work-load, which in effect meant writing and typing their own letters to their bank managers, their stock-brokers, their travel agents and their wine clubs. Ned kept his supply of private stationery (an elegant grey printed by Smyth-sons) in the bottom left-hand drawer of Vicky's desk, well to the back and concealed under an old, well-thumbed *A-Z*. Geoffrey was happy to use company stationery with the address crossed out and an 'as at' typed on the upper right-hand side of the sheet. Martin was a Basildon Bond boy and very little trouble at all.

The door of the office flew open and a squash bag hit the floor just in front of Vicky's desk, or, as they would all be forced to admit by the end of the day, what used to be Vicky's desk.

'Hello, Martin,' said Kate.

'Morning, Kate. Vicky about?' asked Martin. 'I left a note for her last night asking her to book me a squash court for tonight. Do you know if she has got round to it yet?'

'Well, I think you may be disappointed. The note is just where you left it, and, speaking of leaving things, she's left.'

'What do you mean, "left"?'

'What I said: left. As in "gone".'

'What, without giving notice and without booking my squash court? I call that really irresponsible. That's what I call it.'

'Possibly,' said Kate.

'What are we going to do?' said a troubled Martin as he sat down in the nearest chair, drew it up to Kate's desk, put his elbows on a pile of files, and cast a wistful look at his squash kit.

'Ned,' said Kate.

'Yes,' he answered, though from the distance, as it were. He was deep in thought, really deep. What particularly troubled him was the letter to the travel agent. He had been banking on stocking up on Italian shoes.

'The telephone's ringing.'

'Yes.'

'Well, answer it! I'm thinking.'

'All right, all right. Calm down. Don't get yourself into a state,' advised Ned.

So, all was humming at Major Events. Kate was formulating a plan that she thought would work, Martin was turning the pages of his diary, checking up on his squash fixtures, Ned was chatting merrily into the telephone and Geoffrey was somewhere outside, hot and puffed, pounding the pavements desperately searching for a copy of *Sporting Life*. All seemed to be in fine order when Michael opened the door to his office and stuck his head out to check on his staff.

'Vicky! Can you come in for a moment?' he called and then, seeing that she didn't immediately come running, all expectation, he said, 'Vicky not about? Kate, be a darling, and when she finishes whatever she's up to, would you ask her if she sent off the cheque for Andrea's Harrods account?' (What Vicky was actually up to at that moment was perfecting her spinning and raking techniques and wondering just what to pack for a life on the ocean wave and as many late nights as she could handle.)

'Martin,' said Kate.

'Yes,'

'You're supposed to be the accountant. Stop moping and go and get busy with your calculator.'

'I suppose that would be the best thing to do. It might take my mind off the ladder,' moaned Martin, as he roused himself from his chair and shuffled off. In his present mood, no one would have guessed he was an athlete.

'Can you beat that?' thundered Geoffrey, falling into the office in a state of near exhaustion. 'I had to go all the way to South Ken tube to get my *Sporting Life*. I think I'll have a quiet cup of coffee and do a bit of studying. Where's the coffee kept? We do have a kettle, don't we?'

'Geoffrey,' snapped Kate.

'Yes.'

'You're the technical genius. Shape up and sit at Vicky's desk and answer the telephone.'

'Right-ho, Katy. Can I read my paper while I work?'

'Yes, of course you can.'

There was a decisiveness about Kate, an ease of command, that was so attractive and comforting. If only they had had girls like that in the ATS, it might have been a very different kind of war for Geoffrey.

'OK, Chief, I will be at my post.'

Ned had considered his holiday, he had also considered the consignment of wine he would have liked to have ordered, he had dealt with the bank manager, and had even spent a few minutes thinking about his stockbroker. He was now ready to move on to delegation of duty.

'Kate.'

'Yes, Ned?'

'You'll have to tell him.'

'Tell who?'

'Tell Michael.'

'Tell Michael what?'

'You know, that Vicky's leaving. That Vicky's left.'

'Why me?'

'I think it would be better coming from a woman.'

'Why a woman?'

'Well, you know, staff and things. It's woman's work.'

'Oh, phoo. Go and boil your head.'

'I say, Kate,' said Martin, strolling over from his corner, which was stuffed full of ledgers, calculators, invoices, both in and out, costings and worksheets, 'Have you seen *Roget's Thesaurus*?'

'What do you want that for?' inquired Ned.

'Don't interrupt, Ned,' snapped Kate.

'I'm writing a report.'

'Katy!' called Geoffrey across the office from the reception area, where he had taken control. He had put on a green eyeshade. 'I say, Katy, can you hear me? Call for you on two.'

'You don't write reports,' said Ned.

'Oh, yes I do.'

'Oh, no you don't.'

'Yes I do!'

'Stop arguing you two. It's on the shelf behind Ned's desk. Don't forget to bring it back,' said Kate.

'Thank you, Kate.'

'Katy!' tried Geoffrey again. 'Call for you on two.'

'Vicky still not back?' observed Michael, as he emerged from his office to do a turn round his staff's laden desks. 'She still tied up? Do you know if she's done anything about Andrea's Harrods account yet, Kate? Get on to it, will you, when she's finished whatever she's up to. Also, be a darling and book me a car. I'm going out to lunch at the Ritz.'

'You'll have to tell him,' whispered Ned, as he watched Michael out of the corner of his eye.

'Katy!' called Geoffrey. He was standing up and waving. 'Call for you on two.'

'You're supposed to tell me that via the telephone. I will then say whether I am prepared to accept the call, and then you will put it through. Got it?'

'OK, Chief. Got it. Call coming right up.'

'Hello,' said Kate into the telephone while she covered her right ear to cut out the din developing between Ned and Martin.

'Kate. Is that really you? It's Nick,' he said, as if she needed to be told. 'I miss you so much.'

'Piss off, Nick!' screamed Kate, immediately followed by a decisive slamming of the telephone receiver.

'Guys,' she said.

Ned, Martin, Geoffrey and Michael turned to look at her stand up, leave her desk, grab her leather holdall and struggle into her Burberry.

'Carry on without me. I'm going out to lunch.' Which she did, without delay, and in a taxi too.

What a morning, thought Kate, and, more importantly, what a narrow escape. Though she could have cheerfully throttled Vicky on more than a dozen occasions during the past few hours, she had to admit that had it not been for her doing an unexpected runner, her own day might well have taken a very different course. Imagine what might have happened had she been listlessly flicking through her *Daily Mail* when Nick's telephone call had come through. Had the day been progressing in its usual uneventful and smooth fashion, she might well have agreed to have a drink after work, sure that it was only civil to discuss old times; and from discussing old times it was only a skip and a jump to a demonstration of same. And from there it was all too clear where the evening would end. No, right now, it looked as if it was a case of 'Here's to you, young Vicky, and sorry about the leaving party.'

A lunch with Louise and Jill had been planned, but because of her sudden and dramatic exit from the office, Kate had arrived in the restaurant fifteen minutes early and had filled in the time perched on a bar stool. It was not the first time Kate had put in a few hours on a bar stool. She had spent quite a few waiting for Nick. On this occasion she was happy that she was not waiting for him and was relieved to note that the hot and cold feelings had subsided, as had the pounding of her heart, which had for several minutes shifted location and lodged itself in her throat, thus making it impossible to breathe, swallow or sing. As there was nothing going on at the minute that merited a cheerful chorus, the lack of a tuneful doh-ray-me was not causing any undue distress. Her breathing was now firmly back under control and she was successfully keeping time and breathing in when she should have been breathing in and breathing out when she should have been breathing out. As for swallowing, she was in the midst of testing that particular faculty and had a marguerita lined up in front of her. There was already one inside her.

It was a mixed lunchtime crowd and there seemed to be rather a lot of young men in baggy trousers and oversized, rumpled jackets, which would have looked fine on Don Johnson, but on present company passed as baggy trousers and oversized, rumpled jackets. Hanging on their every word and, in some instances, their arms, were several young girls, a great many of whom were sporting brightly coloured headbands tied in witty knots. When they weren't hanging on to words and arms, the girls were doing a lot of gazing into the eyes of the baggy young men who, if appearances were anything to go by, were all in various ways connected to the world of advertising. Dotted amongst the crowd were examples of the older and more distinguished elements, who were the clients, trying to enjoy a spot of lunch after a morning staring at story boards. It was easy to sympathize with their looks of concern as it dawned on them that, not only were they paying for lunch, they had already paid for the baggy trousers, the rumpled jackets and the headbands.

An extremely handsome young barman passed by Kate and asked her, very politely, if she would care for another drink, an offer which, on this occasion, she chose to decline. For the moment, she decided to bring all her concentration into play and try and look like a woman of her times, dressed for a career and going places.

'Oh, there you are,' said Louise, peering through the gloom and trying to make herself heard above the enthusiastic sales patter. 'It's dark in here, isn't it?'

'Hi. Yes, it is a bit gloomy. Where's Jill?' inquired Kate.

'She's parking the car. She dropped me off, as we seemed to be running a bit late.'

'Do you want to go to the table or shall we have a drink here at the bar?'

'Oh, let's wait here. We can catch Jill as she comes through the door.'

'OK. Pull up a stool. What will you have?'

'White wine, please. Actually, on second thoughts, make that a kir. No, make it a kir royale.'

'Coming right up. Well, as soon as I can attract the attention of that good-looking young barman.'

He was an extremely good-looking and extremely young barman and with those qualifications he was perhaps a little too used to having his attention attracted. While he had been very polite and attentive to Kate earlier in the proceedings, things were now hotting up and he was deeply involved with two baggy young men at the far end of the bar.

'Excuse me,' said Kate, hand raised. 'I say,' she called, adding a smile. 'Excuse me,' she tried again, raising herself up off her stool. 'Oh, I'm no good at this. I say. Cooee!'

'Let me try,' said Louise. 'Tom, do you have a moment?' she said in a level and firm tone. It immediately had an effect, and with one bound the youthful Tom was by her side.

'Hi, Louise,' he said, all smiles and sun-tanned arms. 'We haven't seen you for a long time. I was sorry to hear what happened between you and David. Quite honestly, I don't know what he could be thinking of,' he confided. 'Now, what are you having?'

'A kir royale, please.'

'Good girl. Have this one on me. I must say, you're looking wonderful,' he said sincerely, leaning over the bar and gently touching her wrist for just the right length of time.

It was all extremely moving and very likely would have made a whole chapter in a thick soppy novel.

'I say, are you known here?' asked Kate.

'Yes. David and I used to come here quite a lot,' said Louise.

'I'm terribly impressed. I've always wanted to be known in a restaurant, but have always secretly feared that the only way I was going to be remembered was as the lady who spilled the red wine, collided with the dessert trolley or threw sugar on the floor.'

'Actually, today is the first time I've been back since you know what. I was rather apprehensive when you suggested coming here, but now that I am here, I'm determined to enjoy myself. Cheers.'

'Of course you're going to enjoy yourself. So am I. Cheers.'

'I wonder if David comes here with Jacqui?'

'Now, stop it. Don't do that to yourself.'

'What if they come in here for lunch?'

'I told you, stop it. You're going to get morbid and weepy. It won't do, not in a public place. Anyway, she's not the type to eat lunch. She probably stays in bed all day recovering from the night before.'

'Perhaps you're right.'

'I know I'm right.'

'You think I shouldn't dwell on them.'

'I most certainly do. Concentrate on enjoying yourself. I've had the most terrible morning. I really didn't enjoy it.'

'What happened?' asked Louise, getting into her kir royale, out of her morbid mood, and smiling her thanks to Tom.

'Well, to start at the end,' said Kate, waving clenched fists in the air, 'Nick telephoned.'

'He didn't.'

'Yes he did.'

'The nerve.'

'Exactly.'

'You didn't talk to him, did you?'

'Briefly, sharply and to the effect that he should get lost.'

'Well done. Very courageous. I'm impressed,' acknowledged Louise. She put her champagne glass down on the bar and remained silent for a few moments in honour of the occasion.

'But that isn't all. It came on top of a very difficult morning.'

'Isn't it always the way? They always seem to know when we're feeling vulnerable. Men.' Louise paused again. 'What happened?'

'Well, Vicky, our secretary, left, just like that, without giving notice. Can you believe it? I couldn't believe it and what I really couldn't believe was the way I just listened to her on the telephone while she told me she was off on a far more exciting adventure than we could ever offer her. Why didn't I scream at her and tell her to get herself into work and to hell with anything else?'

'Why does she want to leave?'

'She's got a job working as a croupier for a cruise line. I suppose it beats working for us, but she might have let us know. She's really landed me in it. I'll have to find someone to replace her, and she was an absolute gem, so I'm not sure how easy it will be.'

'Is it a difficult job?'

'No, not really. Sometimes it can be quite hectic and at other times it can be quite slow. And there is an awful lot of running around after everyone, me included. Michael, our boss, can be demanding at times. In fact at times he can be an absolute pain. Come to think of it, most of the time he's a pain.'

Louise was beginning to wonder if this wasn't a case of fate stepping in and throwing salvation her way. Bells of enlightenment were going off in her head, and she began to see a glimmer of light at the end of her restricting tunnel.

'Are you going to get a temp in?'

'Well, I suppose that's the thing to do, but it's not something I'm looking forward to. You know how difficult they can be at times, being drippy around the place and saying "Sorry, I'm only a temp", and all that. Enough to drive you crazy.'

'I'm a secretary,' announced Louise.

'Yes, you told me,' replied Kate, giving her marguerita a reflective sip.

'Well, I suppose, what I mean is . . .' tried Louise. It didn't seem to be coming out very easily.

'Suppose what?' Kate was not at her brilliant best. She was distracted, and didn't seem to be catching on too fast.

'Well, how about if I came in and worked for a few weeks, until you get things sorted out? I don't want to put you on the spot. I don't want to force you into anything and you must think about it . . .'

'Think about it?' interrupted Kate. 'What a brilliant idea! Why didn't I think of it? You're on. But are you sure you want to? Perhaps you should meet everyone first. As I've already told you, Michael is a pain and, when I say a pain, I mean a mega-pain. Martin is our accountant; he's thoroughly tiresome, as accountants frequently are, added to which, he is devoted to his squash. Geoffrey is only happy when he's on to the bookie and has to be forced to get to grips with his job, while Ned is just Ned and divine with it. And, I should warn you, I can be a bitch. But having said all that, I'd love it if you came in and helped out.'

'I'd love it too. I feel quite overcome. I can't tell you what this means. You wouldn't believe how thrilled I am. I know it sounds silly, but it's work and it means so much.'

'Well, let's not get carried away. I think we should both agree that it's for a few weeks until I find a permanent replacement for the wandering Vicky. Do you think you could do your stuff with young Tom? I'm going to have another drink.'

'And so will I. Sometimes it's good to be alive. Gracious, did I say that?' said Louise, surprised at herself, and breaking into a joyful laugh.

When Jill arrived in the restaurant, what immediately caught her attention was the fact that her sister was smiling and giggling and looking altogether happy. Suddenly, it didn't seem to matter that she had driven round and round in circles unable to find a parking meter and had finally given up and slotted the car into a prohibitively expensive NCP car park. To see Louise happy, she would willingly have parked on a double yellow line and been clamped every day for a week.

'Hello, you two,' said Jill and as she said it she was immediately engulfed in a massive hug.

'Oh, Jill, hello. Let me introduce Kate, and then I've got some big news for you.'

While Jill and Kate were saying hello and having a good look at one another, the head waiter came up and suggested that perhaps the ladies would like to go to their table. Once they were seated he would send an actor, masquerading as a waiter, who was going to tell them the day's specials. The ladies, being ladies, acquiesced and were rounded up and headed in the direction of a table right at the back of the restaurant and quite out of the main flow of activity.

'What's the news?' asked Jill, anxious to know what had made Louise so excited.

'I've got a job.'

'Go on. How thrilling!'

'Well, not exactly a job. What I mean is, I'm going to help out at Kate's office for a few weeks. Isn't it wonderful?'

Jill knew how wonderful it was, Louise certainly knew how wonderful it was, while Kate could see that it was having a wonderful effect, which she hoped would remain wondrous once Louise got to the office, installed herself at the late lamented Vicky's desk and met Michael, Martin, Geoffrey and Ned.

'Well, what shall we have to eat?' asked Louise, all effervescence.

Kate squinted and attempted to focus on the blackboard on the far side of the restaurant on which were marked the day's offerings. 'I can't see a thing,' she said. 'Any suggestions?'

'The waiter will tell us what's good today, but I'm going to have a mixed salad.'

'I'll have a chopped salad,' said Jill, 'with house dressing.'

'I'll have a special salad,' said Kate, falling into line.

'Hello, ladies,' said a waiter, appearing out of the gloom. 'Today's specials are . . .' he started and then hesitated in midflow. Poor thing, he'd got such a lot going on in his head. This waiting on the side was all right for an actor up to a point, but learning new menus every day got to be a bit difficult when you were learning lines for a commercial on Monday next and an audition at Worthing Rep on Thursday. 'Now, let me see,' he said, biting his lips in concentration. 'We've got some lovely fish in a special sauce. And there is some delicious chicken in a special sauce. And er . . .'

'It's OK,' said Louise. 'I'm having a mixed salad, my friend here is having a special salad and this lady is having a chopped salad. We will all have house dressing. Have you got that? And we'll have a bottle of house white wine.'

'Fine,' he said. 'Three salads. Mixed, special and chopped. One of each. House dressing. And a bottle of house white. Got it.'

'Good,' said Kate. 'Bring the wine, please, would you?'

'Coming right up, ma'am.'

'He'll go far, that boy,' said Kate. 'He has a certain style.'

'Now, tell me,' said Jill. 'What's all this about going to work with Kate?'

'Well, the secretary at Kate's office has suddenly left, and they need someone to fill in,' said Louise with bubbly enthusiasm. 'I realized that I could do it and so I suggested to Kate that she give me a chance, and she very bravely said yes.'

'I think you're being the brave one,' commented Kate. 'You haven't checked out the set-up yet.'

'I'm sure it will be great fun,' said Louise, who evidently was not going to be put off. 'Can I start tomorrow?'

Who would have thought the chance of spending your days with Michael, Martin, Geoffrey, Kate and Ned, the force behind the notable concern that was Major Events, could have caused such startling behaviour?

'I'll talk to Michael when I get back to the office and I'll telephone you at home. But if he buys the idea, I can see no reason why not. In fact, I think we'll need you.' At that juncture, the waiter arrived with the house white wine and started to pour.

'Here's to you, Louise. And here's to you, Kate,' said Jill. 'I think this is really good news.'

The salads appeared and there was indeed one of each kind, mixed, special and chopped, with house dressing, though there was a bit of confusion as to which was which and there was some passing of the plates around the table while they were identified and given to their rightful claimants.

'Oh, this is delicious,' said Louise, eating with considerable gusto, an event which was happily noted by Jill. Over the past few weeks, Jill had become quite used to watching Louise spend twenty minutes eating half a boiled egg. She had seen her stir and stir a bowl of soup but not lift the spoon to her mouth. Louise had pushed a piece of halibut around a plate and perhaps, but only perhaps, eaten two mouthfuls. So, to see her chomping her way through a salad, to listen to her call over the waiter and say that she had changed her mind and thought she could do with a baked potato and, yes, sour cream would be great, was a feast for her eyes and veritable music to her ears. When Louise made a snap decision in favour of chocolate mousse, Jill thought she was going to keel over in a dead faint. Louise bubbled on about what she was going to wear, wondered if she shouldn't nip down to Ebury Street and see if Clifford could fit her in for a fast trim and blow dry, questioned Kate on what time she should arrive and should she work all day and, if she did work all day, what time would she finish. She asked Kate time and time again what would happen if Michael didn't want her and was reassured each time that it was highly unlikely Michael wouldn't want her and, if he made any negative noises, Kate promised she would punch him on the nose, but in order to make sure all was decided upon without delay, she would reluctantly have to leave them. Louise insisted that Kate come and have dinner with her that night; she said she would cook something so that they could eat at home and discuss the intricacies of the job.

'Promise you'll telephone me the minute you get an answer, won't you?' urged Louise.

'Yes, of course, I will. Now, I really must go, as it's well past two and I can't push my luck any further. Lunch is on me, by the way. As I've found a new recruit, I'm going to swing this one on my expenses.'

'Oh, are you sure?' asked Jill.

'That's really kind,' said Louise. 'A job and lunch too. I can hardly cope.'

Kate was beginning to feel like the lady who had given Oliver Twist his extra bowl of gruel together with the promise of a stack of luncheon vouchers. 'Really, it's fine.'

'Now, telephone me and don't forget dinner with me tonight. I'm so excited,' said Louise.

'I won't forget. I must go. I'll pay on my way out. Bye, Louise. Bye, Jill.'

The entrance and reception area of Major Events was designed to catch the eye of visitors and workers alike. A large desk occupied the area and behind it were arrayed photographs of some of the more major events Major Events had mounted. If the casual visitor looked hard, they would see Michael with company heroes, Michael with minor sporting personalities, who had been rolled into conferences to add a touch of colour and excitement, Michael with leggy models, who had been rolled in to add a touch of something else, and, at the centre of it all, a photograph of Michael with the medal the Pet Food Producers had given him at the end of a well-received conference in Coventry. Also mounted on the wall were blow-ups of newspaper articles, and wherever Michael was favourably featured, the blow-ups were very blown up indeed. Seated at the large curved desk was supposed to be a young, lovely and efficient girl, who would greet the visitors, inquire as to their name and business, put them at their ease, guide them to a comfortable leather sofa, ply them with coffee or whatever they fancied in the drinks line and shove a newspaper or a magazine under their noses. For ten wonderful months this position had been more than adequately filled by Vicky. Filling the position this afternoon was Geoffrey, jacket off, braces exposed, shirt-sleeves rolled up, green eye-shade in place, and, for some reason known only to himself, sharpening a pile of pencils.

Tomorrow, the position would be filled by Louise.

'Louise, it's me, Kate,' said Kate into the telephone.

'What's the verdict?'

'You're on. Start tomorrow.'

'Oh, that's wonderful. I can't tell you what this means to me.'

'We're the winners, I'm sure.'

'Right, well, I'm definitely going to go and get my hair done. Now, you are coming for supper tonight, aren't you?'

'Absolutely.'

'I do believe things are turning around. I'm beginning to feel as if I'm in the middle of a story that is going to have a happy ending.'

'Well, life's for living, don't you know?'

CHAPTER EIGHT

Patrick, the cat, who was taking a turn round Kate's flat, suddenly arched his back, bushed his tail, squealed, jumped up on all fours and flew out of the room. Perhaps he had been scared by Kate's goldfish. While he was making his speedy flight up the stairs, he narrowly missed tripping up Louise, who was skipping down in happy anticipation of her first day at her new job.

'Oh, poor Patrick. He's in such a state this morning. I'm sure he knows I'm going to be leaving him all day. I do hope the little fellow will be all right. Do you think if I telephone the flat a few times during the day it might help him not to be so lonely?' asked Louise. There is nothing in the world quite like a mother's concern.

'Now, just one more check. I want to make sure I've got everything. Can you think of anything I might have forgotten?' queried Kate.

'What do you usually forget?' asked Louise, trying to be helpful.

'Oh, it changes every day. There's no way of telling.'

'Do I look all right?' asked Louise.

'Of course you do.'

'Do you think this jacket is pretty?'

'Yes, it's lovely.'

'You don't think the blouse is too much?'

'No, it's lovely.'

'I know you said last night that my hair looked good, but does it look all right this morning? He must have cut at least two inches off it. I mean, I like it, but do you?'

'Well, that's what matters, isn't it? If you like it, that's fine. I think it looks great.'

'So, I look all right then?'

'Of course you do.'

And of course she did. She always did. She just didn't know it.

'Now, I think I've got everything, so let's get off. Bye, boys,' said Kate dipping her finger into the aquarium. 'See you tonight.'

Outside it was one of those thoroughly damp and disagreeable mornings. The air was wet and cold, the skies were treacherous and grey and any minute the heavens were going to open and dump everything they owned on any unsuspecting Londoner who had gone out without a brolly. Louise, being in a fine mood, except for her slight misgivings about leaving Patrick, and now sure that she looked all right, was not too concerned about the weather. Kate was too worried about whether she had got everything to give the climatic conditions much thought, but Doug Soper was staring upwards and wondering if the rain would hold off until he had crossed the North Circular. He was going on a trip.

'Hello-o there,' called a happy Doug.

'Morning, Doug,' said Kate.

'Good morning, Doug,' said Louise.

'Well, well, well,' said Doug, as he always did.

Kate mulled this over, wondered what to say and decided that she simply couldn't offer anything substantial in reply.

'Where are you two off to?' asked Doug.

'Work,' snapped Kate. It was where she went every day, well, every weekday, at this time, and there was no reason to suppose that she had suddenly changed her pattern of existence and was off anywhere else.

'And I'm going too,' said Louise. 'To work with Kate, that is. Isn't it exciting?'

'Oh, good news, capital idea,' said Doug. 'Just the ticket. Keep yourself busy, that's what I always say. It's the remedy for everything. Whenever I have been troubled, I have thrown myself into my work. In fact, it's what I did after my sad loss. Climb the ladder, I said to myself, let nobody stand in your way. You can afford to give it your all. Show the bosses at

Kilburn the stuff you're made of. The best thing I ever did. May I say, you have made a very sound decision, my dear. Good luck. Good luck.'

'Thank you,' said Louise.

'And what a fine gesture of friendship and understanding you have made, Kate. To offer Louise a job. What can I say? A splendid thing. Capital.'

'Thank you,' said Kate, shuffling her feet and looking down at the pavement.

Kate was anxious to get on, but Doug, having grasped Louise's arm in a gesture of solidarity amongst the broken-hearted, seemed unable and unwilling to let them go just yet. He obviously thought there was a bit more mileage to be got out of the conversation. Standing there on the pavement as they did, Kate could have reached down into her holdall and taken out her newspaper in order to do the crossword. Six down: a tiresome, retired elderly party: four letters, beginning with an F.

'Of course, keeping on the go and keeping busy are principles I apply to my life even to this day. Now that I'm retired, I make sure I stay active. Take today, for example. I'm off to Huntingdon to see Colin. Well, of course, it's not actually Huntingdon, but near by in the countryside. I'm going to make quite a trip of it and stop somewhere for a bite of lunch. I don't like to miss lunch. A regular pattern is very important to the quality of life.'

'Well, do have a good time,' enthused Kate. 'Just how long are you going to be in Huntingdon, or, should I say, near by in the countryside?' She was a girl who liked to get her facts right. Being quite bright, she should have realized that Doug Soper was a man who *liked* his girls to get their facts right.

'I should say about a week. Colin needs some assistance with his garden, and then, of course, I can always chip in and help with his beer making. I must say, I am anticipating a very rewarding few days.'

'Well, we simply must fly, Doug. It's been lovely to chat, but work calls and, as you always so rightly say, you've got to keep on the go,' said Kate, trying to disengage Louise from Doug's vice-like grip, and then she added on a very sincere note, 'Do drive carefully, won't you?'

'I most certainly will. Well, goodbye, you two,' said Doug. 'Until we meet again!' He waved in their direction and watched them walking down to the end of the road, where he saw Kate's Renault Five parked. He had certainly brightened up their morning, as Kate seemed to be laughing. What charming girls they were. And both single. Would you credit it? It was difficult to understand young men these days. One wondered just what they were made of. They lacked stamina and substance. That's what they lacked. No backbone, that was for sure. Not the types to have made a go of Kilburn and adversity.

'Huntingdon, here I come,' said Doug out loud. He then polished the wing mirrors of his car and gave himself up to a happy and contented whistle.

'Geoffrey, dear,' said Kate.

Geoffrey was wandering around the office looking lost and also looking for something that was lost. He was picking up newspapers and rifling through them, checking under piles of trade magazines and hunting under cushions, all to no avail.

'Morning, Katy,' he called, still on his hunt.

'I was about to install Louise behind her desk, when I found this little black book. As it is called "Time Form", I am making a wild guess and hazarding that it belongs to you. Did you perhaps leave it here after your tour of duty at the switchboard yesterday?'

'Oh, well done, Chief. I've been hunting for that all morning,' said a grateful Geoffrey. He ambled across the main office from his corner and threaded his way past Kate's cluttered desk, happy that he would now have all his valuable reference material around him when he plotted the day's events at Catterick.

'Geoffrey, this is Louise, who is going to be working with us for a while,' said Kate.

'How do you do?' said one.

'How do you do?' said the other.

'Geoffrey takes care of things technical. Don't you, Geoffrey?' said Kate.

'Well, I try. I can but try. I say, Chief, have you seen my eye-shade? I don't seem to be able to lay my hands on it.'

'Is this it?' offered Louise, holding the item aloft.

'The very same. Thanks, Number One.'

'Anyone in?' asked Kate.

'Tillie's been in and says we've run out of Harpic and could you oblige. Michael's in and he says he wants a meeting. He said something about a trip to Chicago. And now that you're in, I'm going to nip out. I won't be long.'

'When?' asked Kate.

'What – the meeting, when will I be back or Chicago?'

'In order. Starting from the top. First, the meeting.'

'Eleven.'

'Secondly, what time will you be back and will you be back in time?'

'I'm only nipping out for ten minutes, so I'll certainly be back in time. I wouldn't miss the meeting for the world. Michael might have a technical question to pose.'

'And thirdly, Chicago?'

'Dunno. I must dash. Catterick looks good. In fact Catterick looks very good. Toodle-pip,' announced jovial Geoff, as he grabbed a checked cap from the hat-stand and added a cheerful wave.

Well, at least Louise had met the technical department, though it was doubtful that he could be relied upon to explain the intricacies of the word processor, loud hailers and tick-tack men being more Geoffrey's chosen mode of easy communication.

'Do you understand these machines?' asked Kate, a note of reverence slipping into her voice.

'Oh, yes, it's the 1986 model. The K-100 mark 2 was good, but this one is fantastic,' said Louise.

'I'm hopeless with them. I'm very attached to my old Olivetti and I refuse to be parted from it. Now, this is the switchboard. Shall I run through the system with you?'

'No, it's fine, I've used one of them before. They're quite straightforward and I see everyone's extension number is easily decipherable.'

'The photocopier is over there, behind the kitchen. Do you want to have a look at it?'

'No, I'm sure it won't be a problem,' said Louise. 'So that's the kitchen. Shall I make some coffee?'

'That would be wonderful,' said Kate, thinking that she was in contact with a whirlwind. 'My desk is over there. I'll be going through the post.'

'Shall I make Michael a coffee too?' asked Louise.

This girl was good. This girl was very good. Vicky had been a gem, but Louise was quick to show initiative and get the general drift of what was required.

'Well, yes, I suppose that might be an idea.'

The accounts department announced its arrival as it always did, with its squash bag dumped in front of what had been Vicky's desk, but what was now, and had been since 9.30, Louise's desk. In addition to the squash kit this morning, there was a Lillywhites carrier bag, which, had anyone chosen to inspect it, would have revealed one new pair of Reebok shoes, four Fred Perry shirts, in a range of pastel shades, three pairs of extra-absorbent socks and half a dozen squash balls, yellow spot. Louise walked round to the front of her desk, picked up the squash bag, then the carrier bag, looked at them and then replaced them on the floor.

'Where shall I put these?' she inquired, anxious to get her list of duties correct at the outset.

'Don't do anything for him. Martin, pick up your squash kit and your carrier bag, take them to your desk, and get busy. Michael wants a meeting at 11. Geoffrey says it's something to do with a trip to Chicago,' said Kate.

'What, we're all going to Chicago?'

'No, Martin, no.' She shook her head and then lay her forehead on her desk with her arms outstretched in front of her. 'Michael's going to Chicago.'

'Oh.' For a moment he had thought he would have to telephone the Association and get a list of squash clubs in Illinois. 'So, it's just another meeting,' agonized Martin.

'I'm afraid so.'

'Morning, Kate,' said Ned, as he entered the reception area. 'Oh, hello,' he said, noticing the newcomer, who had found a watering-can from the dark recesses of the kitchen and was restoring an ailing rubber plant to life. 'I'm Ned. You must be Louise. Welcome. It's a madhouse, but you'll get used to it.'

'Hello,' said Louise. 'I've got some coffee on the go. Would you like one?'

'That would be lovely. Yes, I would thank you,' said Ned.

'Martin,' called Louise, 'Would you like a coffee?'

He looked up from his ledger. 'Oh, yes, that would be lovely.' His eyes did not return to his ledger, they stayed with Louise. He thought she was quite delightful.

'I'm back,' said Geoffrey, as if there was any need to announce his arrival, bounding as he did across the reception area and into the main office, all tweed jacket and *Sporting Life*.

'Geoffrey, would you like a coffee?' asked Louise.

'How very civil, Number One. I'd love one, thank you.'

'Kate,' said Ned, who was just settling into his chair and the morning papers.

'Yes?'

'I didn't know you knew such a nice class of person.'

Louise had a unanimous vote of approval. The only member of the group left to meet and impress was Michael.

'Kate,' said Michael, sticking his head out of his office. 'Meeting at 11. Would you let everyone know?'

'Certainly.'

'Thank you,' he mumbled, retreating back into his office.

'Meeting at 11!' she shouted. 'Meeting at 11!'

'Kate, I'm going to give you a gavel for Christmas,' said Ned.

'I think I'd prefer a bell. Oyez, oyez, meeting at 11!'

Louise took Michael's coffee into his office. She had put the cup and saucer on a tray, together with a small jug of milk and a napkin. She knocked before entering and, when told to come in, went in, whereupon she announced herself.

'Hello. I'm Louise. Thank you so much for giving me the chance to work here. I really appreciate it.'

Michael looked at Louise, he looked at her lovely dark hair, her brown eyes, he looked at the blouse and the jacket, he looked at the tray, which was placed on his desk, he looked at the cup and the saucer and he looked at the small jug of milk and the napkin.

'The pleasure is mine, I assure you. I hope you will be happy here.'

'I'm sure I will. Now, is there anything I can do for you?'

'Well, there is one niggling problem, which came up yesterday, and, what with no Vicky, I'm afraid nothing was done about it.'

'What's that?'

'Well, it's to do with my wife's account at Harrods. There seems to have been a mix-up with last month's account and cheque and the balance on this month's account, and Andrea can't fathom it out.'

'Oh, don't worry. I'll telephone the accounts department. They're very helpful. There's one really sweet lady there who always helps me out when I have a problem with my account. Mind you, there seldom are any problems, as they are so efficient and it's such a lovely shop.'

'Yes, Andrea likes it. In fact, we both like it.' Michael was impressed with what he saw. He was very impressed indeed.

'Right, I'll get on to that and I'll let you know how I get on,' said Louise as she took the account from Michael's outstretched hand.

'Anything else?'

'Well, there's a meeting at 11,' he stuttered.

'Yes, I think everyone knows. But I'll make sure.'

Michael sipped his coffee. It was just how he liked it. It cleared his head and enabled him to think of his meeting, when he was going to discuss his forthcoming trip to Chicago and the impact of the meetings he was planning with business associates in the Windy City. He thought he would just pop out and see how things were going in the main office; besides, he wanted to have a quick word with Kate.

'Kate,' he said.

'Yes, Michael?'

'I like your friend. I think she's quite charming and very efficient. Well done.'

'Why, thank you.'

And as he walked back to his office deep in thought about his meeting and Chicago and its implications – he was after all a very hard-pressed executive – he turned. He seemed to be in a reflective mood. 'Meeting at 11. Kate, you'll be a darling, won't you, and let everyone know?' He closed his office door, a happy man. He liked a meeting, he like efficiency, he liked good-looking women, and Louise was certainly that, and, damn it all, he liked Harrods.

'Meeting at 11, meeting at 11,' boomed Kate.

'I know,' said Martin sternly. His finger had slipped on his calculator, and he would have to start all over again.

'Cut it out,' said Ned.

'What was that?' asked Geoffrey.

'Meeting at 11.'

'O K, Chief. I'll be there. Number One, there's a meeting at 11.'

'Yes, I know,' said Louise.

'Just checking,' said Geoffrey and then, on a more hopeful note, he added, 'Do you know anything about horses?'

As everyone knew, Michael wanted his meeting and he wanted it at eleven o'clock, and when a meeting man wants a meeting he usually gets it. It was now approaching midday, and Michael had barely paused for breath. He had certainly not posed any technical questions to Geoffrey and neither had he discussed anything with the accounts department. Kate had not been required to comment, and neither had Ned. Michael was droning on, and had reached such a pitch that it was almost like a religious chant about the opportunities afforded by a connection with a company in Chicago. They had all heard it before and were deep in their own thoughts. Geoffrey was thinking about Catterick, and, specifically, the possibilities of the 2.30; Martin was dissecting, point by point, last night's squash game, which he had unfortunately and un-characteristically lost; Ned was wondering if he would have time that afternoon to get over to Jermyn Street to pick up his new shirts; and Kate was trying not to think about Nick.

'So, you see that I simply have to go to Chicago. I have tried, but there seems to be no way out of it. But I am sure that all of us here today will realize that this opportunity represents a landmark in the history of Major Events. I am hoping that after this trip to Chicago I will be able to persuade Cindy to find a few days in her hectic schedule to come over here and find out exactly what we are about.'

'Sorry, who?' asked Kate. She was afraid she might have missed something.

'Cindy. Oh, I haven't mentioned her before, have I? I suppose I haven't.'

'No, you haven't,' said Kate as she discreetly dug Ned in the ribs. She was going to get to the bottom of the Chicago connection, no matter what.

'She and her partner, Lou Bolt, run the highly successful Chicago-based company, Bedliner and Bolt. they have worldwide connections, and I think we could have a very useful working relationship.'

Poor Andrea. All those years worrying about his shirts and that's what she got. It wasn't right. Cindy might well be convinced of the need to come over here and find out exactly what they were about. But what of Andrea? What would she do when she found out about working relationships and precisely what Cindy Bedliner was up to? And you could bet she would be up to something.

'And now, coming to you, Ned, for a moment, if I may. I am going to have to ask you and Kate to take over the arrangements for the conference with the Sunrise Group.'

'Well, I don't think that's going to present a problem. How do you feel, Kate?'

'Fine with me. No problem at all.'

'Of course, I have already done most of the groundwork and, indeed, I had lunch the other day with Dermot Dessistropoulos, who is manager at the host hotel, and he is now fully apprised of the situation.'

'Well, perhaps we could go and check out the site?' offered Ned.

'Good idea,' said Michael. He had a good team around him. If only he could have Cindy around him and the benefit of a working relationship. With her expertise, drive and flair, things might be even better.

'Where is the conference to be held?' asked Kate.

'At the Sunrise Motor Inn,' said Michael.

'Where's that?' asked Kate. The Sunrise Motor Inn not being an establishment of which she had heard a great deal, she was therefore unable to place it immediately.

'It's near Huntingdon,' continued Michael.

'Huntingdon?' She was sitting on the edge of her chair.

'Well, not exactly Huntingdon. It's just outside.'

'Anywhere near Newmarket?' piped up Geoffrey.

'Well, that would depend on which direction you're coming from,' said Martin, a reply that was typical of an accountant. Never any help when you need them.

'How near Huntingdon?' asked Kate. The level of her voice had gone up a few notches.

'Quite near,' offered Michael.

'I suppose it's in the countryside?' she said, her voice still on the rise.

'Yes, that's right. Dermot says it's an idyllic setting; I have seen some of the plans of the hotel and the conference facilities and I must say they have certainly done an outstanding job. The hotel has recently been totally refurbished, and that is why they want to hold their inaugural conference there. I have every confidence that we are going to be able to mount an impressive and memorable event,' said Michael, who would probably be cavorting in the Windy City with Ms Bedliner, flashing his gold American Express card and oblivious to all else.

'Now, Martin, which route would you suggest for getting to Huntingdon?' queried Geoffrey.

'There are several things to be weighed up here before we can reach a final and satisfactory decision. First of all, it's important to bear in mind at the outset which part of London we are travelling from. Once we establish those facts, we can consider the merits of either the M11 route via Cambridge, or the A1, which has the benefit of a dual carriageway all the way.'

'Cambridge is near Newmarket, isn't it?' said Geoffrey, at long last sitting up and really taking notice.

'Indeed, it is. But the A1 goes all the way to York.'

'Does it, by Jove!'

'Where in the countryside?' tried Kate again.

'What – Newmarket or York?' asked Geoffrey.

'No!' screamed Kate.

'Well, you interrupted. I thought it was something important.'

'Where is it?'

'Where's what?'

'The Sunrise Motor Inn!'

'Does it matter?' said Ned. 'Huntingdon is a very small place.'

'That,' she said, 'is precisely what I am afraid of.'

CHAPTER NINE

'Hello,' said a sleepy and hesitant voice.

'Why did it take you so long to answer the phone?'

'I couldn't find it.'

'I couldn't find mine either.'

'Oh.'

'It's eight o'clock.'

'Yes.'

'You told me to ring you at 8.'

'I did? When?'

'Last night, after dinner. You said ring me at 8 and we'll have breakfast together. In fact, your exact words were "Promise me you'll ring at 8".'

'They were?'

'Yes, they were.'

'Gracious, is it 8?'

'Yes, that's why I'm ringing.'

'Well, I'm sure you're right. I'll just have a couple of Aspirin and I'll be right down. I'll meet you in the restaurant. Order me some tea, would you?' said Kate, her voice slightly less sleepy.

She replaced the receiver of the telephone, checked the bedside clock and her watch to make sure it really was 8, because it certainly didn't feel like it, and looked around the hotel bedroom. She knew it was a hotel room because it was a rectangular shape and she was in the middle of a king-sized bed. Right at this minute the only thing she wanted to do, apart from finding some Aspirin, was to sink back into the pillows for another hour. Directly opposite her against the far wall was a low-level chest of drawers, and placed above it was a mirror, in which she could see her reflection. She rather wished she could not.

Perhaps it was an interior designer's cruel idea of a joke. The room was pleasantly decorated in shades of grey and peach, and around the walls were scattered three all-purpose pastel prints framed in all-purpose grey steel. The fabric of the curtains (which did not quite meet in the middle) matched the fabric of the bedspread, which in turn matched the shades on the two large lamps placed on the tables on either side of the bed. On a round table near the window was a basket of yellow and white roses, a gift from the management. The bathroom was to the left of the door as you came in. It was to the bathroom that she headed in search of Aspirin.

When away from home and staying in a hotel it is always a good idea to have a decent breakfast. The same holds true if you are travelling on a train and are fortunate enough to find the restaurant car open. It's a prudent move to tuck in when you can, because you can never predict when you might have another opportunity to eat something. Now, if you happen to be staying in a hotel as a guest of the management because they are trying to butter you up and swing a bit of business, then it is a particularly good idea to plunge in and have a substantial breakfast and sample everything that is on offer – to hell with the expense.

Sadly, in these days of convenience and high-pressure marketing, there are fewer and fewer hotels that adhere to the old breakfast rules. There used to be a time when you knew exactly what you were getting in a British hotel between the hallowed hours of seven and nine, when all was quiet except for the distinguished waiter at your side gently easing you to your table, where you got straight into *The Times* before your eggs arrived. Today, anyone descending or ascending – depending upon the quirks of modern architecture – to the restaurant anxious to polish off their sausage and bacon is likely to be greeted by the sight of a groaning buffet table. And so it was with the Sunrise Group. They had done their market research, they had had their meeting, they had canvassed opinion, and, since their flagship hotel, their pride and joy situated in the vicinity of Huntingdon, had been refurbished, done over and revamped, breakfast had changed. There in the midst of that gracious dining-room, which overlooked rolling parkland and a lake, stood an oblong table covered in a red gingham cloth.

On the table, surrounding a centre-piece of dried flowers and corn, which contributed an autumnal flavour befitting the time of the year, were packets of cereals in little boxes, ranging from Cornflakes for the die-hards through to bran for the more fickle who had read their diet books, a massive basket of fresh fruit, bowls of prunes, figs and apricots, a variety of bread and rolls and large jugs of orange and grapefruit juice. They were the type of jugs that came with a guarantee to drip.

Anxious to outstrip their competitors, the Sunrise Group had added taped country and western music to the breakfast-room of the Sunrise Motor Inn, Huntingdon. They had also added a smiling, neatly *coiffured* and uniformed individual, whose duty it was to greet the early-morning traveller, weary after a night in a strange bed, and encourage them to help themselves from the 'boofay', after which they could sit down and wait for their waitress, who would be along for their order.

'Thank goodness you telephoned, Ned. I'm not feeling at all well this morning. Did you get me my tea?' said Kate.

'It doesn't work like that.'

She didn't understand. Her early-morning headache rendered her perplexed.

'What do you mean, it doesn't work like that?' she demanded.

'They like you to have selected your fruit juice and cereal from the buffet before they give you your tea.'

'To hell with the buffet. I want a cup of tea,' groaned Kate. She could be very petulant in the mornings, and although the old banjo-pickin' music might have been great in Kentucky, it was not helping to get the day off to a great start in Huntingdon.

'Calm down, old girl. A waitress will be along any minute.'

'Have you got tea?'

'No, I've got coffee, but quite frankly all it's doing for me is to make me wish I'd ordered tea.'

'Have you ordered your breakfast?'

'Yes.'

'What?'

'A fisherman's wave.'

'A what?'

'It's a kipper.'

'Oh. That'll be nice. How long will I have to wait? I'm feeling very seedy.'

'What would you like for your cooked breakfast, madam?' inquired the young waitress, all got up in frilly red gingham. It didn't suit her at all. Somone should have told her.

'I'd like some tea, please.'

'And to follow?'

'No. What I mean is, I would like some tea now and then I will decide what I will have to follow.'

'I have to take your order first and then I will bring you your tea.'

Kate put her head into her hands and looked as if she was about to clench her teeth and let out a slow hissing noise. Ned knew the signs, for he had seen her do exactly the same thing when their plane had been diverted to Prestwick because Heathrow was fog-bound and a ten-hour coach journey had separated her from Nick, who had got a weekend pass from his wife. Still, it was probably best not to bring Nick up at this point.

'My friend will have the Sunrise Good Morning Cheery Platter. That is, she would like fried eggs, bacon, sausage, tomatoes, mushrooms and tea. And if you could possibly bring the tea as soon as possible it would be much appreciated, not only by my friend, but also by me,' said Ned in his role of intermediary.

'And toast?'

This wretched waitress in red gingham had learned her script and she was going to stick to it.

'Yes.'

'Brown or white, sir?'

'Brown.'

'Thank you, sir,' she beamed at Ned and then turning to Kate she said, 'Please help yourself to juice and cereals from the buffette.' Whereupon the gingham turned and flounced off to the kitchen, not to place an order for a Sunrise Good Morning Cheery Platter, or for tea, or for brown toast, but to have a good, old-fashioned moan.

'Good dinner last night, wasn't it?' remarked Ned.

'Lovely. May I pinch some of your coffee while I'm waiting for my tea?'

'Believe me, you'd be much better off waiting for the tea.'

'Is it that bad?'

'It's that bad and more.'

'I'm not sure I like this place.'

'It will do. By the way, Dermot fancies you.'

'Oh, really?' asked Kate, brightening up considerably. Perhaps she might find a way to like this place after all.

'Your tea,' said the waitress, putting down a welcome pot on the table.

Kate poured herself a cup, drank slowly and began to feel much better. The tea helped, as did the Aspirin, and so did the enlightening bit of information concerning Dermot's wandering eye, which seemed to have rested for the moment upon Kate.

'I didn't notice,' she said, adhering to the rule that it was often a good idea to be very cool at the outset of any new relationship.

'You rarely do. Anyway, I'm not sure you were in the right frame of mind to notice anything last night.'

'Thank you for your confidence, Ned. You know how to wound, don't you? Anyway, let's not get excited, he's probably married.'

'No, he's not. I checked that out. I have your well-being at heart, you know. When we are in his office later this morning, you will notice a photograph of a Titian-haired beauty and two equally beautiful little girls. The elder beauty is their mother and his ex-wife. The children are still his.'

'Your kipper, sir,' said another red-ginghamed waitress. It didn't suit her either. 'And your fried eggs, bacon, sausage, tomatoes and mushrooms, madam.'

For a while the conversation turned from Dermot to the delights of kippers and fried eggs, bacon, sausage, tomatoes and mushrooms. However, it was not for long.

'What time are we seeing Dermot?' asked Kate, though she cleverly did not betray herself and blush at the mention of his name.

'Do you want to try some of my kipper?' offered Ned.

'No, thank you. You didn't answer my question.'

'What question?'

'What time are we seeing Dermot?'

'At about 9.30. We're just going to run through the requirements for the conference, check the technical side of things and then I believe lunch is planned. Are you sure you don't want to try some of my kipper?'

'Quite sure.'

'Suit yourself.'

'Actually, I don't know why we are here for two days. We could have driven up for the afternoon and got everything done.'

'Oh, come along, Kate, relax and enjoy it. The group wants to show off the hotel. It's a public-relations exercise for them. We know we don't need to be here, but let's just go along with it. What would we be doing at the office anyway? Michael's away in Chicago and Louise is coping admirably with everything.'

'Yes, she is, isn't she? I'm delighted with that. I wonder if we can persuade her to stay permanently.'

'She's great, but she's too good for us. I really like her.'

'I'm so pleased you like her. I was wondering if you and James would like to come over for dinner towards the end of next week. It's coming up to the weekend when she and David were supposed to be getting married, so I think we ought to be extra specially nice to her.'

'Of course. We'll be there. Should she have some time off work?'

'No, it's best if she keeps busy.'

'You're probably right,' agreed Ned.

Kate finished her second cup of tea, ate most of her Cheery Platter, looked at the ready-sliced toast and managed to refrain.

'Now, I think I'll go back upstairs to my room and smarten myself up.'

'Good idea. Your tights are laddered.'

'Thank you,' said Kate. She was used to Ned's little ways.

'Nine-thirty in Dermot's office. Don't forget.'

As if she was likely to. No, she would not forget. She would be there on time, smartened up and very cool, even though she would steal a look at the Titian-haired beauty.

All morning they checked lists, they looked at plans, they examined menus, they were shown into bedrooms, which were just like the ones they'd slept in, they had coffee in the lobby overlooking the fountain, they looked at the dining-room and agreed that it was indeed a most handsome room, they were shown the view of the rolling parkland and the lake, they checked video machines, plugs, leads, carousels, projectors, screens, sat on hard chairs, soft chairs, were introduced to the chef and complimented him on last night's dinner (though Kate was not sure what she had eaten and had Ned been questioned closely he would have been pushed to remember) and they even went into a small dark room and looked at a photocopier. In the midst of it all, just when Kate was thinking she would have to slip away and find another Aspirin, she could have sworn Dermot cupped her elbow as they walked into the conference room.

The thing about hotels is that there is always something going on, and a good manager, as undoubtedly Dermot was, is always on call. Just when he is about to turn the conversation around to something he has been burning to discuss, someone interrupts and asks him if he might just pop along to reception as there's a problem with the arrangements for the wedding on Saturday. At about the time when he can see lunch on the horizon, there will be a request that he try and sort out the double booking in the function room. It never stops, what with the Rotary Club wanting the Dawn Room on the fifth instead of the tenth and the Conservative Ladies Luncheon Group about to kill in order to gain possession of the Sunset Suite on the fifteenth. But a chap lacking in initiative does not a good manager make. The directors of the Sunrise Group were very pleased with their choice of Dermot Dessistropoulos, and one thing they had noticed about him at his interview was that he was decisive.

'I think we might take a break now,' he said to Ned and Kate. 'Let's get away from here for a while and have lunch in the local pub. I'm sure you'll like it.'

'Oh, I'm sure we will,' said Kate.

'We'll take my car. It's parked around at the back by the coach-house. That's where I live. In this sort of job one simply has to be available twenty-four hours a day.'

So he lived on site. Kate found herself going quite weak at the knees at the prospect of seeing the reverse side of his curtains. It was just as well she had put on a fine show at the breakfast table. Lack of nourishment at this juncture might have resulted in an unfortunate fainting fit.

'I'll get in the back,' said Ned when they reached Dermot's car. Bless him. 'You sit in the front, Kate, next to Dermot.'

'Isn't the countryside beautiful? I had no idea,' cooed Kate.

'It is beautiful, isn't it?' said Dermot. He was talking to Kate and ignoring Ned.

'What a lovely car,' she said.

'Yes it is, isn't it?'

'What is it?'

'It's a BMW.'

Just like Michael's. In fact, it was the same model and the same colour.

'Oh, what a beautiful cottage,' she said.

Ned would have liked to grab her wrist, twist her arm, kick her ankle or thump her on the back, but as he was sitting in the back, firmly trapped by the car's kiddie locks, he was powerless to act.

'Oh, what a beautiful pub,' cooed Kate.

'This is one of my favourite haunts,' said Dermot. 'I think it is so important to have a place away from work, away from the pressure, where one can relax and recharge the batteries.'

'Oh absolutely,' she agreed and then added a look of compassion.

Dermot opened the heavy wooden door of the pub and beckoned Kate to go in, followed by Ned. As Kate turned to watch Dermot come through the door she noticed that he was so tall he had to stoop in order to miss knocking his divine head on the beams.

'Now, what would you like to drink, Kate?' he asked, casually placing his left elbow on the bar.

'What are you having, Dermot?'

'Oh, a beer.'

'I don't usually drink beer, but I think I'll try one.'

'Right, half a pint of bitter for you, and what about you, Ned?'

The third member of this lunchtime expedition had remained silent for some time but now said, 'A beer, please.'

'Right, you two go and sit down and I'll bring the beer over,' said Dermot. 'There's a free table over by the fireplace.'

Ned guided Kate in the direction of the ingle-nook fireplace (where surprisingly there was indeed a free table), not because he felt inclined to be a gentleman, but because he knew she wasn't concentrating on the business at hand. The pub was dark and was full of lunchtime drinkers who only had sixty minutes in which to down their bitter and sandwiches, and they certainly wouldn't relish colliding with Kate and having to spend valuable minutes mopping up and queuing for replacement pints.

'Oh, isn't this fun?' enthused Kate.

'Sit down,' commanded Ned.

Seated, Ned would at least be able to administer an advisory kick on the ankle, should it become necessary. He thought it might. When Dermot arrived with the beer, demonstrating that he must have worked in a bar during his hotel training, since he was expert at juggling two and a half pints of best bitter through a crowd, Ned saw a look of awe lodging itself on Kate's face and he knew that a kick was ominously near.

'Dermot.'

'Yes, Kate?'

'There's something I've been dying to ask you.'

'Fire away.'

'Well, how did you get a name like Dermot Dessistropoulos?' He had been asked the question before. 'It's so unusual. It is unusual, isn't it, Ned?'

'Yes, it is unusual,' agreed Ned over the top of his beer.

'Well, my mother was Irish and worked in a pub, behind the

136

bar, and my father was Greek and worked in a pub in front of the bar selling whelks.'

Oh, how thrilling. So really your family has always been in the catering business. It's sort of in the blood, you might say.'

'You might say that, yes. I always wanted to be in hotels. Even as a child I knew exactly what I wanted.'

'How wonderful,' she sighed.

There was no other way, Ned was going to have to give her a kick. Which he did. Unfortunately Kate, being a woman in love and a bit slow on the uptake, thought it was an enthusiastic Dermot carrying on from where he had left off with the cupped elbow.

'Now, how about a spot of lunch?' suggested Dermot.

Kate knew that when romance is in the offing the first thing it strikes is the appetite. 'Well, for some reason, I'm not all that hungry. I'll have some potted shrimps and perhaps just a slice of brown bread.'

'Ned?'

'Shepherd's pie and some brown sauce.'

'I'll have the same. I'll just go off and organize things. Shout if you want more beer or anything. Perhaps some crisps, Kate? Cheese and onion or smokey bacon, some Twiglets, a few peanuts, cashews, or smoked almonds?' A good hotel man never leaves his job. He knows how to please the customers.

'No, thank you.'

'Okey-dokey.'

There was no dealing with Kate when she was in this mood, smiling and cooing all over the place. It was so unlike her. However, Ned being Ned thought he had better have a go and give her a few words of cautionary advice. He was just about to take advantage of the fact that Dermot was occupied at the bar ordering up potted shrimps and shepherd's pie twice, when a fellow in a tweed jacket and cavalry-twill trousers came up to join them. He was grinning in a demented manner, but then so was Kate.

'Well, hello-o there. What a surprise,' said a voice known only too well to Kate. 'No, don't get up. Well, well, well.'

'Oh, hello, Doug,' said Kate, and, because she was trying to be charming and wonderful and to show her best side to Dermot, it came out as being charming and wonderful to Doug Soper.

'What are you doing here, Kate? Well, well, well,' said Doug. He was in his element. He had told Colin all about Kate and here she was, and here he was, and here Colin was, though he didn't know that Dermot was here too or would be in a minute.

'We're here on business. Doug, let me introduce my colleague, Ned,' said Kate and as Dermot returned to the table she was able to say, 'And this is Dermot Dessistropoulos of the Sunrise Motor Inn. You might know it, it's just down the road.'

'I most certainly do. Well, how do you do? Delighted to meet you. And delighted to meet you Ned. Well, any friend of Kate's and all that,' said Doug, grinning and jumping about on his Hush Puppies. 'And this is Colin,' he said, dropping the grin and switching to a proud father look, though what he thought he had to be proud about was anybody's guess. Colin was Colin, and that's about all that can usefully be said of him, other than that he was rather puny.

'Now, let me get you some drinks. This calls for a celebration. What a turn-up for the books. Beer all round, is it?'

While Doug, dressed for a fatstock sale, was striding around the pub, bumping into people and apologizing, Beryl was at the hairdresser. Beryl – who was first introduced when Doug was a soul in torment trying to fathom out the workings of his troubled heart concerning Kate and Louise – had been considered by Doug. Poor Beryl, that stalwart of the bookkeeping department, Kilburn, who had devoted all those years to Doug, had been dropped, just like that, with no warning at all, and he had gone off to Huntingdon. So, as Doug was thinking that life can be strange at times and perhaps he had made the right decision after all, Beryl was with Lawrence having a perm. She would have been interested to learn that Doug did have some misgivings about throwing her over, but would have thought it typical that he was now making light of the fact and was rapidly switching his thoughts to the workings of fate in throwing Kate into his path, and in Huntingdon, in the countryside, of all places. Beryl had been very brave and had decided that she would not let the likes of Doug Soper upset her. No, Beryl was plucky, and it takes more than a Doug to upset a plucky woman. So, there she was sitting under the dryer, Lawrence having done her perm and also her roots. To hell with it, when the spirits are in need of uplift, there are no limits. 'I'll have the colour done,' she said. And Lawrence, being a sensitive hairdresser and highly tuned to the needs of his customers, had whipped out the *acajou* (that's French for mahogany – he knew his tints) and had given her a thorough overhaul and thrown in a neck massage as well. Had she known that Doug was just about to down a second pint of the pub's finest bitter, she probably would have willed him to choke on it. Well, put Doug behind you, Beryl, she had said to herself, tonight you are going out. Doug or no Doug, don't let it put you off your square dancing. She was going to put on her cowboy boots and do her do-si-do, and if anyone wanted her to be his partner and swing her around, he jolly well could.

Back at the pub they had polished off their shrimps and shepherd's pie. Doug joined in with the pie while Colin had a bowl of soup. There were remnants of it on his beard.

'And do you know what? Colin and I have been to a different pub every day and tried a different beer each time. Quite amazing. Well, well, well,' said Doug.

Colin nodded but said nothing. Perhaps he was always that way or perhaps the real ale man had had enough beer and had had enough Doug.

'Well, we must be getting back,' said Dermot. 'Duty calls.'

'Yes, we must,' agreed Kate.

'Well, this has been a delightful surprise,' said Doug, who was looking even more demented than ever. He was either very excited, or very tight, and possibly both.

'Yes, what a surprise,' said Kate, going along with the drift of the conversation.

'Mmm,' said Colin.

They all said goodbye in turn to each other and Colin entered into the proceedings by giving Kate a hesitant handshake. Just what had Doug told him about life in Vaucluse Road? The barman waved jauntily and called out to Dermot that he would see him later, which allowed Doug to suggest that it would be wonderful if they all met up for a drink at six o'clock. In the general hubbub of leave-taking, the suggestion was not followed through, but Kate, knowing Doug so well, thought it likely that he would be on the telephone before the afternoon was out; if that gave him no satisfaction he would be in the cocktail bar of the Sunrise Motor Inn as the doors were opened and the shutters raised for evening trade.

'Ned, get in the back of the car,' whispered Kate out of the side of her mouth.

'All right. But don't make a mess of it. You know what you're like,' he whispered back, though, being a dignified chap, he did not find it necessary to enter into contortions of the mouth.

'Yes, I'm afraid I do,' agreed Kate reluctantly.

The drive back to the hotel was quick and the return journey past all those lovely cottages and trees, like all return journeys, seemed faster than the outward one. The conversation was quieter and more subdued, and the walk from the car, parked by the coach-house, was all too brisk. A flood of messages awaited Dermot when he entered the reception area and, as there is something very appealing about seeing a man conduct his business, especially when he is in command, it added more to Kate's glowing picture and made up for the fast drive and the brisk walk. Dermot was definitely a man with responsibilities, and, when he suggested that Kate and Ned might like to carry on working in the conference room because he had so much on, they readily agreed. Not that they had any work that needed doing, but the free hours would at least allow them to return to their rooms, and although they talked about catching up on some paperwork while they were in the lift, Ned looked forward to reading his book (he had a John D. MacDonald on the go) and Kate thought she might have a face mask and a little nap. Dermot had mentioned a cup of tea at 4.30, and it was something they all looked forward to with anticipation of varying degrees.

At 4.35 Kate sat down in the lobby, where afternoon tea was being served and a pianist tinkled on a white grand piano. She noticed that Dermot was running a bit late, but happily realized that it was probably due to taking his work so seriously. Poor lamb, he was undoubtedly snowed under with paperwork. No matter, she had taken the precaution of bringing a paperback with her and she opened it up and carried on where she had left off. It was the stirring tale of Etta from Bingley, who had been sadly orphaned when she was only eight years old and was put into a life of servitude in the big house by her disagreeable Aunt Hestor. Little Etta had started off in the laundry washing smalls which, as anyone who reads thick historical romances will know, is about as bad as it can get. Such had been her beauty and determination that she had caught the eye of young Roderick, the son of the master. A voice interrupted Kate's reading.

'Sorry I'm late, Kate. I got caught up with some telephone calls. You know how it is,' apologized Dermot.

She looked up with a start to see him standing there beside her chair, the light pouring in through the plate-glass window behind him and throwing his craggy features into shadow.

'Oh, yes, I do. But I've been quite happy here reading my book. I think that's a sign of a good hotel, when a single woman can feel comfortable on her own,' said Kate congratulating herself on slipping that bit about the single woman into the conversation. Quite subtle, she thought. 'I do like your hotel,' she continued.

'I'm delighted you do. I was wondering . . .'

'Yes?' said Kate, betraying nothing.

'I was wondering if you and Ned would like to have dinner with me tonight?'

'Why, yes, I'm sure we would. I mean, I would and I'm sure Ned would too,' said Kate.

'Mr Dessistropoulos. Telephone call for you,' called the receptionist.

Kate watched him walk towards the reception desk and pick up the telephone. He had a lovely back. She wondered if she could get him a bleeper for Christmas. He would probably appreciate it.

'Hello, Kate. Sorry, I'm late,' said Ned.

'That's quite all right. I've been very happy here. Dermot has asked if we might have dinner with him tonight.'

'Sorry, I won't be able to manage it. I'm going out tonight.'

'You are?'

'Yes, I am.'

'It's a bit sudden, isn't it? Where are you going?' asked Kate, for she believed that there should be no secrets between them.

'A gay bar in Huntingdon.'

'Really!' she said, sitting up with a start. 'You do surprise me, but then, in this day and age, one shouldn't be surprised. When did you hear about it?'

'Colin told me about it at lunchtime. He's picking me up at 7.30.'

'Colin!'

'Yes, Colin.'

'You don't mean to tell me . . .'

'Yes, I spotted it immediately.'

'Does his father know?'

'I shouldn't think so.'

'But what about Doug? Won't he want to come too? I can't imagine him letting Colin out of his sight.'

'Doug's gone back to London. Some friend of his called Beryl apparently telephoned to say that she had slipped as she came out of the hairdresser's and broken her ankle. Doug's gone dashing off to St Thomas's on an errand of mercy.'

Ned had removed himself from the picture and Beryl had removed Doug from the picture; Colin was never in the picture and even if he had been, subsequent information had proved that he was a non-starter.

'So, I'll have to have dinner with Dermot on my own,' said Kate.

'It looks like it.'

Just when he was needed, Dermot returned, his brow furrowed with the pressure of sorting out the Conservative Ladies Annual Lunch.

'I'm afraid Ned can't manage dinner tonight, Dermot.' How she liked the sound of his name. 'He's going out. Of course, I would love to have dinner with you.'

His brow unfurrowed, his eyes lit up, his spirits lifted and all problems concerning Conservative Ladies in hats disappeared.

'Wonderful.'

'What time?'

'About eight o'clock. I'll ask Chef to cook something special for you. And let's have a quiet drink beforehand. You do like champagne, don't you?'

'I love it.'

'Which is your favourite? We have a fine selection in the cellar, and, of course, I also have my private collection.'

Ned at this point thought it might be the right time to wander off, either in search of an evening newspaper, a cup of tea, a quiet place to put in a few hours' practice kicking ankles or, if that failed, throwing up.

Kate narrowly stopped herself from saying that anything would do for her and managed to say, 'Bollinger would be wonderful.'

'It will be done.'

'I look forward to it.'

'And you don't have to be back in London too early tomorrow, do you?' he asked. He had lowered the pitch of his voice and was speaking very slowly and deliberately, eyes meeting eyes.

'No, I don't have to be back at any special time,' she said, her voice also low and mellow. 'I have nothing planned for tomorrow.'

Dermot reached to the display of pink roses and gypsophila near his chair and from the centre of the arrangement he plucked out a fine rose. He moved purposefully. The late afternoon sun was now pouring through the window and on to the fountain, and they heard only the music of the pianist, who seemed to be playing solely for them.

'This is for you,' said Dermot, moving closer and ever closer.

From somewhere in the distance came the sound of a foot meeting a potted palm with some strength.

CHAPTER TEN

No, they didn't. She was very disappointed.

CHAPTER ELEVEN

Although Kate was alone in the office, she was saying quite a bit and had let her opinion be known to the desks, the chairs, the filing cabinets, the wall-charts, the surrounding air and her old Olivetti typewriter. She had been particularly voluble when dealing with her calculator, the general drift being that she had never met such a thoroughly disagreeable piece of machinery in her life. She was in the midst of a troublesome costing, which she had to have ready by three o'clock for one of Michael's tiresome meetings. Try as she might, she just could not get the figures to come out right; she had worked on them until seven o'clock the previous night and had put in a very early start that morning on the basis that with no distractions she would whizz through them.

There had not been many distractions, but still the figures were proving impossible. Tillie, cleaner of offices, had been in and done quite a bit of singing while she worked, at the end of which she announced that everything was shipshape and she was 'orf'. Louise would be in next. She had taken to her job, and certainly everyone had taken to her. She no longer asked if she looked all right every morning, though she may well still have wondered to herself. Outwardly at least she seemed to have a bit more confidence. Kate had not broached the subject of her taking the job permanently, as she tended to agree with Ned, that Louise was far too good for them.

'Good morning, Kate,' said Louise breezily. 'How is it going?'

'Terribly. I can't get these figures to add up. They come out differently every time.'

'Shall I have a go?'

'Would you? Sums have never been my strong point.'

'Where shall I start?'

'It starts here and runs over on to this second page,' said Kate, indicating the columns she had gone over and over time and time again.

Louise studied the figures and mumbled to herself as she tapped the calculator with her beautifully manicured and polished nails.

'Well, I get 25,620.'

'I think I might have got that once, but I can't be sure. Last time, I know I got 22,430.'

'Well, isn't that odd?' conceded Louise. 'Shall we have a cup of coffee and then have another go?'

'What a good idea. Perhaps I should take a break.'

'I saw Doug this morning. He says Beryl's back on her feet now and he's lent her a walking stick,' called Louise from the kitchen.

'That's nice. Perhaps she'll hit him with it when she's better.'

Louise was looking quite happy and relaxed as she brought the coffee to Kate. She had unwound quite a bit in the past few weeks and was delighted that Kate was planning a dinner party on Friday. It would have been her wedding at the weekend, but she was trying to be very proud of herself for the way she was handling things. The job had helped tremendously in restoring her confidence, and she found herself warming to everyone and even had a soft spot for Michael. Ned was adorable, but then everyone thought Ned was adorable. Geoffrey was very amusing and Martin had his good moments when he wasn't thinking about his next match.

'Oh, there's a telephone call,' said Louise. 'Excuse me a moment.'

'Sure, I'll just start this second page again and see what I get this time around.' Kate concentrated on the second page, which was the shortest and therefore should have been the easiest, but she had to abandon her work when the telephone on her desk rang.

'It's Lizzie for you,' announced Louise.

'Oh, thanks. Hello, Lizzie. How are you?'

'I'm fine. Look, I was wondering if I could come and stay for a few days?'

'When?'

'At the end of this week. Say Thursday night until Monday morning.'

'That's fine. No problem.'

'And, Kate, one thing. If Peter ever happens to mention anything, would you please say I was with my mother in Bath? I mean, that's what I've told him, so if you would stick to the same story.'

'Yes, of course.'

'If he thought I was coming up to London on my own, he would think I wanted to get away from him for a few days.'

'But doesn't he think you want to get away from him for a few days because you are going to Bath?'

'No. I've told him that my mother has water on her ankles and I'm going to look after her.'

'Why do you want to come to London then?'

'To get away from Peter for a few days.'

'But what happens if he telephones your mother?'

'She won't hear the telephone. She's as deaf as a post.'

That seemed to settle things.

'OK, so I'll see you on Thursday evening. Come at about eight o'clock, as I never know what time I am getting home from work.'

'Oh, Kate, thanks so much.'

'Don't mention it. I just hope that one day I have an intriguing life and I can ask you to do the same thing for me. Things are pretty quiet on the social front.'

'Oh, really, nothing happening at all?'

'Well, not strictly true. There was almost a minor flutter in Huntingdon but sadly it came to nothing. He was absolutely divine too. Divorced, or so he told me. At least I have my work, I must remember that,' said a brave and courageous Kate.

'Well, I must dash,' said Lizzie. 'See you on Thursday, and you can tell me all about everything.'

'All right. I'll try and think of something. Bye-e.'

The thump of a squash bag hitting the floor just in front of

Louise's desk announced the arrival of Martin, though neither Kate nor Louise looked up to acknowledge his presence when he entered or, indeed, when the bag arrived at its destination.

'Martin, could you help me for a moment? I'm in a bit of a bind with these figures. I can't seem to get them to add up.'

Well, if there's one thing an accountant can do, apart from playing squash, it's add up a column or two. Always eager to flex his arithmetical muscles, Martin was only too happy to oblige.

'What's the problem?' he asked.

'Well, every time I add them up, I get a different total.'

'Let me have a look,' said Martin. He was coming over all masterful. 'Have you remembered to carry over the balance from the previous page?' Martin always found it best to start at the most basic level when talking sums to a woman.

'Of course I have. I'm not that stupid.'

'All right. Just checking. Now, let me have a go. I'll use my own calculator,' he said, preferring his own professional tools. Being clever with numbers, he was able to flick through the figures, tap the calculator and talk, all at the same time. 'When do you need to have this finished?'

'By three o'clock. Michael's having a meeting and he wants the costing so that we can meet about it, discuss it, thrash it to death, agree with it, disagree with it and start at the beginning again.'

'You'll be lucky.'

'Oh, thanks a lot.'

'Right, now. I get 24,320.'

'Well, I've got nothing like that.'

'Oh. Let me have another go. We'll soon sort this out. OK. I've got 25,450.' The accountant paused. 'Now, isn't that odd?'

'I got 25,000 and something, didn't I?' said Louise.

'Yes, but you got 25,620. I marked it down for future reference,' said Kate, more mystified than ever.

'Well, this is very odd,' said Martin.

'Do you think that perhaps my calculator needs a new battery?' asked Kate.

'Well, that wouldn't help, because it runs off electricity.

Anyway, I know my calculator is accurate – it's the top of the range – and I've just got two different totals. It's very odd.' Martin took the top-of-the-range calculator in his hands and shook it and then sat down opposite Kate. They both thought it was very odd. Kate had been thinking it was very odd all night, and Martin had been thinking it was very odd for less time but would doubtless go on thinking it was odd until the close of business. They were about to combine forces and have another go when the telephone on Kate's desk rang again.

'Kate, it's Peter for you,' said Louise.

'Peter who?'

'He just said "Peter".'

'Oh, it must be that Peter.'

'Very possibly. Shall I put him through?'

'Yes, do,' said Kate remembering water on the ankles and Bath as being important.

'Hello, Peter. What a lovely surprise,' said Kate.

'Hello there, Kate. Everything all right with you?'

'Yes, everything's all right with me. Is everything all right with you?' When in doubt it's always a good idea to stick to safe subjects and the well-trodden path.

'Yes, everything's all right with me too.'

'Well, that's good.'

'Yes.'

'Mmm.'

'Kate?'

'Yes?'

'I was wondering. I have to come up to London at the end of the week, and Lizzie suggested that I should meet you for dinner.'

'She did?'

'Yes, poor thing. She's got to go off to Bath to look after her mother, who's got water on the elbow, so she won't be able to come up with me.'

'Oh, dear.'

'Yes, we hope her mother will be better soon.'

'No, I was meaning "oh, dear" as in "oh, dear, I'm sorry Lizzie won't be able to come to London with you". I don't think the water will last long on Mama's knees; it doesn't usually.'

'Did you say knees? I could have sworn it was her elbow.'

'Did I say knees? Sorry, I meant ankles.'

'Might be. She's got an arthritic wrist too. And, of course, she's as deaf as a post. Poor thing. Anyway, what about dinner?'

'Well, Peter, I really don't think I can. I have to go . . .' and it hurt her to say this, but when in trouble a girl simply has to grab on to the nearest thing possible, 'to Huntingdon. It's to do with a conference we are mounting at the Sunrise Motor Inn.'

'Oh, what a shame.'

'Yes, isn't it?'

'Ah, well.'

'Yes, sorry about that.'

'Another time perhaps?'

'Mmm, perhaps.'

'Well, I'll be off then. If things change you'll let me know, won't you?'

'Of course, and please give my best wishes to Lizzie and please say I am sorry to hear about her mother.'

'Yes, she's been having trouble with her hip for some time now. Better say goodbye then.'

'Goodbye then.'

Back to the figures and also a bit of fast sorting out of who was telling what and to whom. Oh, what a tangled web we weave, when first we practise to deceive and land others well and truly in it.

'Martin, I've just got 25 something,' said a delighted Kate.

'25 what?'

'25,201.'

'No, that's not right. It can't have a one on the end.'

'Why not?'

'It's a mathematical impossibility. Look at your figures.'

'I've been looking at them for hours,' moaned Kate.

'Kate, what sort of school did you go to?'

'Well, it was very good for needlework and other subjects in the field of domestic science.'

'Let me have another go,' said Martin. 'Well, this is very odd. I've now got 25,740.'

'We do seem to agree on 25,000. Shall I round it up or down or call it a day?'

'No, I can't allow you to do that. This is very odd.'

'I think it's very annoying.'

'Yes, I'm inclined to agree with you there.' Whoever said two heads are better than one was clearly off the one he'd been issued with and was casting around for a transplant.

When Geoffrey arrived at the office, he first of all wanted to see his Louise, who had induced in him a kind of tender protectiveness such as he had not felt since he had spent a mellow afternoon watching a favourite filly he had been following running in the Oaks. He knew that it was a difficult and significant week for her and he wanted to do his little bit, so accompanying him on his usual fast and furious dash across the reception area was a bunch of chrysanthemums.

'Morning, Number One. These are for you,' he said as he shoved the flowers under her nose in order to hide his embarrassment. He knew he wanted to give her flowers, he was just not skilled in the execution of the act, not having given many during his lifetime. Rosettes, yes, flowers, no.

'Oh, Geoffrey, how sweet,' she said and then leaned forward and pecked him on the cheek. 'Kate, look at these lovely flowers from Geoffrey.'

'Oh, how sweet,' said Kate, looking up from the figures.

'Ridiculous waste of money,' said a huffy Martin.

'Spoil-sport.'

'Just practical. I've got 24,470. Have you had anything like that?'

'No, I think I got a 70 once, but I got a 21,000 in front and I know that can't be right.'

'No, that can't be right.'

'That's what I said.'

Geoffrey was a keen and helpful chap and always happy to muck in and assist wherever necessary. As long as he could nip out every now and then to Joe Coral's little hideaway to place a bet or pick up his winnings, all was sublime in his world.

'Can I be of assistance, Chief? What seems to be the trouble?'

'We can't seem to get these figures to add up to the same total. Every time we get a different answer.'

'Shall I have a go? I worked on codes during the war, you know.'

'Did you? How fascinating. I didn't know that.'

'Well, it's the kind of thing one likes to keep confidential. But it is the sort of training that comes in handy.'

'I can imagine. Would you like your eye-shade?'

'Yes, I would. And my pipe.'

'Coming right up,' said Kate rushing off to Geoffrey's technical corner.

'Right, now,' said Geoffrey, gently easing himself into Kate's chair and surveying the pages of figures. 'Where do we start?'

'Here, and it runs on to a second page, and don't forget to carry over the balance,' said Martin.

'I was a code-breaker, you know. That stands for something, young man. We were a very select group at Bletchley. Right, here goes.' Geoffrey mumbled to himself, rolled up his sleeves, flexed his fingers, scratched his head and thought that he must remember to tell Kate and Louise about the night Ping Latimer cracked the big one. Martin was an insolent young chap and didn't deserve to hear.

'Right, Chief. I've got 206.3 recurring.'

'What on earth does that mean?'

'A big raid over Bradford. It's been too quiet for too long,' confided Geoffrey while scratching his chin and drawing meaningfully on his pipe.

As Ned entered the office he came upon Louise sitting behind her desk with her nose in a bunch of chrysanthemums, Kate in an exasperated state with her head on the desk while she gently groaned, Martin shaking his top-of-the-range calculator and Geoffrey pacing the office mumbling about Ping Latimer.

'Ned,' said Kate as she lifted her head from the desk, 'we're having a spot of trouble with these figures. You wouldn't like to have a go, would you?'

'I never touch figures, I'm the art department.'

'Well, Geoffrey's the technical department and he's had a go.'

'Did he come up with the right answer?'

'No, but that's beside the point. Oh, go on, have a go.'

'No, I absolutely refuse to get involved. I know my strengths and I know my weaknesses. Figures are not what I'm good at.'

The telephone rang on Kate's desk. It was developing into a busy morning.

'Kate, it's Dermot for you.'

'Oh, all right, put him through.'

'Be cool.'

'I most certainly will. Just watch me.'

'I'll put him through. Go for it girl.'

'Hello, Dermot.'

'Hello, Kate.'

'How are you?'

'I'm just fine, thank you. How are you?'

'Fine.' Well, that's got the preliminaries over with. Now let's see what he does.

'I was wondering . . .?'

'Yes?'

'I was wondering if you would like to come to Huntingdon for the weekend. You know, relax, spend some time in the countryside, perhaps go to the Jolly Shearer for lunch, have a lovely dinner. Chef tells me he's got some lobsters coming in from Felixstowe.'

'Will they keep until the weekend?' Salmonella poisoning is not an attractive affliction for a woman in love.

'Oh, they're not caught yet.'

'Oh. I see.'

'Well, how about it? Would you like to come for the weekend?'

'Dermot, I can't.' She was going to remain very cool. 'A friend of mine is coming up to London and I simply have to see him.' She hoped he noticed the 'him' and she hoped it hurt. 'We haven't seen each other for ages, and he only gets up to London occasionally, so I simply must see him. You do understand, don't you?'

'Oh, yes. Ah, well, in that case, perhaps another time?' said Dermot, sounding quite cheery and not in the least put out.

'Yes, perhaps another time. Do keep in touch.'

'Absolutely. Well, we've got the conference to look forward to, haven't we?'

'Of course we have.'

'I've reserved a special room for you.'

'Oh, how lovely.'

'A very quiet room.'

'Oh, really,' she giggled. Whatever happened to the cool approach?

'Well, I must go. Talk to you soon.'

'Yes. Bye.'

'Bye.'

Oooh, this tangled web was getting positively snarled, matted and, on top of that, dipped in tar. Now remain calm, she told herself, take a deep breath and, if necessary, go all the way back to the beginning. A girl never gets anywhere by betraying her emotions.

'I'm not going to let this get the better of me,' said Martin. It was an approach he used whenever he was 2–9 down in the league final. Like that time when he'd fought all the way back and eventually taken the fifth game 16–14. 'I'm going to have another go.'

'That's the style, Martin,' encouraged Geoffrey.

'Right, well, I get 25,640.'

'There's a drop over Antwerp,' said Geoffrey, puffing on his pipe and tweeking his eye-shade.

'What?' asked an incredulous Kate.

'By Jove, this is interesting,' said Geoffrey.

'It's not interesting. It's odd. Very odd.'

Geoffrey started to pace the office again. He kept stopping and looking over his shoulder and muttering. 'There is something very interesting going on. I think I'm going to put through a call to Ping Latimer. I'll have to scramble it, of course. Unfortunately, I no longer have any contacts in MI6, but Ping will be fascinated by this. He'll know what to do. We saw some curious things at Bletchley. Of course, I'm not allowed to divulge any information. Keep yourself to yourself was one of the first things we learned when we started training school. Keep your head down, but keep your eyes and ears open. By Jove, it's all coming back to me.'

'I can't stand this,' said Ned.

'Well, neither can I,' agreed Kate.

'How do you make these things work?' said an exasperated Ned as he grabbed hold of the calculator.

'Tap out the figures, bash the plus sign and if luck is on your side – and it certainly isn't on mine – out should come the answer,' instructed Kate.

'Right, well, I've got 2,102.'

'That's not right at all. You're hopeless. You've left a zero off somewhere.'

'Of course I have. Zero stands for nothing, so I didn't think I needed to bother with any of them. I left them all off. Best place for a zero.'

'I can't stand this. I really can't take any more.'

'I told you I was artistic.'

'Well, go and play with your paintbox and crayons and stop butting in.'

'There were times when it got to be pretty tough in ops,' reminisced Geoffrey. 'I remember when Ping and I were on duty for days.'

It was getting pretty tough in this particular operations room too. It felt as if they had had a raid over Bradford and masterminded a successful drop over Antwerp. What Kate could do with right now was a replacement shift coming on duty, and, if they'd got stuck in the air-raid shelter, perhaps young Richard Attenborough might like to wander in and give everyone a mug of cocoa. Come to think of it, Jack Hawkins and Nigel Patrick might like to polish up their braid and brass buttons and do a turn. And perhaps Phyllis Calvert would like to slip into uniform and have a go with the ready reckoner.

'How about some coffee?' suggested Louise. 'Why don't you all take a break? You're getting nowhere.'

She was absolutely right. Nowhere was where they were getting. They all readily agreed that a coffee was a very good idea. After several hours of battling yesterday and several hours of a less than fruitful morning, Kate was ready to give up and felt like saying so.

'I've had enough. That's it. I'm going to tell Michael we're up against it and he can shout if he likes. I simply can't go on.'

'That's right, Kate. Tell it how it is,' cheered Ned.

'Don't be ridiculous. Let me have another go,' said Martin. 'OK, this is it. I know it's going to be it this time. I feel it in my fingers. Right, 25,000 . . . ?'

'We all agree on that,' said Kate.

'Don't interrupt. 25,830.'

'Fog over the Channel,' said Geoffrey. He was rather dreamy and had a faraway look in his eyes. He was thinking of Simone, who had been parachuted into France with a packet of sandwiches and a pair of bicycle clips. She had been wearing silk underwear by Eva, a trench coat, tightly belted, and a navy-blue beret. She was never heard from again. They had found her bicycle clips and her parachute, but not her sandwiches. They had been grated carrot because carrots help you see in the dark.

'It's odd how one remembers the details,' he murmured.

'It's very odd.'

'Yes, they were grated carrot.'

'What?' asked a bewildered Kate.

'Not even corned beef. She was a brave girl.'

'Oh, shut up, Geoffrey.'

'Leave him alone, he's very happy,' said Martin. 'Now, Kate, concentrate, pull yourself together and try again.'

'Oh, all right,' agreed Kate, though not with good grace. 'And this is the last time, it really is. Right, I've got 25,740.'

'I got that once, I'm sure I did,' said Martin enthusiastically. He might have jumped up and down, but he reserved those kinds of demonstrations for after the match.

'High flyer over Rotterdam,' said Geoffrey. 'Good God, there's a horse called High Flyer in the four o'clock at Sandown Park. I think I've got my Yankee. I'm just going to nip out for a minute. Toodle-pip. I won't be long, Chief. Keep at it, Number One.'

'Really, I did get 25,740,' said Martin again. 'Didn't I?'

'Yes, you did. I'm sure you did. I think we've cracked it. Shall I run the figures through once more just to make sure?' queried Kate.

'No, that would be too risky.'

Not quite liking to admit that they had found their solution, they stood looking at the calculator, which announced the total in green, and then at the thumbed pages of figures. Michael saw them standing there as he opened the door of his office.

'Kate, could you come in for a minute?' he asked.

'I'll be right with you,' she said, almost standing to attention.

'Close the door and sit down,' said Michael. 'I'm afraid I've got some bad news.'

Even the attractive pink shirt failed to brighten his appearance, and the loosened well-chosen tie showed that here was an executive under pressure and deeply concerned.

'Oh, dear,' commiserated Kate. She sank into a leather armchair and waited. He seemed unable to frame the words to express the turmoil in which he found himself.

'Yes, I'm afraid I have to see a client this afternoon, and we won't be able to have our meeting.'

'Oh, dear,' she repeated.

'Yes, I've tried, but there's nothing I can do.'

'Ah.'

'Sorry about that.'

'I quite understand. Shall I tell everyone?'

'Yes, would you be a darling and break it to them, please, Kate?'

'Of course.' Kate sounded as if she was talking to a little boy who had fallen over in the playground and grazed his knee. Any moment she might offer to kiss it better.

'I've been thinking about Louise,' he sighed.

'Yes?'

'Well, I realize it's a bad week for her, so I wondered if I shouldn't take her out to lunch on Thursday. What do you think?'

Kate was quite overwhelmed and forgot about Michael and his meetings, Michael and his clients, Michael and his BMW, Michael and Andrea and her Harrods account, Michael and his costing and Michael and Cindy, and thought what a nice chap he was.

'I'm sure she'd love that.'

'Right, well, I'll ask her then.'

'What about the costing?'

'Oh, yes, the costing, that went clean out of my mind. I was thinking about something else,' said Michael, a certain misty and distracted look entering his steely blue eyes.

'Chicago?' hazarded Kate.

'Yes, Chicago,' he faltered.

'Nice place I'm told.'

'Wonderful place. Vibrant, full of life.'

'Take Al Capone, for example,' offered Kate.

'Or the speakeasies.'

'Mrs O'Leary's cow,' chuckled Kate.

'The Great Fire.'

'The Water Tower.'

'Ah, yes, the Water Tower,' sighed Michael.

'The Loop.'

'The Chicago Bears.'

'What a team!' agreed Kate. 'Soldier Field. Quite a stadium, wouldn't you say? Excellent hot dogs.'

'The Chicago Cubs.'

'Indeed. Wrigley Field. Now, there's a handsome ball park for you. The Boys of Summer. Oh, the Boys of Summer.'

'An evening walk along the shores of Lake Michigan,' sighed Michael. 'You seem to know Chicago very well, Kate. Have you been there?' he asked, brightening up considerably. 'I wonder, have you ever met Cindy?'

'No, unfortunately, I've never been there. But I did read a thrilling book set in Chicago. It was all about a gangster's moll. It was really gripping. Anyway, in the end she gave up her life of crime and married a clerical gentleman who was dedicated to temperance and spoke eloquently in favour of Prohibition. She was called Sindie.'

'Cindy?' queried Michael hopefully.

'No. Sindie. With an "S" and an "ie". It's a play on words. Life of crime, cleric, get it? Not like Cindy at all.' All that Kate could hear reverberating around the room was her own hollow laugh.

'Oh.'

'So, what about the costing?' she asked delicately.

'Ah, yes, the costing. Don't worry about that. I'm sorry, I should have told you before. I somehow forgot. I don't seem to be myself at the moment. Perhaps I've got flu coming on. Anyway, where was I? Oh, yes, the costing. I've submitted an estimate to the Sunrise Group of 25,500 and I don't think the odd couple of hundred either way is going to upset anyone. Chicago can get very windy at times.' He was off again. 'The winds come in off Lake Michigan, you know. That's why it's known as the Windy City. Fascinating really.'

CHAPTER TWELVE

Throughout the week, everyone who knew Louise had been extra specially caring, attentive and very nice. The members of staff of Major Events knew that it was a difficult and sensitive time for her and were anxious to make it as easy as possible; they had all therefore rallied to the cause. Perhaps Martin hadn't quite known how to express his concern – suggesting that Louise take up a sport, just as he had so successfully done when he had failed his accountancy exams first time around, had not been quite what was needed, but he had at least tried and his motives had been of the purest. Geoffrey had blustered through with his bunch of chrysanthemums and had also taken Louise out to lunch at the local pub, where they had had an uproarious time talking horses and codes. Michael had also done his bit and had taken Louise to Le Caprice for a very long lunch. When he discovered that she knew half of the clientele and most of the waiters, he wished he had taken her there for dinner. Perhaps next week, and, if that went well, they could go to Alistair Little's the week after.

Kate had planned her dinner party for Friday night and she knew that Roger and Jill were taking Louise to the theatre on Saturday night. Something light and entertaining. A musical would be good. A heavy night at the National wouldn't be on, not when she was feeling shaky. The evening was filled, but the day was empty and Kate thought she might suggest a session of Christmas shopping in Harrods. A lazy day and a late lunch was pencilled in for Sunday. And, if Louise was feeling up to it, Kate was invited over for drinks with Roger and Jill in the evening.

The gritty problem that beset Kate and refused to go away

was what to do about finding an extra man for her dinner party. It would be lovely to see Lizzie, and she was very good company, but Kate had told her that there weren't enough men to go around. Had Lizzie been in any doubt, she was soon going to learn the accuracy of those well-chosen and all too wise words. Martin had been asked, but was playing an important club match and wouldn't be able to manage dinner, though he thought he might be able to come over for an orange juice later. When invited, Geoffrey had found himself quite torn between spending an evening with Louise, and a weekend stalking with Ping Latimer. As the stalking weekend with Ping was an annual fixture and had been long booked, Geoffrey was reluctantly dusting off his plus-fours and catching the sleeper to Edinburgh. Angus of the family McTavish (gillies for generations) was collecting them in the Land Rover and driving them the rest of the way. Dermot might have been enticed up to London, but had expressed an interest in staying in Huntingdon, in the countryside, preferably with Kate, and sampling the bill of fare at the Jolly Shearer. That left Peter, who had said he would be free for dinner on Friday night, and in London too, but as his partner across the table would be his wife Lizzie, whom he thought was in Bath caring for her ailing mother, Kate knew that wouldn't do. If he turned up as a spare man for Friday night, he would know that Lizzie wanted to get away from him for a few days, and she would know that as soon as she did get away for a few days, the first thing he did was nip up to London for a bit of fun; and everyone would know that Lizzie's mother, poor thing, was left in Bath to cope with her troublesome water on the ankles all by herself. If anyone was good enough to give her a passing thought, wondered just how she was managing all by herself and telephoned to inquire of same, she would not hear because she was as deaf as a post, so the heartfelt inquiry would remain unanswered.

The awful truth had dawned on Kate on Friday morning. And when truth dawns at an early hour in its raw clarity, it can be a difficult moment for a girl.

'Well, hello-o there.'

'Good morning, Doug. How marvellous to catch you.'

'Well, well, well.'

'Indeed. Doug, I'll come straight to the point.' There was no reason to prolong the agony. This way it would give her more time to get used to the idea. 'Might you by any chance be free for dinner tonight?'

'I most certainly will,' he replied as quick as a flash. There was no need for him to dig down into his breast pocket and consult his Bowling Association diary.

'I'm giving a small dinner for Louise . . . and . . .' – she almost stumbled over her words – 'it would be so lovely if you could join us.'

'Always ready and willing, if you'll pardon the expression.'

'Wonderful. So, you'll be able to come?'

'I most certainly will.' He had said he most certainly would the first time, but perhaps Kate hadn't heard him, or perhaps she had been hoping he would say he most certainly couldn't. However, what he had said, twice, was that he most certainly would.

'Oh, good,' she said bravely with a sinking heart. This was absolutely killing her. Added to everything else, she realized, she would have to watch him eat.

'Now, what time would that be? I have to take Beryl to see the physiotherapist at five o'clock, but I'll be home before seven I should say.'

'About eight o'clock would be tremendous.'

'Oh, good, that gives me time to have a bath.'

Kate didn't want to know. She really didn't want to know. He would probably change his socks, too, and use lashings of Dr Scholl's footpowder.

'Well, I must get off to work. I'll see you later.'

'Louise not with you this morning?' questioned Doug. 'Is she at home at the moment? Perhaps I might just pop round and see her and give her the good news that I'm coming for dinner tonight. Cheer her up a bit maybe.'

This early-morning discussion on the pavement was doing nothing to cheer Kate up, and though the possibility of Doug managing to brighten up Louise's day was anyway remote, he would have to wait, since she was out attempting to be cheered up somewhere else.

'No, Doug. She's gone to the hairdresser's.'

'Well, yes, of course she would. Specially for tonight, I should imagine. I know you ladies like to look your best for special occasions and tonight is a special occasion, is it not? Are you going to the hairdresser's later?' He grinned, bounced back and forth on his toes and knew that only he understood women so well.

'No, Doug. I'm not going to the hairdresser's at all. Well, I really must get on my way to work. See you later.'

'Yes, absolutely. See you later. What a turn-up for the books. Goodbye, my dear.' Doug moved forward and took her hand in his. Kate barely managed to conceal a look that could loosely be described as squeamish. It was the sort of look a person might give when they uncovered a dish of tripe that they had been inadvertently served when what they had ordered was a nice fresh brown egg, boiled for four minutes, and soldiers.

'Thank you so much for thinking of me,' he said in a smarmy way. And to think they were going to have to endure four hours of it. 'Until later.'

Kate stood with a white linen and lace tablecloth and napkins and cutlery for six clasped in front of her while she studied her dining-table, which was designed to run to intimate dinner for no more than four. Lizzie was standing beside her. She held a charming centre-piece of white roses, which was her contribution to the evening.

'I'll take one end and the leg,' said Kate magnanimously. 'It's only right, as hostess. Besides, I need to get out easily to the kitchen.'

'I can help in the kitchen,' offered Lizzie, worried that she was putting Kate out and that she should earn her keep. She was also conscious that had there been only four for dinner, they wouldn't have been having all this leg trouble.

'No, you can't. You're going in there against the wall and to get out you'll have to climb over Doug. You won't like it. Of course, he might. I suppose there is that to be considered.'

'Couldn't you put Louise in against the wall?'

'No, I really think I should give her a comfortable place between Ned and James. I'm going to put Ned at the far end of the table, with the other leg; you're between Ned and Doug, and I'm between Doug and James with,' she sighed, 'the leg.'

'What about chairs? There are only four.'

'I hadn't thought about extra chairs.'

'They're important.'

'I realize that.'

The kitchen chair could be brought into play. It could be used on the far side of the table, against the wall and with a cushion to pad it out a bit. Lizzie or Doug would have to sit on it; but that seemed only fair. She couldn't give it to Ned, as it had a wonky leg and he already had the table leg to cope with. It would probably be best if Lizzie sat on it, for she could be briefed about the hazardous fourth leg and be relied upon to deal with the situation with discretion. She had after all shared flats in her youth. She knew all about shillings in gas meters, paper cups, communal washing facilities and borrowed cutlery. Doug would only keep referring to it throughout dinner and try to make jokes. But what to do about a sixth chair and a safe parking spot for Doug? She could ask Louise if she could borrow a chair, but that would mean bothering her and the dinner was supposed to be in her honour. She shouldn't be disturbed with the trivial details. The trouble was, if she did have to resort to bothering Louise and a chair was forthcoming, it would mean having to hump it downstairs, and one or other or both of them would be bound to bash an ankle or scrape a shin on a strut.

'Shall we have a drink?' suggested Lizzie, anxious to perform an act of human kindness and pull her weight at the outset of the evening.

'What a good idea. I'll just finish laying the table.'

'Don't worry, I'll get them. I think a glass of white wine would be in order,' she said as she purposefully made her way towards the kitchen and the bursting fridge. 'You sit down for a moment. You've been rushing around all day.'

Lizzie felt in need of a refreshing drink herself, because she too had been doing quite a bit of rushing. Although she had planned to get up early and hit the shops, she had stayed in bed for a while, as she and Kate had had a very late night talking nonsense, drinking wine and being very silly. Louise had joined them briefly, but had gone off upstairs to bed at 10.30. It must have been at least one o'clock by the time Kate and Lizzie had finally got to bed, and, when Lizzie woke in the morning, she hoped that Kate was feeling better than she was, because Kate had to go to work, while she, at least, could lie in bed and recover. She had wanted to try and find something new and wonderfully exotic to wear over Christmas, but she thought that she should really deal with her responsibilities first. After her wickedly late night she was feeling repentant and guilty and, in order to exonerate herself, rather than taking an irresponsible and self-indulgent turn down Bond Street, she had gone to Marks & Spencer's and spent two hours blearily buying sweaters and trousers for Charles and Robert and underwear and socks for Peter. Such was the wandering state of her concentration that she hadn't even bought a nightdress for herself, checked out the new line of knickers, or been able to determine whether Marble Arch did in fact have a better selection than Oxford. But as the family wouldn't worry about that and wouldn't be impressed either way, why should she? The one thing she did manage to buy for herself was a giant economy-sized bottle of bubble bath and she had wallowed in a bath full of it for half an hour before Kate came home. Lizzie agreed with Kate that it was indeed a lovely bathroom.

Dressed in a pair of black velvet trousers and a grey beaded evening sweater, which she had bought because the sales lady had told her she could wear it anywhere (and she had, again and again and again), Lizzie was happily looking forward to the evening and was also quietly admitting to herself that she missed Peter. It was quite a revelation. Perhaps a few days away was a good idea, and perhaps she should try it more often. Not too often. Just every now and then. Oh, it was all so confusing. One minute they drove you mad and the next minute you missed them. And, of course, there was Kate missing Nick. They'd talked about it last night and ended up hoping that Nick was missing Kate more than she was missing him. Then there was poor Louise. Now she really was missing David. Perhaps Peter missed her a bit. There again, perhaps he was watching television with his feet up, eating a sandwich and not giving a damn. Well, perhaps Charles and Robert, packed off to boarding-school before their time, missed Mummy just as much as she missed their dear little scrubbed faces. Perhaps. Just a bit.

Lizzie remembered that she was trying to make herself useful, and, while her offers to help with dinner had met with an adamant refusal from Kate on the grounds that she was in control of everything, she could at least organize some drinks. As she turned from the fridge, in which she had just replaced the bottle of wine (it had taken quite a time because it was a congested area), to carry the glasses of wine into the sitting-room, she saw a curious red-faced fellow knocking on the kitchen window, peering between the cheerful curtains and asking if he could please come in.

'Kate, I think you'd better phone the police. There's a madman at the back door!' shrieked Lizzie and she rushed out of the kitchen.

'Oh, that'll be Doug,' said Kate, taking a glass of wine from the trembling Lizzie.

'You mean that . . . that . . . that's my dinner partner?'

'I've come to the conclusion that we shouldn't think of this evening in those terms,' said Kate, tapping Lizzie on the shoulder. 'It's a mixed social bag, what with Ned and James devoted to each other, Louise feeling shaky, me feeling exhausted and trying to put on a good show and you feeling as if . . . well, how are you feeling, old girl?'

'As if I'm up from the country and can't recognize a madman when I see one.'

'Oh, you did see a madman. I'd better go and let him in. Sit down and enjoy your wine.' Kate paused and then added, 'I won't be long. I hope.'

Kate was wearing her faithful old dressing-gown, six inches above the ankles, and had her hair in rollers. Doug took it as a sign that she felt relaxed in his company.

'Well, here I am,' he announced. 'I've taken Beryl to the physiotherapist and I just thought I'd stop by and see if there was anything I could do for you.'

'How kind, Doug. Actually, there is one thing.'

At long last. He was needed. He had known that the moment would eventually come and here it was. It was music to his ears and poetry to his heart. He looked at Kate dressed in her funny little dressing-gown and her woolly slippers and was overcome with tenderness.

'Your wish is my command.'

Kate paused for a moment, not to gather her thoughts but because the roller behind her left ear was hurting her and she really would have liked to have given it a good tug.

'Do you happen to have a spare dining chair I could borrow? I'm afraid I only have four, and we are six for dinner.'

'I've got the very thing.'

'Splendid.'

'You can borrow my piano stool. In fact you can keep it,' he trilled in a moment of munificence.

'I didn't know you had a piano.'

'Well, I don't. I used to have a Pianola, but no longer. However, I do still have the stool and I keep it in the cupboard under the stairs. I'll just nip back home and dust it off and Bob's your uncle. Anything else?'

'No, that's all.'

'Righty-ho. I'll be over as soon as I can. I'll have my bath and change and then I'll be right back. Now, don't worry, I'll be over early enough to help with the drinks. I know how you young ladies like to have a reliable man around to help with the pre-dinner sherries.'

What a night it was going to be, and to think he was going to be getting out the old Pianola stool! What memories that brought back. The nights he and Jean had practised their waltzing while the Pianola tinkled its Danube Selection. Still, it was no good looking back. Life was for living, and the future beckoned invitingly. So, dust down the stool, throw away the old sheet music, the Gilbert and Sullivan favourites they had loved to sing together and the Pianola cylinders. What were they, after all? Only memories. Splendid girl, Kate. Absolutely splendid. Perhaps she liked to waltz, though, come to think of it, she was probably better at the polka.

Kate and Lizzie agreed that Louise looked really stunning in her tight black silk skirt and fuchsia-pink jacket. Her long hair was piled up, and she looked altogether relaxed and as if she felt a good deal more optimistic than Kate. She had arrived fifteen minutes before the appointed hour of eight o'clock, because she thought they would all enjoy a quiet slurp of champagne before the men arrived. She was carrying a bottle of Moët et Chandon expressly for the purpose.

'What a lovely outfit, Louise. Where did you get it?' asked Kate. Lizzie was also dying to know but had thought it might be rude to ask.

'Yves Saint Laurent.'

Hardly surprising. It had the look of somewhere special about it.

'I went to their sale once,' said Lizzie.

'Did you buy anything?' asked Kate.

'No, they didn't have anything in my size.'

'Isn't it always the way?' commiserated Kate.

'I thought we should have a quiet drink beforehand, and so here's some champagne,' said Louise handing the bottle over to Kate.

'Oh, well done. You two have a glass. I really think I ought to get changed.'

'Are you sure everything's under control in the kitchen and there's nothing I can do?' queried Lizzie. It sounded suspicious to her and not quite like the disorganized Kate she knew and loved.

'Honestly. It is. I'm quite impressed with myself, actually. I made an avocado mousse last night before you arrived, Lizzie. Just like that, no trouble at all. And we're having a chicken thing, which is bubbling away and seems fine. I'm going to cook some noodles to go with that, plus some green beans – frozen, I'm afraid, but as a working woman I'm allowed some short cuts. And after that it's some salad and cheese. I'm not doing a dessert. I'm dieting, you know. I lost a pound last week. Can't you tell?' There was no immediate response to this new information. 'Well, it's one of the three pounds I put on the week before so perhaps you wouldn't notice it instantaneously. Anyway, I'm not at all hurt. Must go and change. Enjoy yourselves.'

Lizzie went to the kitchen to try and find some champagne glasses, and Louise followed behind her. Just as Louise was about to start saying how much she appreciated Kate's giving the dinner party, the front doorbell rang.

'I'll get it,' offered Louise. 'Do you want to carry on opening the champagne?'

'I'll give it a go,' said Lizzie as the bottle was handed over and Louise turned to go to the front door.

Doug had had his bath, he had changed his clothes, he had used a double dose of footpowder and brushed his teeth, he had swilled down with Listerine and had been lavish with his application of Old Spice deodorant and aftershave. He had put the dusted-off piano stool outside Kate's back door but felt that, as it was a dinner party, he should announce himself at the front door, greet Kate, take her through to the sitting-room, soothe her troubled nerves, go to the back door, move the piano stool into position and then surprise her with the bottle of sparkling Italian white wine he had been saving for a special occasion (and if this wasn't a special occasion he didn't know what was).

'Louise, my dear, well, well, well.'

'Good evening, Doug. Won't you come in?'

'Kate is busy, is she?' he asked as he was ushered into the sitting-room.

'She's just changing. We're having a glass of champagne. Won't you join us?'

'How charming. Yes. Delighted, I'm sure,' he said as he nodded wildly first at Louise and then at Lizzie.

'Doug, have you met Lizzie, a friend of Kate's?' said Louise.

'How do you do?' said Lizzie. Close up he didn't look any better than he had looked when he was grinning through the kitchen window.

'How do you do?' said Doug.

Another charming young lady. How his cup did runneth over. And how splendid Kate looked when she came into the sitting-room. She had taken out her rollers, applied her make-up – she'd tried to pick up a few hints from Louise – brushed her hair, anchored it down with hairspray and put on a cleverly cut dress in a Liberty print, which concealed quite a lot and exposed a delicate throat. Doug jumped up, while Lizzie and Louise observed him with amusement from their position on the sofa and Kate tried to quell her quite understandable revulsion.

As Doug had an audience, he thought it imprudent to speak at great length and they were therefore mercifully saved from hearing just how wonderful, splendid and charming Kate looked, how honoured he was to be included in the evening, how delightful Louise was looking, how delicious the dinner was going to be, what a rip-roaring time he knew they would all have and how charming he found his new acquaintance, Lizzie. He stuck to the subject of the piano stool, which was quietly waiting outside the back door.

'Shall I get it now?' he whispered, not wishing to let Kate down in public and refer to her lack of adequate furnishings in front of guests.

'Sorry?'

'You know, the piano stool,' he whispered, eyes wide and getting wider.

'Oh, yes. Shall I help?'

'No, no, I'll do it. Where shall I put it?'

'In this place here, against the wall,' said Kate, indicating the place at the table that was set, just like the other five places, with Habitat cutlery and glasses, but lacked a chair.

'Righty-ho. Leave it to me,' he declared and he sloped off in his well-polished, squeaking brogues to the kitchen and the back door. As he left the room he flashed what he thought were one or two conspiratorial looks, which he assumed displayed an intimacy understandable only to Kate and himself.

Kate sipped her champagne and perched herself on the arm of the sofa in order to have a quiet word with Louise and Lizzie before Doug blustered his way back on the scene dragging a piano stool behind him.

'I do hope this evening's going to be all right. How are you feeling, Louise?'

'I'm absolutely fine. At least, I seem to be. It's so good of you to give this dinner. I do appreciate it. I promise I'm not going to embarrass you and cry. I feel wonderful. Honest.'

'Well done,' said Kate, raising her glass.

'Here's to you, Louise, and here's to you, Kate,' said Lizzie.

Kate thought that she really should go to the kitchen and check that everything was bubbling well and all was still under control. That was the trouble with cooking: one minute you could say it was under control and the next minute control had slipped from under your wooden spoon. But if she went to the kitchen now she would find Doug grappling with the piano stool. She had worked out that the only way to get through the evening was to rise above it, to put her distaste for Doug behind her and at the end of it all congratulate herself on her social fortitude. It was not going to be easy for a girl whose emotional map appeared on her face and was as easy to decipher as a painting by numbers set designed for six-year-olds by the gentlemen at Fisher-Price.

From the kitchen came the sound of Doug manhandling the stool through the door, knocking over the brush and mop, which were concealed behind it, propping them back into position twice, colliding with the pedal bin and then realizing that, because he had backed himself into the kitchen, dragging the piano stool behind him, he had left insufficient room to manoeuvre himself and the stool through into the sitting-room.

'Do you need any help, Doug?' called Kate.

'No, everything's just fine. Don't worry. I'll be with you in a jiffy.'

Kate, perched on the arm of the sofa, and Louise and Lizzie, both comfortably settled in its cushions, hoped it would take a little longer than the threatened jiffy for Doug to reappear. They were having a very pleasant time and could happily have sat there for a while longer discussing clothes from Yves Saint Laurent (if they happened to have your size), working for Michael Major and Major Events, Kate's hopes for the devastated little patch that was the garden, all their hopes for a better and fuller life and the difference between the stock of Marks & Spencer's, Marble Arch, and Marks & Spencer's, Oxford, were it not for a ring on the doorbell and the realization that it must be Ned and James.

'Hello, you two. Come in,' said Kate as she opened the front door.

'Evening, Kate,' said James, bending down to peck her on the cheek; he was ever so tall and good-looking with it.

'Hello, you old bag,' said Ned, giving her a massive hug and a kiss on both cheeks.

'I see you're all on the champagne already,' said James. 'Just as well we brought along extra supplies.' James opened another bottle of champagne, while Kate made sure the glasses of those who had already started were replenished and that everyone knew each other.

'Good evening, Doug,' said Ned, recognizing the form of the hot and flushed individual dragging a piano stool in behind him. 'We met at the Jolly Shearer, near Huntingdon.'

'So we did. Well, well, well. What a surprise. Nice to see you.'

'Can I help?' offered Ned. 'Is that stool supposed to be going somewhere or do you normally travel with it?'

'I've lent it to Kate,' he whispered confidentially to Ned. He knew that Ned was a friend of Kate's, so he thought that it was permissible to involve him in the secret and that he would think none the worse of her for knowing that she was lacking in chairs. 'She needed an extra chair. She's only got four,' he added meaningfully.

'I see,' said Ned seriously. 'Let me just move the table a touch so that you can slide the stool in.'

'Thank you so much.'

With the piano stool safely in position, Ned and Doug were able to join the main group gathered around the sofa at the other end of the sitting-room. Doug latched himself on to Lizzie, who had rather pleasantly asked him about his garden, which she had noticed through the kitchen window, while Ned and James talked to Louise and told her, among other things, that she looked simply stunning. Kate played the good hostess and made sure glasses were kept full, hers amongst them, passed nuts and olives, dipped in and out of conversations and nipped out to the kitchen just to check that the control of which she had so loudly boasted was indeed still hers for the asking.

'Shall we all sit down?' asked Kate. 'Ned, if you would sit at the end, but don't sit down until Lizzie and Doug have got into their seats, as they have to file in that way. That's right. Now you can sit.' She paused for a moment and then whispered in Ned's ear that he should be careful of the leg. He had obviously already found it, as his eyes closed in what was a swift and vivid acknowledgement of pain.

'James,' she continued, 'you sit next to me, and Louise, you are between James and Ned.'

'Well, isn't this cosy?' said Doug. 'I must say, there's nothing like a few friends getting together for dinner.'

Kate raised her eyes to the ceiling but, realizing that she had better get used to it now because the entire evening was likely to continue in the same vein, she collected herself, decided to trust in her own merit as a hostess and brought her green peepers back down to table level, where she was just in time to catch Louise's brown beauties in the process of moving upwards.

While her guests were settling into their seats, Lizzie on the kitchen chair with the wonky leg, Doug on the piano stool, Ned, James and Louise on proper dining chairs, Kate made three trips back and forth to the kitchen to collect the avocado mousse, which was already served on glass salad-plates, and two bottles of Sancerre. She didn't believe in holding back in any areas of life, and particularly not tonight.

'I must say, this is very tasty,' said Doug obsequiously through a mouthful of mousse. 'What is it?'

'It's avocado mousse, Doug,' said Kate, smiling and betraying none of her mounting revulsion.

'Advocado. My, how exotic. I've eaten it once or twice before, of course, but usually with prawns and some cocktail sauce. But this is very different and very tasty. Did you make it yourself?'

'Yes,' she said in a clipped manner.

'My, my, how talented you are. What did you say it was?'

'Avocado mousse.'

'Yes, yes, advocado. I must remember that. Very tasty.'

It was only to be hoped that Kate was just as talented in the laundry department. Doug was so excited and overwhelmed that he was spraying the surrounding area with avocado mousse. There were spots of pale green all over the beautiful white linen and lace tablecloth. She'd bought it in Florence, that heavenly time when she had been there for a week with Nick and they had discovered the little shop when they were wandering back one evening from the *duomo* to their divine pension overlooking the Arno. The air had been heavy with emotion, and the old lady, dressed in black, who had served them had so easily recognized they were in love. Kate had got quite carried away with it all and had bought the tablecloth thoroughly convinced that it was just the sort of thing she should have for her bottom drawer. Oh, well, soak it in Persil overnight and hope for the best.

'I understand you are retired,' said Ned, coming to the rescue.

'That's right.'

'But he keeps on the go,' added Louise quickly.

'I most certainly do. Since my retirement I have thrown myself into countless activities. Local discussion groups, square dancing, the church, bowling and my visits to my son, Colin, to help with his beer making. Take my bowling, for example. I'm Chairman of the Joint Social Committee for the entire North London area. Now, here's something that might interest you all.' Doug put down his fork on the side of his plate. Kate watched it fall off the edge and hit the tablecloth. 'Following the success of the past two years,' he continued, 'I am organizing a New Year's Eve Dance and I wonder if you might be interested in having some tickets. I should warn you, it's a popular event and the tickets sell like hot cakes, so I would advise you all to come to a swift decision in order not to be disappointed. Like last year, and the year before that, it is being held at the church hall of All Saints, Cricklewood, and by acting firmly early in the year I managed to secure the services of that popular act, Roy "Harmony" Harmon and the Pinner Players.'

'Incidental Music by the Harrow Horns, I presume,' squealed Lizzie, proving that once a girl gets away for a few days and then has a few she really lets her hair down.

'I don't think I've heard of them,' said a bewildered Doug, returning to his mousse, or at least what remained on his plate

174

and was not sprayed around the surrounding area. 'I must ask Roy. This is very tasty.'

Lizzie was still giggling to herself, and Louise was having difficulty keeping herself under control since she was positioned directly opposite Lizzie and between Ned and James, who were determined to wind her up. Indeed, the seating had been arranged expressly for that purpose, so at least some elements of the evening were coming together successfully.

'Now, Kate, do tell us how you make this mousse,' demanded James, a study in seriousness.

'I can't quite remember,' said Kate, casting round for a prop. 'I made it up as I went along.'

'How absolutely amazing,' said Doug, thoroughly impressed, open-mouthed, and wanting to know more. 'It's so very tasty. Advocado, you say. Very tasty.'

'James, would you be an angel and help me get these plates into the kitchen?'

What had been safely bubbling on the kitchen stove for the past two and a half hours was one of Kate's trusted and favourite recipes. She didn't want to risk doing anything too new and complicated and thought that her guests would appreciate something simple, and if they didn't appreciate it, tough, because that's what they were getting, together with some Beaujolais *nouveau*. They did appreciate it, however, particularly Doug.

'I must say, this is very tasty. What is it?'

'It's chicken paprika.'

'Now, what might that be?' he tried again. He had travelled extensively since his retirement, but had not come across chicken paprika on his winter breaks.

'It's chicken, breasts of, cooked in a sauce of onions, stock, tomatoes, the spice paprika and some mixed herbs and finished off with sour cream. It's Hungarian, though I got the recipe from my Sainsbury's cookbook.'

'Well, I do congratulate you, Kate. It's absolutely delicious. Very tasty.'

Spots of paprika red were now joining the specks of green on the tablecloth, and, as Doug strived to keep up with the conversation, which ranged from opera, to politics, to holidays, to theatre, to films and restaurants and bounced around the table from Kate, down to Ned, to Louise, to James and across to Lizzie, the spots reached further and further away from Doug and covered a greater area. Doug looked at Kate's plate. He then looked at his own, stabbed a noodle and held it aloft.

'And what are these called?' asked Doug. 'I think I've eaten something like them in Italy. I went to Lido di Jesolo last spring. Did I tell you about it?'

'No, you didn't, Doug. These are noodles. Though I think if you ate something like them in Italy, you probably had tagliatelle.'

'How absolutely fascinating. Oh, the lives you girls lead,' said Doug and then, looking again at Kate's plate where there lay an untouched chicken breast, he added, 'Are you eating that?'

Kate felt a kind of restriction in her throat, almost as if a fishbone were lodged there, but as she was not eating fish and had been eating chicken, and boned breasts from Sainsbury's at that, she knew that what she was feeling in her throat could not at one time have been part of a cod's vital structure.

'No . . .' hesitated Kate.

'Do you mind if I . . .?'

Her eyes widened as she looked on while he leaned across, stabbed his fork into her chicken and wafted it on to his plate, whereupon, without looking left or right, he plunged in and carried on eating.

'Salad, anyone?' she hazarded to the rest of the table.

'Have you got any Heinz salad cream?' cried an elated James, adding a wink, which was quite unnecessary. It resulted in Kate having a coughing fit.

'It's probably that paprika making you cough,' said Doug, the international traveller, while he chewed Kate's chicken breast. 'You can never trust spices. They upset the stomach.'

'But it's not her stomach,' said Lizzie, a mother of two and quite up on childhood ailments. 'It's a cough.'

'Have a glass of water,' suggested Louise.

'Give her a glass of red wine,' said Ned. 'She'll be all right in a minute.'

'Have you tried breathing into a brown paper bag?' called James.

'That's for hiccups, silly. She's got a cough,' said Louise.

'A slap on the back sometimes helps,' suggested Lizzie.

'Oh, shut up,' wheezed Kate.

'I've told you, a glass of wine is the only thing. More Beaujolais anyone?' proposed Ned, the helpful playmate.

They toyed with their salad and they all remarked on the dressing, which was quite delicious, and then moved along to a selection of cheeses, brie and stilton proving to be the most popular, with which they drank port. Doug thought Kate was being very continental by not serving what he was pleased to call a sweet, but was further confused when he was told rather briskly that she gave up serving puddings years ago.

And so calm descended and coffee was served, though Louise had a camomile tea. Doug, not used to staying up late with such stimulating company and certainly not used to eating avocado mousse followed by chicken paprika and in such vast quantities, began to fade by 11.30 and thought that he might wander off home. Louise was not good past eleven o'clock as she tended to tire easily after straining herself beyond reason to appear happy, so she also felt inclined to drift off. Lizzie had continued to let her hair down and was feeling like dancing the night away and longing for Ned and James to suggest going on somewhere. She had never been asked to go on somewhere and she rather thought that it was now or never. But when it was put to her by Kate that they had to be up early to do some shopping in Knightsbridge and that it would be a pity to waste her weekend in London, she agreed that they should probably go to bed. However, she had not lost her grip to such an extent that she could not reflect, rather sadly, that she must be thoroughly middle-aged if going on somewhere and missing the shopping because she was holed up in bed recovering with an Alka-Seltzer was now considered to be wasting a weekend in London. Ned and James gallantly offered to help with the washing up, but Kate told them that they really shouldn't, there wasn't enough room for them all in the kitchen and she could easily cope with it herself. And anyway, that was the whole point, it was her dinner party. She got to do the cooking and she got to do the washing up.

Louise left quietly, thanking Kate sincerely for having given the dinner and promising her that she felt much better and very protected. Doug left loudly and thanked Kate effusively for the evening, which he thought had gone absolutely splendidly. And everything so tasty too. He hoped it was the first of many such special occasions, as he was always ready and willing to stand by for the next time. Ned and James left discreetly and gave Kate a fond farewell with a kiss on the cheek, a squeeze of the shoulder and a ruffle of the hair.

While Kate tidied up the flat, puffed up cushions, cleaned out full and revolting ashtrays, scraped plates (though Doug had done a fine job in scraping his own and hers, and perhaps would have scraped everyone else's if he had not had to stretch a little too far), Lizzie emerged from the second bedroom to fetch a bottle of Perrier water. She was a great believer in the benefits of a glass of water on retiring if one had indulged, especially when one was due to shop in the morning.

Now that everyone had gone, the flat was quiet and it felt cold. Well, it was November, after all, and Kate remembered that she foolishly hadn't fixed the plug on the electric blanket, so she thought she would have a hot-water bottle. A good old-fashioned hottie on the feet and a cup of Earl Grey were just what she needed before she drifted off to sleep. She hoped Louise was going to be all right. The evening hadn't gone quite as she'd planned; she hadn't had enough time to talk to Louise and to make sure that she was not brooding too much, she was being distracted and was enjoying herself. It certainly hadn't turned out to be the elegant evening she'd envisaged, and she thought Louise deserved a touch of elegance – so did she, for that matter. With a sigh she picked up the stained tablecloth and dropped it in a red plastic bucket full of foaming Persil.

She moved quietly around the flat and went to have a look at the aquarium. She dipped her finger in the water and tickled the fish. Kate glided into the kitchen to fix her hot-water bottle. The kettle had boiled, and she bent down and pulled out the hot-water bottle, covered in pink towelling, from the cupboard under the sink. She tried to open the top, but it wouldn't budge. She took a deep breath and then tried again. Still no luck. She paused and tried to think of a solution. She took a screwdriver from a drawer and inserted it through the top and hoped that with the greater leverage she would be able to shift it. No use. It was stuck fast.

There are times when the degree of initiative and strength of character a person brings to the fore in a crisis is all important. Independence and self-reliance are laudable qualities, but sometimes it is more valuable to see a wider picture and understand that we all have our part to play in the sweeping panorama of life.

'Doug,' she said as he peered around his back door, concerned as to what the late-night knock on his window was about. 'I can't seem to open my hot-water bottle.'

CHAPTER THIRTEEN

They had made a valiant effort, but, what with one thing and another and particularly Doug popping round to say he had had a wonderful time and he had meant every word he had said about the New Year's Eve Dance and why didn't they make up a table, they were running a shade behind their schedule. By the time the three of them had discussed and organized the seating in the car, settled upon Lizzie in the back, Louise in the front and Kate driving since it was, after all, her motor, they were running even later when they finally embarked upon their expedition to Knightsbridge. As they eventually fell through the doors of Harrods, having struggled with considerable style through the Saturday morning traffic and discovered a place to park in Rutland Gate, they were running about an hour late. And after they had battled through the throngs of ill-tempered shoppers, pressing close and complaining, all the way to the Christmas decorations department, they realized that it was going to be one of those days.

'I think I'm having an anxiety attack,' declared Kate as she stood on the edge of the fray with a giant red box of Christmas crackers clasped in front of her like a shield. 'I've come over all hot and peculiar and I can't breathe.' She winced as a large lady, up for the day from Canterbury, dressed in a thick camel coat for the occasion and not coping very well with either her umbrella or her tartan shopper on wheels, reversed into her.

'So have I,' said Lizzie, glowering at a child who had lost its parents and had decided to attach itself to her coat. 'Do I look like the motherly type? Why did it choose me? How can it tell? Why didn't it choose you, Kate, or you, Louise? I mean, has it come to this? Don't I look in the least bit reckless or irresponsible? Am I so safe, boring and comforting? Why won't it go away?'

'I'm feeling quite odd,' said Louise with a sigh. 'In ten minutes from now I should have been walking down the aisle.'

'Oh, Louise, I'm sorry. Try and hang on, we can have some lunch soon.'

'Be brave, Louise,' said Lizzie, making a face at the little brat.

'Oh, dear. I can't imagine how awful it must be for you, Louise. I'm feeling very hot and peculiar,' said Kate. 'I really am.'

'I think everyone is,' said Lizzie, who was now getting very testy and wondering just how she could shake off the clinging child without being overtly cruel in a public place and inciting the wrath of the NSPCC. 'We're all wearing too many clothes. I've got to take off this scarf.'

'This woolly hat is getting horribly itchy,' complained Kate.

'Well, take it off then.'

'I can't. My hands are full of crackers. Are you all right, Louise? You seem very quiet.'

'I think so. I'm hanging on by a thin thread, but I do believe I shall make it. I'm taking off my gloves. Phew, that's much better.'

'We'll be out of here soon,' said Kate hopefully.

'Oh, there you are, Tracy, you naughty girl,' said a worried voice, which identified itself as belonging to one of the clinging child's parents. As first one parent emerged from the crowd and then the other followed, it became abundantly evident why the child preferred to stick fast to Lizzie's thighs.

'Put that fairy down. You can't have it,' commanded the second anxious parent, who then grabbed the child, replaced the tree novelty made in Taiwan and hauled the squealing kid off into the heaving mass of humanity, which had also dressed in too many coats, gloves, hats and scarves.

'They didn't even say thank you,' seethed Lizzie as she watched the horrid child and its equally horrid parents disappearing amongst the crowd. 'Can you believe it?'

'And in Harrods, too,' commiserated Kate. 'I think we ought to abandon this project. We've been in here for fifteen minutes and there's no chance we are ever going to find what we want and even if we do, we won't be able to fight our way through to the cash register. There's bound to be a queue there anyway. What do you think, team?'

'I'm inclined to agree. Actually, why did we come in here in the first place?' wondered Louise.

'It's all under one roof. It says so in the catalogue. It's supposed to be easier,' said Lizzie.

'Kate, put the crackers back and let's move on,' said Louise.

'Agreed,' said Kate, shoving the big red box of crackers on top of a swaying pile of gold boxes. 'And do you know something? I don't care if these go on the wrong pile or not. I've had enough. Where to next?'

'Let's get out of here first and think about that later,' said Lizzie hurriedly. She had just spotted the odious little child on its way back to her. It had found a packet of balloons.

As they were now running even more behind their schedule after the fruitless, hot and noisy fifteen minutes in the Christmas decorations department, they decided that it would be a good and productive idea to divide and attack. Lizzie wanted to go down to the grocery department and buy a Christmas pudding and a cake.

'Are you sure about that? They're very heavy?' said Kate. 'Why don't you order them by post and let the Post Office do the humping for you?'

'I'd love to, but I daren't risk it. Harrods let me down last year and the pudding didn't arrive.'

'Oh no!'

'How awful!'

'I had to make do with a very inferior version from the Co-op in Ottley, which was all I could get at the last minute. Peter's mother got very beady after lunch on Christmas Day. It was touch and go until she had her mince pie and some extra brandy butter.'

'Harrods isn't what it used to be,' said an informed Kate. 'Mind you, I think the postal department must get very over-stretched, what with sending all those puddings to families posted to Sri Lanka and Zanzibar. It must be an awful job. Just imagine, all they see for months on end are piles of stamps and yards and yards of puddings and crackers. It's hardly surprising that puddings destined for tables in Ottley-on-the-Edge and the like tend to get left to the last minute and are then overlooked. So, you're probably right, Lizzie. You'd better get downstairs and select your pudding right now. We can't have Peter's mother disappointed again.'

'Shall we meet you in the lingerie department, Lizzie? I fancy buying myself a treat. I don't really need a pudding,' suggested Louise tentatively.

'Excellent idea,' said Kate. 'All right with you, Lizzie?'

'Fine with me. I'll see you in about half an hour. I might be quicker, but you never can tell with these crowds. Isn't it awful?'

'Ghastly.'

'Hideous.'

The lift down to the first floor was crowded, but not as crowded as the decorations department, which had been seriously in need of ventilation. They weaved their way into lingerie, and although they found it busy, it was an oasis compared with the war zone around the tree lights, angels, enchanted grottoes and pixies.

Kate and Louise wandered around, happily looking at the exclusive bits of satin and silk with bows and lace bodices. They adored all the embroidered detail, the ribbons, the appliqué and the tucking on the Swiss cotton nightdresses. They stroked the fabrics, they lingered, they dreamed, they took down some of the nightdresses from their hangers and put them back, they admired and desired and came to the conclusion that they were all hideously expensive for what they were, though eventually Louise decided that she would splash out anyway. She needed to be kind to herself, and Kate had been very encouraging. While she was in a changing room trying on a slip of something in ivory crêpe de Chine with shoestring straps and a matching négligé, Kate was ogling a camisole in pale coffee satin with lots of mushroom-coloured lace and a pair of French knickers with even more. She was wondering if she ever could.

'Kate?' said a rather embarrassed male voice.

'Peter?'

'Hello.'

'How extraordinary,' said Kate. She was thinking very fast. 'What on earth are you doing here?'

'Well, I was at a bit of a loose end, so I thought I'd come up to London and try and find something for Lizzie's Christmas present.'

'Why, it's Kate,' said a figure with a bouncing blonde ponytail, heavily made-up eyes and eyelashes, a silver-fox fur around the shoulders and an overpowering whiff of Giorgio. It was enough to knock you sideways. 'How wonderful to see you. I would never have recognized you in that hat.'

'And I bumped into Asta,' said an even more embarrassed Peter, 'and she very kindly offered to help me. Choose the Christmas present for Lizzie, that is.'

'Well, isn't that nice?' said Kate, hoping that it would still stay nice when Lizzie, all hot and bothered, struggled up from Christmas provisions weighed down with a pudding ready for steaming and a mixed fruit cake iced with a happy snow scene.

'Yes, very nice,' said Peter, shuffling his feet.

'I was so surprised when I saw Peter,' trilled Asta. 'And now it's a lovely surprise seeing you, Kate. That hat is so cute. Do you wear it often?'

You don't know what a surprise it is, Asta. There could be even more surprises on the way for you, honey, thought Kate.

'Yes, it is a surprise,' Kate agreed. 'Have you found anything you like so far?'

'Well, I've found this darling pink towelling robe studded with rhinestones, but Peter's not sure it's quite Lizzie,' confided Asta. 'It's got a matching turban.'

'Perhaps not,' said Kate.

'I've gone completely mad and decided to get it,' said Louise. 'It's being packed at the moment.'

'You have?' Kate collected herself and recalled that Louise was shooting for the shoestring straps in ivory crêpe de Chine with négligé and not the pink towelling with rhinestones and matching turban.

'Louise, do meet Peter, Lizzie's husband,' said Kate, squeezing

184

Louise's wrist as she said the important words so that she would grasp the full significance of who they were talking to over the French knickers and racy garters.

'I'm delighted to meet you,' said Louise. 'I had the pleasure of meeting Lizzie a couple of weeks ago. Such fun.'

Kate was tremendously impressed with this awesome display of quick thinking. Given that Louise in another life had just walked down the aisle wearing her tailored suit with peplum in ecru lace, brandishing a lily and sporting a lovely hat with a froth of discreet veiling, while in this life she was calculating just how much was left in her current account at the Midland Bank, Sloane Square, after the purchase of the little crêpe de Chine number, it really was quite remarkable.

'And this is Peter's and Lizzie's friend, Asta,' said Kate. 'They bumped into each other here. Isn't that a coincidence? And now we've bumped into them.'

'How do you do?' said Louise pleasantly, smiling and pretending she hadn't heard what she had heard, seen what she had seen and sensed what she had sensed.

'Hi,' said Asta, following this up with a cute little wave and a smile.

It was at this moment, as she was hoping to think the best of Peter, trying to believe that he was the loving and constant husband of her dear friend Lizzie, he had only bumped into Asta and had not planned a rendezvous and was indeed trying to find a present for Lizzie, that Kate chanced to glance down and thus noticed the red satin and black lace suspender belt gently held by Asta.

'Um . . .' tried Peter.

'Yes?' said Kate.

'Lizzie's with her mother in Bath. She's not at all well. Her mother that is. Poor thing.'

'So I understand. Water on the ankles, I believe.'

'Yes, that's right.'

There was an agonizingly long pause while Kate concentrated on the knickers, Asta rattled her suspender belt and Peter hummed.

'I just wanted to show Kate something over there,' said

Louise, who seemed to be the only one capable of constructive thought. She was pointing to a distant display of Viyella pyjamas. They were quite a long way away and in a corner, which was perhaps sound marketing practice on the part of Harrods as there probably was not a great deal of demand for these cosy all-concealing garments. 'Would you excuse us for a moment?'

Kate and Louise put on a good show of calmly walking towards the Viyella pyjamas and woolly bedjackets and concealed themselves with considerable relief behind a rack of quilted dressing-gowns in pleasing pastel shades.

'Have you had experience of this kind of thing before?' asked Kate.

'Once or twice.'

'Thank goodness you're on board. What do we do next?'

'I don't know.'

'It might be a coincidence, of course. Peter might be looking for Lizzie's Christmas present. And he might have bumped into Asta.'

'Or he might not.'

'It's a sad reflection on the times we live in or the lives we've led that we immediately think the worst. Oh, dear, I'm feeling hot again and I can't breathe,' said Kate. 'I think I'm having another anxiety attack.'

'Try and keep calm. At least keep a look out. Lizzie might come crashing in at any minute swinging a pudding and, if she sees Peter with Asta, she might get carried away and swing it in his direction.'

'Or she might swing it at Asta.'

'That will be no loss.'

'Quite. Now, let's have a quiet think here and sort out our facts,' said Kate. 'Peter thinks Lizzie is in Bath, so we know he mustn't see her. He'll only think the worst. Lizzie thinks Peter's at home doing a bit of gardening, so we mustn't let her see him, because she's *bound* to think the worst. Asta has been told that Lizzie is in Bath, so we mustn't let them meet, as Asta shouldn't be involved in the secret. She would get it all wrong. She's a silly woman. And we certainly can't let Lizzie see Peter and

Asta together. That would be disastrous. Of course, the other thing we have to think about is that it might all be wholly innocent and Peter might well be buying Lizzie's Christmas present. Even so, we can't let her see him, because it'll ruin the surprise.'

'I don't think we can let any of it happen,' said Louise.

'I totally agree. Are we in a "divided loyalties" situation here?'

'No, I think we're in a straightforward "keep them apart" situation here.'

'Right. Oh, dear, I've suddenly gone very cold,' shivered Kate. 'I think I'd better buy one of those vests.'

Louise peered around the dressing-gowns and saw that Peter was standing doing nothing in particular, other than looking acutely embarrassed, and Asta was fondling the marabou edging on a flimsy bit of lavender chiffon.

'OK, I'll tell you what we'll do,' said Louise, taking command.

'Please do.'

'We'll wander back, chatting happily between ourselves, as if nothing untoward has come to pass and it's lovely that Peter wants to buy Lizzie a present. You'll suggest to him that what Lizzie really would like is a cape; then you yank him off in the direction of the cashmeres before he knows what's happening.'

'What do we do about Asta?'

'I hope she'll trot along with Peter, but if she doesn't go willingly, I'm afraid we're going to have to force her to go with him. I know it goes against the grain, but there's no other way. We've got to make this a safe area.'

'Oh, dear, I don't know if I'm hot or cold now,' mumbled Kate. 'OK, here goes.'

Gathering themselves up, they did just as Louise had suggested, managed to look thoroughly absorbed in their own conversation and acted as if it was a perfectly normal Saturday and they were barely concerned with Peter or Asta or both of them together and what they might or might not be up to.

'I've been thinking,' said Kate with only the slightest tremor in her voice. 'What Lizzie would really like is a cashmere cape. I don't think she wants a nightdress at all. She showed me a picture of a cape in Vogue when I was down at your house, Peter. That one was grey, but she might like one in cream or one in black or even navy blue perhaps. There's quite a good selection over in cashmeres.'

'Are you quite sure she wouldn't prefer a nightdress?' asked Peter.

'Quite sure,' said Kate.

'I got her a nightdress last year, and she liked it.'

'All the more reason to get something different this year,' said Kate briskly.

'There's a really cute teddy over there in banana yellow. Come and look at it,' suggested Asta, gliding back on to the scene when she wasn't wanted and dazzling everyone with her teeth.

'Kate says she thinks Lizzie would prefer a cashmere sweater, murmured Peter vaguely.'

'Oh, that's so boring,' said Asta with a pout.

'I didn't say a sweater,' corrected Kate while gripping her patience by the scruff of the neck. 'I said a cape. A lovely big cape, which she can fling around her shoulders with gay abandon and keep herself warm.'

'Oh, that is a good idea,' encouraged Louise, who was looking at her watch and getting very anxious about the time factor. 'I think a nightdress would be boring. So predictable.'

'It doesn't have to be a nightdress,' whined Asta. 'What about the teddy in banana yellow silk? It's got the sweetest lace trim you ever saw.'

'You can never go wrong with cashmere.'

'Do you think so?' asked Peter. He was getting very confused by all this conflicting advice.

'Yes, I do,' said Louise firmly.

'And so do I,' said Kate even more firmly. 'Actually, I want to go and have a look at the cashmeres myself. I have to get something for my mother, so why don't you come along with me now and I'll help you?'

'Are you sure?' asked Peter.

'Yes, I'm sure,' said Kate, linking Peter's arm and attempting to move him off in the right direction without appearing actually to manhandle him away from the petticoats and frills.

'Oh, all right then,' he agreed. 'Let's go and have a look at them. I can always come back if I ultimately decide on a nightdress.'

'But the teddy might be sold,' whimpered Asta.

'Now, come along, Asta. Why don't you come with us?' asked Kate, trying to seem very charming and pleasant and not to sound like she was feeling. 'Your advice would be very helpful and most welcome. I'm sure they'll still have lots of things here when you come back. There's always the robe with the rhinestones.'

'And the turban.'

'Yes, and the turban,' managed Kate through tight lips.

Louise, who was standing behind Asta in an attempt to keep one eye on the way she thought Lizzie would be coming and one eye on Peter, gave up for a moment, focused both of them on Kate and tried to flash her a look that would say, 'Get moving now. Hang around any longer and everyone will be in trouble.'

'I suppose I might as well come too,' said Asta rather huffily. It was the first indication she gave that she could ever let her cute, bubbly, charming demeanour slip. Being put out did not become her, and the poor girl even forgot to bounce her ponytail when she flounced off, leaving a heavy cloud of Giorgio in her wake.

'I think I'll wait here for you, Kate. I've got to pick up my carrier bag from the cash register and I'll just wander around and see if there's anything else that takes my fancy.'

'Go and have a look at that pink towelling robe with the rhinestones,' called Asta as she reluctantly followed Peter and Kate in the direction of the cashmeres. She didn't quite know what was happening and why she was going when her soul wasn't really in it. She would much rather have stayed amongst more intimate apparel, but she had better stick with Peter. They were to have a nice little lunch later. She added in a final thrust, 'It's absolutely darling. I think I'm going to ask Greville to get it for me for Christmas. In my estimation it is never boring to have beautiful things.'

Fortunately, Asta was looking at Kate when Louise was mouthing 'Ugh' and at Louise when Kate was doing likewise, and Peter noticed nothing at all, because he was thinking that a nightdress would really be best and wondering if he could remember the way to that little out-of-the-way restaurant in Chelsea.

Louise looked at her watch and realized that they had spent a full forty-five minutes in lingerie. She was just about to come over all misty-eyed as she calculated that they would have been out of the church by now and on their way to the reception with two hundred of their closest friends when it struck her that she hadn't heard from one of them. Where were they all now? It was best not to dwell. She would only get upset. She simply had to get through the day and be brave.

Lizzie was concerned that their schedule would be running extremely late by the time she managed to fight her way from groceries and get back to lingerie, which she had left an hour before. She hoped that Kate and Louise hadn't been too bored waiting for her and that perhaps they had found something to buy. She had bought her pudding and also her cake, but the trouble was that just as she'd been whizzing through groceries, her eyes had suddenly been drawn to a display of Keiller marmalade and she found herself becoming wistful and re-flective. It was Peter's favourite, and Sunday morning wasn't Sunday morning unless he had his toast and marmalade. In fact, he made quite a thing about it and had been decidedly grumpy when Lizzie had insisted upon a household economy drive and had taken to buying Tesco's own brand. It wasn't the same, and after two jars Lizzie had given up and returned to Keiller's best. The incident had rather annoyed her at the time, but today she looked back on it with affection and good humour. She decided to buy Peter a jar right there and then. She got him three fruits – orange, lemon and grapefruit. He'd like that.

As she continued on her way back to lingerie, her thoughts stayed with Peter, and she began to think again of how she was missing him and of how she was so looking forward to seeing him and hearing all about his weekend. What was he up to at the moment? Perhaps he'd done a good morning's work in the garden and had gone to the Goat and Shuttle for a lunchtime pint; probably this afternoon he would watch *Grandstand* on television. Well, why not? – he deserved it. While she was in Harrods, Lizzie thought, she really should take the time to buy Peter's Christmas present. She should try and get him something different this year. Something he would appreciate. Resorting to a cashmere sweater from the Burlington Arcade and a book on gardening, courtesy of W. H. Smith, every year got to be a bit predictable.

'Oh, Louise, there you are. I'm sorry I took such a long time. Have you been all right?' puffed Lizzie, who was, as predicted, finding the pudding and the cake rather heavy.

'Yes, I'm fine, thank you.'

'Have you bought something?' asked Lizzie, fixing immediately upon Louise's carrier bag.

'Yes, I've splashed out and bought the most gorgeous nightdress and robe. It's stunning. Hideously expensive and a great extravagance, but what the hell? I decided I deserved it.'

'And so you do. Peter always gets me one for Christmas. I rather look forward to it. He's got very good taste. Isn't it a surprise? I don't know where he gets it from. Where's Kate?' asked Lizzie, looking around and not seeing Kate in the immediate vicinity.

'She's in cashmeres, looking for a present for her mother. She won't be long, I'm sure.'

'Shall we go and join her?'

'No, I think it's best if we wait here. We might not find her and then we'll waste more time wandering around in circles.'

'I bought Peter a lovely Mont Blanc pen. I hope he likes it.'

'I'm sure he will.'

'I usually buy him a cashmere sweater.'

'You can't go wrong with cashmere,' said Louise, hoping that Kate would happen along soon and neither of them would go wrong with their dialogue.

'That's what I always say.'

Just as Lizzie was beginning to wonder if she shouldn't have a stroll around and see if there was anything that caught her eye

– she could do with some new thermal underwear – Kate came rushing headlong up to them.

'I hope you haven't been waiting long,' she said, still in a rush.

'No, only a few minutes. Did you find something for your mother?' asked Lizzie.

'No, I didn't. I wasn't concentrating,' answered Kate for the benefit of Louise and then, for the benefit of Lizzie, she said, 'I was worried we were running late.'

'Oh, I don't think it matters too much. Do you, Louise? Do you want to go back and have another look? Shall we come with you and help?'

'No,' said Kate decisively. 'It's very crowded in there. Let's go downstairs to cosmetics and see if there are any special offers that look interesting.'

'Oh, good, I can buy Peter some aftershave. I'm quite keen on him today. Are you feeling all right, Louise?'

'Yes, I'm fine,' said Louise, who had been coping admirably with the morning's events, but was now beginning to feel decidedly shaky.

While Lizzie was off trying to find the perfect aftershave for her man (who was otherwise engaged in sweaters and capes and not at the Goat and Shuttle with the lads), Kate and Louise were hanging around the Estée Lauder counter trying to attract the attention of someone who would be pleased to sell them a lipgloss and a mascara, thus making them eligible for a gift package containing samples of shampoo, neck cream and a lipstick in a colour that promised to be next season's smash. It might turn out to be a long wait, as there were several big spenders around the counter who were buying up large jars of special creams that would give them a perfect skin and increase the day's takings considerably.

'What a day,' said Kate. 'You've no idea what I had to go through in cashmeres.' It had been quite an ordeal and Kate had had to employ a great deal of initiative, outright lying and deception. However, Asta had rallied and had forgotten her discontent when she found some beaded sweaters in hues of violet and peacock. She had got quite into the swing of things and was busily bossing Peter around; as Kate had made her discreet exit she had turned back to see him surrounded by Ballantynes and elbow-deep in Pringles.

'It's not over yet. I've just spotted Jacqui's ex-husband, or the most recent ex, to be more precise.'

'Oh, no,' groaned Kate. 'Has he spotted you?'

'Yes, I'm afraid he has. He's coming this way.'

'Oh, dear. Well, I'm now way beyond an anxiety attack. Shall I go into the perfume hall and try and pick up some lavender water and eau-de-Cologne? I wonder if they still stock smelling salts?' For support, Kate propped herself up against the Estée Lauder counter and watched the altogether distinguished gentleman in his late sixties. Even in November he had a marvellous sun-tan, but today he had chosen to wrap up warmly in a wonderful coat with an astrakhan collar. It was a most attractive picture.

'Louise. How wonderful to see you. I've so wanted to know how you were.'

Louise took a very deep breath, paused for a moment and, when she was ready to reply, she said, 'Hello, Kurt. This is my friend, Kate.'

'Hello, Kate,' purred Kurt, who had had a bit to do with ladies in his time and was still at it.

'Hello,' said Kate.

He smiled a lingering 'nice to meet you' smile, before turning his full attention back to Louise.

'I tried to find out where you were, but no one seemed to have your telephone number. I'm so sorry about things.'

'Ah, well.'

'You're looking wonderful. We must have dinner sometime.'

'Yes, that would be nice.'

'Where are you living now?'

'I'm staying in my sister's flat until I find my own place.'

'Yes, I'm very sorry about things. If there's anything I can do . . .'

'Yes, thank you.'

'Well, it didn't last.'

Louise hesitated. 'What?'

'David and Jacqui.'

Kate picked herself up from the counter and moved a step nearer.

'Sorry, what are you talking about?' asked Louise. She felt she did know what he was talking about, but was too confused to admit it to herself.

'Well, I thought you'd be the first to know. But then, of course, no one seems to have your telephone number.'

'The first to know what?'

Kate had moved even closer and was staring at Kurt, her eyes set, quite prepared to shake him until his teeth rattled if he didn't answer soon.

'That David and Jacqui split up.'

'They did? When?'

'About two weeks ago.'

'Really?'

'Yes. I'm surprised you didn't know.'

'What happened?'

'Oh, she's gone off with some Greek who owns a boat.'

'You're kidding.'

Kate quietly moved closer to Louise with a supportive arm. She thought it was the kind of thing that was going to be useful.

'Well, we must have dinner sometime soon. I must dash, as I'm having lunch with one of my ex-wives. I think she was the second. Keep in touch,' said Kurt as he kissed Louise farewell. He didn't think to take her telephone number, however, and since he hadn't got it and neither had anyone else, it looked as if their dinner was going to have to wait.

'Are you all right?' asked Kate.

'Yes,' replied Louise.

'You can't be. I'm not.'

'Well, actually, I am feeling very shaky and rather peculiar and not a bit all right,' said Louise, speaking the truth.

'I think we'd better go and have something to eat and, more to the point, something to drink. Where's Lizzie?'

'Here I am,' she said on cue. 'Who was that gorgeous-looking man you were talking to?'

'It's a very long and complicated story,' said Louise in a flat voice.

'Let's go and have a glass of wine. It's been quite a busy morning, hasn't it?' chuckled Lizzie, full of energy and counting her carrier bags.

Kate considered this statement. 'Yes it's been quite a morning. Are you feeling all right, Louise?'

CHAPTER FOURTEEN

'No, Geoffrey, it says open the other end.' Geoffrey pulled himself up to his full height of five foot six and scratched his head. He looked at the cardboard box and then he looked at Kate and then his eyes were drawn back to the large and battered box, which was covered in stamps, customs stickers and directions to handle with care, which, in his opinion, was advice that had not been adhered to in the annual Christmas rush at the Post Office.

'Which end?'

'The one I'm pointing to.'

'Is that the other end or the end? Be precise, Chief. I've got other commitments, you know. I can't hang around here all day playing postman.'

Kate tried to remain calm, poised and in control and to appear to be the person she longed to be.

'I'm pointing to the end that says open the other end, which means that the other end, the end you should open, is the end face down on the floor. Got it?'

'I'll have to turn it over then.'

He'd got it.

'Yes, you will.'

'Ridiculous. You'd think they'd have the sense to put something on the box to say it was this end up. What's the point of them telling you which end to open when the end you want is down and not up? It doesn't make any sense at all. Utter stupidity. Here goes. Come along now, Katy, grab the other end! Don't just stand there.'

Kate jumped to it, did as she was told and grabbed the other end.

'This side has collapsed,' said Geoffrey, indicating the beatenin side with his foot. 'Pass me the scissors, Chief. This is one of the worst packing jobs I have ever seen. It's absolutely disgraceful.'

'We're not worrying about how it was packed up, Geoffrey. What we're concerned about is opening it.'

Geoffrey plunged the scissors into the top of the box at the end that was up and supposed to be opened. 'Right, that's got it open. Now all we've got to do is get it out.'

'You've got to do it, Geoffrey, not we.'

'I've got to do it?' mumbled Geoffrey, resigned to his task.

As Louise came through the kitchen from the photocopying room, where she had been doing nothing more exciting than a bit of photocopying, she flicked on the kettle, thinking that Kate could probably do with a mug of coffee. She was still on the camomile tea, since it was supposed to have a calming effect. She had suggested to Kate and the others that they might like to try it, but so far had had no takers. Louise went on through to the reception area to see if anyone else had arrived and if they too would like a coffee; she was making it anyway and it wouldn't be any trouble at all to make some more. She was greeted by the spectacle of Geoffrey, wearing a pair of loud checked trousers, waist size forty-six, and a green and salmon-pink striped shirt with braces to match, bending over a large cardboard box. The movements he was making from right to left and back again seemed to indicate that he was involved in a struggle to extricate the contents of the box. Had she been able to see the front of his top half, she would have noted that he was wearing a green bow tie with salmon-pink spots. He had bought the shirt, the braces and the tie as a set, though from which shop he couldn't quite remember. But as his top half was for the moment working hard in the box she was unable to behold the full effect of his snappy co-ordinates.

'Got it!' cried a triumphant Geoffrey.

'Well done, Geoffrey,' said Kate as she applauded.

'Got what?' asked Louise, wondering what on earth was going on.

'We're not quite sure. This box arrived about ten minutes ago. The postmark is Chicago, and the senders are Bedliner and

Bolt. I rather think it's their way of saying Happy Christmas,' Kate sighed and added, 'What a shame we didn't send them anything.'

Louise was a very good secretary and, above all, extremely discreet, so she was unable and unwilling to tell Kate that they had indeed sent a token of the season to Bedliner and Bolt, more specifically to the Bedliner end of the partnership. Ms Bedliner would be receiving three dozen sterling roses done up in Cellophane decorated all over with little white stars and dramatically tied with a large silver bow. She had been receiving one dozen long-stemmed red roses every Friday afternoon for the past four weeks, and they had been much appreciated. But Louise would say nothing. Her lips were sealed. She would also say nothing about the person-to-person telephone calls that came in regularly from Ms Bedliner for Michael and went out regularly from Michael to Ms Bedliner. The ones placed by Michael were usually made early in the morning, London time; the time difference between London and Chicago was six hours, which meant that Cindy should have been sound asleep and away in dreamland, but as she never snapped an abrasive 'Doesn't that jerk know what time it is?' and instead purred a husky 'Hi', Louise had drawn the conclusion, not unnaturally given the facts, that not only was Cindy expecting Michael to telephone, but that she was also pleased to hear from him. But, of course, she would say nothing about any of it. Nothing at all.

'It's in bits. All that work and it's in bits,' said Geoffrey, stamping his foot. He was, after all that unnecessary exertion, quite exasperated.

'Is there a card?' asked Kate.

'What's the point of a card? It's in bits,' moaned Geoffrey. 'I told you it was a bad packing job.'

'Let me have a look.' Kate was not going to let it rest at that. She knew that there would be a card tucked in there somewhere and she wanted to know precisely what it said. 'Here it is. And here are the instructions. It's not in bits at all, Geoffrey. We have to assemble it.'

'I think I'll go and make some coffee,' said Louise. 'I think we need it.'

'I most certainly do, Number One,' commented Geoffrey. 'I suppose you want me to assemble the damn thing now, Katy. I've wasted half my morning already, you know.' Geoffrey glowered at Kate and she glowered back at him until he couldn't resist breaking into a genial smile and giving his green and pink braces a fast twang. The truth of the matter was he would do anything for Kate and even more for Louise. He would have walked on burning coals for her, even if she hadn't arrived with a welcome mug of coffee right at that very moment.

'It seems to be some sort of table decoration,' said Kate, looking at the instructions. 'Perhaps they're under the impression that we have an executive dining-room. It'll have to go in reception. The card says, and I should point out that it's handwritten – now gather round everyone – the card says,' and, putting on a very bad American accent, she read out, 'From the offices of Bedliner and Bolt to all at Major Events to brighten your office and your hearts over the Holiday Season.'

Silence reigned supreme.

'Shall I repeat that?' asked Kate of her audience.

'No, it's quite all right, I heard it the first time,' remarked Louise.

'Very nice coffee, Number One,' said Geoffrey gravely.

'What do we do now?' asked Louise.

'Clear a space and try and put it together. The base seems to be this bit of frosted log. I hope it's not an endangered species. Isn't it hysterical?' Kate appeared to be alone in her opinion.

'What on earth are you three up to?' queried Ned as he entered reception and very nearly lost his elegant footing in a piece of string, which trailed across the floor.

'Oh, just in time, Ned,' said Kate. 'We've got this thing to assemble, and, as you're the art department, I'm sure you're just the person we need.'

'I walked right into that one, didn't I?' observed Ned, kicking a piece of brown paper in the air. 'All right. Let me settle in and I'll give it a go. Any coffee around?'

'I'll go and make you one right now,' offered Louise, rushing off to the kitchen on winged heels.

'Oh, don't go to any trouble on my account. Only if you're

making it,' said Ned mechanically. He edged his way through the reception area and stepped over the chewed remnants of the box, which littered the floor, and made his way to his desk. Once there he flung his jacket, which was a lovely Giorgio Armani and shouldn't have been treated like that, down on his chair, had a swift scan of the front page of Kate's *Daily Mail*, which was lying unread on her desk, and then gently ambled back to reception.

'I've found the base,' said Kate helpfully. 'It's this bit here. And here are the instructions.' She paused and added hesitantly, 'It looks fairly straightforward. I'm sure you'll be able to do it.'

'Here's your coffee,' said Louise, handing him the welcome brew. She led him to the deep-seated leather sofa. 'Sit down and make yourself comfortable.'

While Louise was busy fussing over Ned, puffing up cushions for his back and making sure he had a good light behind him lest he have to squint while reading the instructions on how to put Cindy's table decoration together, the telephone rang.

'I'll get it,' said Kate, leaping over half a cardboard box. 'Good Morning. Major Events.'

'Kate, don't put the phone down, it's Nick.'

She didn't put the phone down. She waited. She could hear her heart beat.

'Are you still there?' he asked.

'Yes.'

'Don't put the phone down.'

'I won't.'

'Listen to me.'

'I will.'

'Promise?'

'Promise.'

'Kate, listen to me.'

'I am listening.'

'It's Christmas.'

'Yes, I know,' said Kate. She rather wished he would get to the point. For an intelligent chap, he was taking his time.

'Christmas is a time for communication, for friendship and understanding.'

'Oh, really? Ha!'

'Kate, are you listening?' he asked sharply.

'Of course I am, this is riveting stuff. I wouldn't want to miss a word of it. Please go on.'

'Kate, just let me say what I feel, which is that you are my best friend and I miss you. Forget about the other stuff. Quite simply, you are my pal, and I miss my pal. I really do.'

That was it. She went. Completely. He'd got her. He was right. He missed her and she missed him. And yes, he was her best friend and it was Christmas and, oh, how she missed him, and he was her pal too and how right he was, and how could she resist? And how very sensible of him to call.

'Oh,' she choked.

'And I thought that I would like to see you, my best friend, sometime over the next few days. I promise I won't put any pressure on you. You do understand what I'm saying, don't you?'

'Yes, I do,' said Kate as she fumbled for Louise's chair and gratefully sank into it. 'I miss you too, Pal. I miss hanging out with the lads and I miss man-talk. How are Manchester United these days?'

'You don't change, Kate.'

'I would hope not, Nicholas.'

'Can we meet for dinner?'

'Nope. Dinner is for lovers and we are friends. Best friends. You said it yourself. How about lunch?'

'OK. When?'

'How about today?' It was not that she was eager, it was more that she was booked solid for the rest of the week. That was her story and she was going to stick to it.

'Fine, I'm free.'

'I'm free,' said Kate.

'How about San Frediano?'

'Splendid. But promise me that we are meeting as friends and that you won't try piling on the pressure. We will be grown up, won't we?'

'Of course. Kate, I told you, you are my friend, my very best friend. We've known each other for ten years. Why throw that away and lose all that friendship and understanding?'

She listened with an increasingly heavy heart.

'Will you tell your best friend all your secrets?' she asked.

'Some of them.'

'Oh, goody, I can't wait. Shall I see you there at 12.30?'

'Twelve-thirty would be perfect. Until then. Bye.'

'Bye,' said Kate, aiming at a very friendly manner. She slowly replaced the receiver and as she did so she saw that Louise was watching her from the other side of the room, and it was with a considerable degree of interest and concern that Kate was being observed. Above all, it was with a clear recognition of exactly who it had been on the telephone.

Had anyone happened to ask Kate thirty minutes previously what she was doing for lunch, the last thing she would have thought she would be doing was lunching with Nick. But that was what she was going to do and she wasn't kicking herself, nor was she saddened by her own weakness. She *was* feeling foolish, not because of her reaction to the telephone call, but because she had allowed herself to become emotionally blinded and it had taken her so long to recognize the importance of companionship. Thank goodness Nick was sensible enough to understand its value and how fortunate that he had persisted with his telephone calls and had made her see that she too missed her best friend, her pal, her buddy. She could meet him, talk to him, laugh with him, delight in being with him and, as he had so rightly put it, forget all the other stuff. As she sat behind the reception desk, although she was aware that Louise's quizzical eye was still upon her, she began to feel calm and free. Things were going to be all right. She sighed softly and gave herself over to a few moments of mellow meditation.

In a busy office time moves relentlessly on, so it was no good sitting there and dreaming away the rest of the morning, there were things to be done in addition to the assembling of Bedliner and Bolt's festive offering. There were letters to be written, telephone calls to be made, travel arrangements to be confirmed and an excessive phone bill to be checked. There seemed to be an extraordinary number of long-distance telephone calls and many of them person-to-person to a number in Chicago.

Martin would have flung down his squash kit on the floor in

front of the desk, but, as there were so many bits of wrapping paper and pieces of polystyrene packing already strewn there, he decided to hold the bag in front of him.

'Morning, Kate.'

'Morning, Martin,' she replied, adding a big 'and how are you today' cheerful smile.

'I wanted to have a word with you about something. Do you have a moment?'

'Not just now, Martin. Can we talk later?'

'All right. I'll be over in my corner. I've got an awful lot on.'

Before getting to grips with all the trying things she had to tackle, Kate decided that the first thing on the list was a fast few words with Louise. She could well afford to take a few minutes out from her hectic schedule, besides which her energy level had soared and she knew that she would be able to conquer her pile of work in no time at all. She hadn't felt like that when she had first encountered her in-tray at 9.30 that morning, but she was certainly feeling good now. She raised herself up off the swivel chair and walked over to Ned and Louise, who were working well together on the table decoration. Louise was holding some glue and a pair of scissors. Ned was carefully placing a golden sledge on the piece of frosted wood.

'That looks lovely, Ned. Is it very difficult?' asked Kate, thinking it was only fair to take an interest.

'It's quite easy, actually,' admitted Ned. 'I've decided to change it a bit, so I've put the sledge at a slight tilt so it gives the impression of Santa whizzing down the mountain side. The instructions had him dead centre. Thoroughly boring. No imagination, you see, no imagination at all.' Ned got up from the sofa and stepped back, all the better to admire his handiwork.

'What happens next?' asked Kate, still taking an interest.

'All the parcels go in the back of the sledge. Now, the instructions have them piled up uniformly in the back of the sledge, but I'm going to put them in in a random fashion and have some of them scattered on the ground as if they've fallen out.'

'Sort of as if they fell out while Santa was whizzing down the mountain at great speed,' added Louise.

'I'm going to see if I can fix it so that some of them are actually in the process of falling out. It will add more movement to the whole piece. If I can find some wire, I'm sure I can do it,' said Ned confidently.

'Louise?' asked Kate, a tolerant smile fixed in position.

'Yes?'

'Could we have a word?'

Louise, who was very intuitive by nature and who had been watching across the littered room as Kate had giggled, smiled and sighed her way through the telephone call, had rather expected that a heart-to-heart was due. The kitchen seemed like the right place to exchange confidences.

'Shut the door,' said Kate. 'Draw up a stool. Are you all right?'

'I'm fine,' said Louise.

'Are you sure? You're not thinking about David too much?'

'Well, every now and then, but I'm fine really,' asserted Louise, though, of course, it wasn't strictly true. She was just good at covering up. Sometimes too good.

'That's wonderful,' said Kate. She glanced around the room before drawing her stool closer. 'That was Nick on the telephone.'

'I thought it might be.'

Kate registered the tone of concern in Louise's voice.

'Don't worry, everything is all right,' began Kate, anxious that Louise know the facts lest the tone of concern turn to a tone of criticism. She was paranoid about people finding fault with her. Had she ever undergone hypnosis she would have learned that it dated back to the time Brown Owl was beastly to her at Brownies about her table setting in front of the rest of the pack. 'I'm having lunch with him.'

'You're having lunch with him.' Louise did not add a clipped 'I see' at the end of her comment, though she might well have done; the tone of concern had turned not to one of criticism but of resignation. 'When?'

'Today.'

'Ah.'

'But everything's fine, really it is.'

204

'In what way?'

'Quite simply, we are going to be friends. Nick pointed out to me that we've known each other for years and years and after all that time we have become best friends, which is what he misses most: the companionship and the camaraderie. And do you know something? I realize that is what I miss too. It's the friendship that he wants to re-establish, and I think he's right.'

'I can see that, put like that, he has a point. How loose is the interpretation going to be?'

Kate was about to draw her stool even closer, but was unable to tell Louise how strongly she felt and how sure she was that this was indeed the right thing to do, because there was a persistent knocking on the kitchen door.

'Oy, you two,' called Martin. 'Michael wants to have a word with Kate.'

'Be with him in a tick,' answered Kate, acknowledging that duty called.

Michael had already asked Kate to close the door and she had already done so, so it seemed logical that the next step was to ask her to sit down. He had, after all, asked her to have a word, and with Michael's record there was no knowing how many words that might mean. Kate settled herself in the leather armchair she knew so well.

'Kate, I've been thinking about Louise.'

'Yes,' said Kate. She thought she ought to pay attention, as you never could tell exactly what Michael had been thinking.

'I know she's far too good for us, but have you thought about the possibility of asking her whether she would consider taking the job permanently?'

'Well, I hadn't, actually. I did ask her if she would think about staying until after Christmas and into the New Year because it's always a bad time to find staff, and she did say yes, and she does seem happy, and I must say she's frightfully good. But quite honestly, like you, I'd always thought of her as being far too good for us and so I thought it might be insulting to ask if she wanted to stay permanently.'

Michael remained silent, but, fortunately, it was not because he was insulted by the idea that Louise might be insulted by being asked to join the staff of Major Events on a permanent basis. It was just that his focus of attention had momentarily drifted to something else.

'Well, do you think you could? Or do you think I should?' he asked.

'Perhaps I should sound her out, and then you should ask her formally.'

'Yes, that's probably the way to do it. So, will you ask her?'

'Yes. Do you want me to ask her now?'

'Why not?'

'Indeed. Shall I report back?'

'Yes, please do.'

'Oh, by the way, Michael, we've received a parcel from Chicago, from Bedliner and Bolt. It's some sort of Christmas decoration.'

'Well, how thoughtful of them.'

'Yes. I feel really bad that we didn't send them anything.'

It was at this moment that Michael realized that Louise hadn't told Kate about the roses for Cindy, like the good secretary she was, and it was only a fraction of a second later that he realized that it was imperative that she be signed on permanently without further delay.

'Well, next year perhaps. Kate, be a darling and go and have a word with Louise, would you? Actually, I think I'll come with you and have a look at what Cindy sent.'

Kate, being almost as discreet as Louise, had said Bedliner and Bolt. She had not said Cindy. It was Michael who had said Cindy. Perhaps he was in really deep, and it was only to be hoped that Louise would accept and would be on hand to mastermind his middle-of-the-night telephone calls and his lovely floral tributes.

'Louise, do you have a minute?' asked Kate.

'Of course,' said Louise, putting down the scissors and the glue. Ned was now on the Santa Claus bit.

'Can I have a word?'

'Of course. Kitchen?'

Kate nodded and they slipped off into the kitchen, while

206

Michael sat down beside Ned, marvelled at Cindy's taste and offered to hold the glue.

'So, you're having lunch with Nick. Where?' asked Louise, picking up from where they'd left off.

'Oh, this word isn't about that. This word is about something else. I'll come straight to the point, there's no need to go beating about the bush. Michael has just been talking to me about you and the job.'

Louise's heart sank. So, that was it. They hated her, they didn't want her, they wanted her out of the office by four o'clock. What had she done wrong? – that was what she wanted to know. She could always offer to try harder.

'Did I do something wrong?'

'Not at all. Quite the contrary. Michael would like you to consider taking the job permanently. I must say, I would be thrilled, but please don't let that tiny consideration cloud your judgement. Ned would be thrilled, Martin would be thrilled, and dear old Geoffrey would be over the moon. Would you please think about it? I know you're too good for us, but I'm just paving the way so that Michael can ask you himself, and, if you want to, you can tell him to go and take a hike, because you are too good for this rabble.'

'Thank goodness. For the past two weeks I've been worrying about what I was doing wrong. I quite expected you to tell me not to come in again. Of course, I'd be delighted to take the job. I adore it here.'

There was a relentless knocking on the kitchen door again, which served to interrupt their flow of thought.

'Oy, you two. Geoffrey's manning the switchboard and he says there's a telephone call for Kate, but he doesn't know how to put it through to the kitchen,' shouted Martin.

'There isn't a telephone in the kitchen,' replied Kate. 'Could that be the trouble?'

She heard Martin tell Geoffrey that there wasn't a telephone in the kitchen and she heard Geoffrey ask Martin to ask Kate to come out and take the call and then she heard Martin bang on the door.

'Can you come out then?'

'I think I'd better go out.'

'I think you'd better,' agreed Louise.

'Oh, there you are, Chief,' said Geoffrey. 'Number One tied up, is she? I thought I'd fill in at the switchboard. There's a call waiting for you on your telephone.' He paused and then added in a stage whisper, 'It sounds like your young man.'

Kate glanced around reception and saw that Ned had noticed Geoffrey's remark but was pretending he hadn't and was instead adding a bit of extra frosting to the piece of log. Michael hadn't noticed anything at all, as he was staring whimsically at Cindy's handwritten message, intent upon memorizing every loop and dot. His heart was probably brightened for the duration of the Holiday Season and more.

'Kate, it's Nick. I can't get into San Frediano. It's fully booked.'

'Oh, hell. Have you tried Meridiana? It's just across the street.'

'I know it's just across the street.'

'Well, have you tried it?'

'Yes. They're fully booked too.'

'There's no chance of getting in Langan's. Not this late.'

'I realize that. That's why I haven't tried.'

'Does that mean it's off?'

'Oh, no. How about the pub at the end of the mews?'

'Geoffrey goes there, it wouldn't be a good idea.'

'Well, how do you feel about the wine bar around the corner?'

'O K' It wouldn't be quite the same, but there you are. When you are going out with friends, you just have to learn to adjust and muck in. Speaking of going out with friends, who was going to pay? 'Twelve-thirty still all right with you?'

'Still all right with me. See you later.'

Kate made her way back to reception, but was waylaid by Geoffrey, who seemed to want to draw her aside for a discreet chat.

'Katy, can I have a word?'

'Of course, Geoffrey. At any time.'

'Was that your young man, Katy? I thought it was all off.'

'It was my young man, though he is no longer my young man, he is more of an acquaintance of mine, a good friend, if you will. So, I suppose it is still off, but sort of on, though under different rules and conditions. Very healthy, don't you think?'

'I'm not sure that I understand.'

'I'll tell you all about it one day,' she said, patting his arm.

'I say, Kate,' said Martin, who was passing by. 'Do you have a moment? I just wanted to have a quiet word about something.'

'Not now, Martin. I'm frightfully busy. Later perhaps.' Kate turned and left Martin, who was looking rather peeved, and returned once again to reception, where Louise had cleared up most of the debris and was just putting the last bits of string and polystyrene into a big black plastic bag. She was proving herself to be indispensable.

'Michael. Can I have a word?'

'Of course, Kate. Shall we go into my office? We don't have things like this in England,' remarked Michael as he eyed the golden sledge whizzing down the frosty mountainside, into which Ned was just sticking a jovial Santa. 'Isn't it a shame?'

'I've had a word with Louise,' said Kate once they were inside the door. 'And she says she'd love to take the job. So, shall I send her in?'

'No, that's quite all right. I'll go and find her myself.' It would give him a chance to go and sit on the sofa beside Ned and think about Cindy again and just how she had decorated her apartment. She had lots of amusing ideas. Very innovative, very innovative indeed.

'Oh, Louise,' said Michael, hovering with intent. 'Could I have a word?'

'Of course, Michael. Shall we go into your office?' suggested Louise as she went in that direction and he trailed behind her. She had style. She was far too good for them. She could have had her own office, if only she'd realized it.

'Shall we sit down?' she said.

'The thing is, Louise, I was wondering if we couldn't persuade you to stay with us permanently. Would you give it a bit of thought over Christmas and give me an answer in the New Year?'

'I don't need to think about it, Michael. I would love the job. I really would.'

'Are you sure?'

'Yes, I'm sure.'

'And you won't change your mind?'

'No, I won't change my mind.'

'So, you're sure.'

'Yes, I'm sure,' stressed Louise.

'That's wonderful.'

'I am very happy here and I'm sure I will be even happier.'

'Oh, good. Shall we go back and see how Ned is getting on with assembling the Christmas arrangement? It's a present. It came from Chicago, you know.'

'Yes, I know.'

In reception Geoffrey was still handling the switchboard, though he was offering encouragement from the sidelines. Martin was in a sullen mood and was leaning against the wall reading the instructions, while Ned was putting the final touches to Santa's flowing coat.

'It doesn't look a bit like the picture,' observed a chilly Martin.

'Exactly. I've added a bit here and there and improved it tremendously,' said Ned.

'I've been thinking, Ned,' said Geoffrey, 'I could rig up a spotlight, if you like. I think with a bit of backlight, it could look even better.'

'You're absolutely right, Geoffrey. Could we put it on a dimmer? It would be good to be able to vary the mood.'

'No problem. I'll just go and sort it out. Martin, man the switchboard, there's a good chap, and stop loafing about,' said Geoffrey.

'I'm waiting to have a word with Kate,' moaned Martin.

'Well, wait at the switchboard. I've got a lighting rig,' said Geoffrey, shuffling off to his tool kit.

Kate returned from her desk and arrived on the scene just as Louise returned from Michael's office.

'Louise,' whispered Kate out of the side of her mouth. 'Could we have a word?'

'In the kitchen?'

'Yes.'

'Oh, Kate, there you are,' said a very disgruntled Martin. 'Can I have a word?'

'Not now, Martin, I'm busy. If anyone wants me I'll be in the kitchen. Make yourself useful and man the switchboard. You've done nothing constructive all morning.'

Together Kate and Louise went into the kitchen.

'Close the door,' said Kate. 'Pull up a stool.'

'Right, where were we?' asked Louise.

'I was telling you that I'm going to have lunch with Nick.'

'Now, are you sure this is wise?' asked Louise, realizing that time was short. It was ten minutes past twelve and they had wasted almost the entire morning on that horrible thing from Chicago.

'Honestly. Everything is fine. I feel so happy and really very relaxed. I am clear in my mind that this is what I should have done ages ago. The affair had run its course, but I couldn't see that there could be something else. Nick put it so well. He said we are friends. Pals. Best buddies. He said, let's be best friends, forget about the other stuff.'

Women never forget, and neither do men, and neither do elephants.

In reception Ned was admiring his handiwork and he was in the midst of deciding where he should place the decoration. Michael and Geoffrey were doing their best to help.

'I think a plinth is the answer,' said Michael.

'That's an idea,' agreed Ned. 'Geoffrey, do you remember that time we had to hide you and the video equipment behind a green drape and a bunch of irises? It was in Coventry, I think, about a year ago. Well, what did you do with that roll of green felt?'

'It's in my cupboard. Do you want me to dig it out?'

'Yes, would you? I think the thing to do is cover the wall with the green felt and place the plinth in front. What do you think, Michael?'

'Excellent, excellent. Well, I must get on, I've got an important telephone call to make.'

'Yes, I must get on too. I've got to chase that plinth. It will only take one telephone call,' said Ned optimistically.

'What colour is the plinth going to be?' asked Michael, who wanted to be able to give Cindy all the details.

'I haven't quite decided yet. It needs a bit of thought. I'd like to see Geoffrey's lighting effect first.'

'Oh, there you are, Kate,' said Martin as he spotted her tiptoeing across reception, intent upon reaching the door and getting to her lunch as quietly as possible. 'Could we have word before you go out to lunch?'

'Not now, Martin.'

'But I've been waiting all morning.'

'Well, you'll just have to wait a little longer, won't you?'

'You off to lunch, Kate?' said Ned. 'Would you pick up a roll of silver foil while you're out? I can't do it myself. I've got to see a man about a plinth.'

CHAPTER FIFTEEN

Like the good friends they were, they agreed on many things, but there was one thing upon which they agreed in particular and that was that they would much rather have been eating some fegato at San Frediano or tucking into an array of antipasto at Meridiana. Either would have been infinitely better than the bowls of substandard onion soup they were reduced to at the wine bar around the corner. The bread and cheese, which should have been on the top, had sunk to the bottom of the bowl.

Kate was, however, thoroughly enjoying her lunch with her friend Nick, and they had discussed all the things that old friends usually discuss when they get together. At the outset of their lunch they had marvelled at how with true friends you just pick up the threads and time apart is of little importance. They had talked about their jobs, what films they had recently seen and urged each other to catch a play they had particularly enjoyed. They had mentioned one or two television programmes they had watched and had talked about the books they had been reading. Kate had lied a bit and pretended she was reading something a touch more upmarket. Still, it was only between friends. Nick had told Kate all about the problem he had had with his car and how he thought he would have to get a new one, and she had told him that her car was just about to peg out. Kate almost told Nick about her experience in Huntingdon, but prudence prevailed and she realized that as an old friend he might not enjoy hearing about her would-be friend, Dermot. She did, however, make sure that Nick heard all about Louise and was kept informed of what Ned, James, Geoffrey, Martin and Michael were up to. The flat had come up in the conversation, and Kate had enthused about her stunning bathroom and how it had a really good shower. Nick was a man who liked a good shower. He had been very interested to hear about the flat and had inquired about the size of the rooms, how many wardrobes she had, where she had put the furniture, what curtains she had chosen and what the kitchen was like. Kate had told him as much as she could and had, as a friendly gesture, invited him round any time he wanted.

'And it's got a lovely garden. Well, it will be a lovely garden. It's a bit on the bleak side at the moment. Louise and I have tried to do a bit each weekend, but the trouble is, whenever we are just getting into our stride, that wretched man from next door, Desperate Doug, comes grinning over the garden fence. He's been going on and on about his New Year's Eve Dance and keeps asking us if we want tickets. I've got a sneaking suspicion he's got two tickets on hold and he's going to try and whisk Louise and me there as his special guests.'

'What are you doing for New Year's Eve?' asked Nick.

'Nothing. You know I always do nothing on New Year's Eve. I can't bear it. I always stay at home. You know, go to bed early and sleep through it. But I think this year Louise is going to join me, and we will give ourselves over to a bout of melancholia together. What are you doing?'

'I don't know. It's a bit difficult to plan at the moment.'

'Oh. Why's that?'

'Well, I don't quite know how to tell you this, but I'll give it a try. I can tell you it came as a bit of a shock when I was told,' said a troubled Nick. He paused, but knew he had to be courageous and continue. 'The truth of the matter is that Yvonne's left me. She wants a divorce. Apparently she's been seeing some bloke for years and now he's got his divorce and they want to get married. She's living with him now. She left me for him. Can you imagine? She's been having an affair for years right under my nose.'

'That's a funny place to have it. Shall I order another bottle of wine?'

'Yes, would you?'

A bottle of house red was ordered, and, when it arrived, the remnants of the onion soup were removed and replaced with plates of stodgy lasagne. The waitress, a bright young thing who would rather have been somewhere else, attempted to take away the garlic bread, but Kate insisted on hanging on to it. When it came to eating the lasagne, Kate found that she had little appetite for it and small interest in the garlic bread for which she had argued so forcibly. She toyed with a green salad.

'When did you learn this, Nick?'

'About a month ago. It came like a bolt out of the blue.'

'Where are the children?'

'Oh, they're with her. Apparently her bloke has got three by his previous marriage, so that makes seven. Anyway, she's got them.'

'I see,' said Kate.

'You know, Kate, I've missed you so much. It's good to talk, isn't it?'

'Oh, it's always good to talk.'

'And I have missed you.'

'Yes, I've missed you too, Nick.' Kate had missed him and she was sure that he had missed her, but she was more interested in getting back to the good news that Yvonne had taken the four little horrors with her.

'But he hasn't got his three with him, has he? Seven kids in one house would be awful.'

'Oh, no, he gets them at the weekend, when I get mine. They do a swap.'

'That's a lot of work.'

'Well, Yvonne's a good mother.'

'But she wasn't a good wife, was she?'

'Indeed. Right under my nose. All those years. I don't know, I really don't.'

'So, where is Yvonne living?'

'He's got some big pile down in Kent. He's a pig farmer.'

'How on earth did Yvonne meet a pig farmer?' asked Kate.

'I've often wondered that myself. But apparently she did and carried on with him for years.'

'I don't see Yvonne down on the farm.'

'Oh, I don't know. She's very capable, you know.'

'People can surprise you, can't they?'

'Well, she certainly surprised me with her news. I never would have believed it of her. To have lived a lie all those years, such a deception.'

'Yes, it must have come as a shock.'

'Yes, it did. It certainly came as a shock.' Nick poured more red wine for himself and then for Kate. 'Sorry, I should have served you first. I'm a bit distracted at the moment.'

'Oh, well, that's what friends are for,' said Kate bravely. 'So, are you living in Kew on your own? The house is a bit big for you, isn't it?'

'Well, I like the house, and, as you know, I'm mortgaged up to the hilt. It's a good investment, of course, but it's going to have to be sold. She's going to milk me dry. She wants half the proceeds of the house, plus support for the children, and on top of that there's their school fees, and now she says she has to have a nanny and I have to pay for the nanny too.'

'Is the nanny going to help with his children over the week-ends or is she going to come to you with your children?'

'Good point, Kate,' said Nick, hurriedly whipping out a notepad from his breast pocket. 'I'll make a note of that and mention it to the solicitor when I see him next week.'

'It's got as far as the solicitors, has it?'

'Oh, yes. And – do you know – that's what really upset me. I heard from them the day after she left and they had all her demands worked out, so she must have been thinking about it for some time and had the whole thing planned.'

'And you had no idea, Nick, no idea at all?'

'No idea at all. You never really know people, do you?'

'Oh, I don't know. I think I know you very well.'

'Oh, yes, Kate, and I know you so well too.'

'Ten years. It's a long time.'

'We're a good team, Kate. A good team.'

'You never thought of leaving her, did you?' remarked Kate, without the slightest trace of bitterness.

'No, you know that. We had the children. And I do believe a commitment is a commitment. Anyway, she would have milked me dry. She would have wanted half the proceeds of the house,

216

not to mention child support and school fees. How could I have done it? You knew how it was.'

'Yes, I knew how it was.'

'How's your lasagne?' asked Nick.

'Awful,' replied Kate.

'It's not too good, is it?'

Nick was about to tell Kate that Yvonne made a really good lasagne, but he realized that those kinds of memories might upset him too much, so he refrained and continued to plough through the flabby offering in front of him. Kate discovered that her appetite was no better, and so continued to play with her salad.

'Oh, it's good to see you, Kate. I've missed you dreadfully. Particularly in the last few weeks. I could have done with your support.'

'Well, you have it now,' said Kate. 'I'm so happy you called. To think you've been going through all of this on your own.'

'We must see each other more often. It's so good to talk, isn't it?'

'Yes, isn't it?'

'I must come and see your flat soon. You say it's got a good shower.'

'Excellent shower with one of those fancy pulsating heads, so you can massage your neck and aching back muscles.'

'It sounds just like my sort of shower. And how much wardrobe space did you say you'd got?'

'Masses. It's so wonderful. I've spread myself out, and for once in my life all my clothes are organized and not crammed into a tiny cupboard. My wardrobe runs the entire length of one wall and I have it all to myself. I could never go back to anything less. Never.'

'The parking good, is it?' asked Nick.

'Street parking, but it's never a problem to find a spot.'

'What are the shopping facilities like?'

'Splendid off-licence just around the corner, a supermarket about ten minutes' walk away, and then there's a wonderful little shop just two streets away that is open until all hours. It's quite a little community, really. I'm very happy there.'

'And a garden, you say. I shall miss my garden.'

'Now, that's something I didn't know. You see, perhaps we don't know everything about each other. I didn't know you liked gardening.'

'Yes, I used to do it every weekend.'

As Kate hardly ever saw him at weekends, Saturday and Sunday being sacred family time, she didn't know whether he did or did not like gardening, but that was what he had told her.

He had lied, of course; he'd done a lot of that in the past; so why should he change now? It was part of his nature. The gardening had, in fact, been done by a willing old-age pensioner named Bert, and what a gem he was. He was a man of the soil, the kind they don't make any more. No, Nick used to spend every Sunday morning at the Golf Club, come rain or shine, and it was one of the many things that had annoyed Yvonne. All week she'd coped with the children and the house and she had to cope with it all weekend, because after the golf he used to come home, eat his lunch and then make some feeble excuse about having to go up to his study to prepare for next week's work. And that was another thing: he was always talking about his career and being boring about a commitment being a commitment. There was never any way of telling what time he would come home and then, on top of that, there were all those times when he used to telephone and say he'd suddenly got to go to Manchester and he wouldn't be home at all. Something unexpected had come up. It was just as well her new bloke wasn't like that. No, Porky Pritchard was a good man and he was going to look after her and treat her well. Yvonne had had enough of the other sort.

'What do you do with the second bedroom, Kate?'

'Well, it's a bedroom. A guest bedroom. Lizzie came to stay a couple of weekends ago. We had an outrageous time. Just like the old days.'

'You've never thought of turning the second bedroom into a study?'

'No, it's a bedroom. What would I want a study for?'

'We're a good team, Kate.'

'Well, we're good friends, aren't we?'

'More than that.'

'Oh, I thought we were good friends,' said Kate rather shakily.

'Best friends who understand each other.'

'Yes, best friends.'

'Do you understand me, Kate?'

'Yes, I think I do.'

'I understand you, Kate. In fact, I love you. Very deeply. I really do.' He took both her hands in his hands. 'Kate, when all of this divorce nonsense is over and out of the way, will you marry me? Things will be tough financially at the beginning, but we'll work it out together. Perhaps we could live in your flat for a while. Will you, Kate? Will you marry me?'

Kate pulled herself out of the passing black-out into which she had unexpectedly plunged, looked at Nick's familiar face and thought of all that he had said, and of how she had longed for him to say those very words for years and years. She pondered his question, reached down into her soul and prepared to say the only thing she could say.

'Certainly not, you lying little wimp.'

CHAPTER SIXTEEN

'Louise,' sighed Kate. She sounded rather bored, and her voice hung in the gloom. 'Would you like another drink?'

'I can't see the one I've got, so I can't tell. I put it down and now I've lost it. How much longer are we going to sit in the dark?' demanded Louise irritably.

'Since I can't see my watch, I can't tell you exactly. Once Doug shambles off to his awful dance and we've got the all-clear, we can put the light on.'

'What a ridiculous way to spend New Year's Eve,' observed Louise, giving the Chanel handbag stuffed beside her in the armchair a disgruntled punch. She wanted to get the whole business over with. She had got through a difficult Christmas, trying to put on a brave face in front of her parents, who had spent the entire time trying not to say the wrong thing. Had they but known it, the right thing to say might have been 'We told you so.' And so, while they hedged around the sensitive issue Louise tried to glean comfort from the recollection that David had never surprised her with a gift but had always suggested that she go out and choose something for herself. The Chanel handbag in a useful shade of taupe had been such a purchase.

'Try and hang on,' encouraged Kate. 'Think how awful it would be if he knew we were here. We'd never hear the last of it. Mind you, I wish he'd hurry up. He's told us enough times he's organized the whole thing. Why isn't he there organizing right now? – that's what I want to know. He should be counting the sausages on sticks and plugging in Roy "Harmony" Harmon's organ. Do you think he's taking Beryl?'

'Apparently not. She's dancing the light fantastic at a rival function. Now that her cast is off her ankle, she's back at her square dancing. Doug was telling me that Beryl wanted him to go to her dance and he wanted her to go to his. He did say that he was very torn, but as he was in charge of his do, he thought duty was duty.'

'I do hope he doesn't come knocking on the door or, worse still, squinting through the windows, doing one of his "well, hello-o there, I thought I'd just see if you were in" numbers.'

'I think I heard something,' whispered Louise nervously. 'It sounded like a door closing. Did you hear it?'

'No, but I'll just edge over to the window and see if anything is going on.' Kate lowered herself on to all fours, and through the dark came the sound of her feeling her way as she crawled across the carpet to the front window.

'Can you see anything?' Louise asked quietly.

'Not a thing. It's pitch-black outside.'

'The same as in here. Can you find your way back? Would you like me to keep talking so that you've got a sound to follow?'

'Yes, would you, please? I can't see a thing.'

'Are you thinking about Nick?'

'Certainly not. I wouldn't waste my time,' asserted Kate briskly. 'Are you thinking about David?'

'A bit,' admitted Louise.

'Right, I'm back at my chair. I can see a bit better now. I think my eyes are getting used to it.'

'Mine aren't,' moaned Louise. 'Are you sure we can't have the light on?'

'Quite sure. Are you all right, Louise? You don't sound yourself. You're not brooding too much, are you? Are you thinking about him a bit more than a bit?'

'I'm quite sure. I'm only thinking a bit.'

'That's the trouble with New Year's Eve, you always start thinking about what a mess the year has been and then you start to think about what a mess the next one is going to be. New Year's Eve never did anyone any good. That's why I loathe it so.' In particular, Kate was thinking of how, on confiding in her mother with regard to Nick's proposal of marriage, she had burst into gales of incredulous laughter. Her mother had then put down her glass of sherry and rushed off to her father's study, calling out through her giggles, 'Frank, you'll never guess what Kate's just told me.'

'Haven't you ever had a good New Year's Eve?' inquired Louise.

'Now you mention it, no.' Kate found it an easy question to answer. 'That's why I always go to bed early and try to forget the whole thing. Have you had some good ones?'

'David took me to Vienna one year.'

'Oh, how wonderful. He must have been very romantic.'

'Not really, just very rich. Anyway, he managed to write it off as a business trip, and I spent three days on my own in the Bristol.'

'I'm surprised he didn't try and get in touch over Christmas.'

'I'm not,' said Louise. 'I'm beginning to realize it's for the best that it's over. Actually, I have begun to admit to myself that he's not that pleasant a person. He's as ruthless with his personal relationships as he is in business. I do feel lonely, yes, but every day things get a bit better and I am enjoying my job, so that's something good, isn't it? What upsets me a lot is the realization that I was beguiled by the life-style. You know, all the clothes and the busy social life. It's an awful character flaw.'

'Oh, come along. Don't start putting yourself down.'

'You're right. I should remember all the running around I did for him. I was forever packing suitcases, unpacking suitcases and making sure he'd got some clean shirts. I think I was used. Six years of being used. Oh, dear. Last year wasn't very good, was it?'

'No, I'm afraid it wasn't one of the best.'

'Do you think it's going to be like this all the time? For ever and ever?'

'No, things are bound to improve. It's the law of averages, isn't it? It can't go on for ever. I like to think that we've just been going through a tiny bit of a barren patch. It'll get better soon, don't worry. There'll be lots of fun and lots of excitement. I'm sure of it,' said Kate, quietly biting her lip in the dark.

'I hope you're right. I wouldn't like to think of spending the rest of my life in the state I've been in for the past three months. Oh, I wish we could put the light on. This is ridiculous.'

'We daren't risk it. Imagine Doug thundering round and trying to do a bit of first-footing. It would put me right off for the whole year.'

'True. Oh, what a relief – I've found my drink.'

'Well done.'

'Are you sure we can't put the light on?'

'Quite sure.'

'Perhaps Doug's ill and he's not going to the dance.'

'If he were ill, he would have called round by now to tell us all the gory details of his affliction. Try and hang on. It won't be long now. My eyes are much better. I can see the bottle and your glass. I'll fill you up.'

'Thank you,' said Louise rather listlessly.

'You're thinking about David, aren't you? I can tell.'

'Well, yes.'

'And Jacqui too?'

'Yes, and Jacqui too. And all the others. I'm sure there were others. It does make me so cross when I go on thinking about it. I do wish I could forget it all. I bet you're thinking about Nick. Now, come on, own up.'

'No, not a bit.'

'I bet you are.'

'Well, all right, a little.'

'I thought so,' said Louise, relieved that she was not the only one.

'But only to the extent that I'm thinking I'm well rid of him. Oh, what a brave statement that is,' said Kate, trying to home in on what she was truly feeling. 'I gave so much of myself to him and all the time I thought I needed him in order to be myself.'

'That's what I thought too,' chipped in Louise.

'What I've found out is that's not true at all. I have myself back now, and, do you know something? I like what I find. I like myself. I don't need someone else to tell me who I am and that it is all right to exist as long as I am existing for them. There are no parts missing. I'm whole.'

'Oh, yes,' agreed Louise fervently. 'I know exactly what you mean.'

'Growing up has taken a long time, and it's been a painful process, but I really do believe that for the first time in my life I can see the way ahead.'

'It's almost as if it has to be painful in order to have any real worth.'

'And now I'm almost there. I'm at the point when I know that I can have a fulfilled life on my own. A man doesn't have to be part of it.'

'It would be nice though, wouldn't it?' sighed Louise.

'Yes, it would be nice,' said Kate, nodding in agreement.

'Can we put the light on soon?'

'In a minute.'